"I didn't kill Lillian Kingsley."

Sara could barely control her voice.

"No?" Nicholas hunched his shoulders in disbelief.

"No," she retorted angrily.

"Then how come she left everything to you? Loosen up, Sara, you can tell me.... A frail little old lady you're assigned to protect ... You wheedle your way into her affections, then decide to send her on a permanent trip—after she'd written a will in your favor, of course."

"That's ridiculous!"

"Is it?" An ominous laugh rumbled deep in his chest. "I think not, Sara Brennan. You're a killer, all right, and I'm going to prove it."

"How?" Sara said evenly.

"You'll be surprised," he promised as he stormed away.

But Sara knew that if anyone was in for a surprise, it was surely Nick....

ABOUT THE AUTHOR

Christine Smith has been a very busy lady. She's been a trade journalist, a public relations consultant, a copy writer, an account representative and she's even owned her own public relations firm. But according to Christine, writing romance fiction is the ultimate thrill—at least as far as careers go. Christine's other thrill is her husband, Ken, whom she married in her mid-thirties. She's happy to say he was definitely worth the wait. Christine and Ken live with their dog and two cats in a house in Toronto.

MURDER MOST STRANGE
CHRISTINE SMITH

Harlequin Books

TORONTO • NEW YORK • LONDON
AMSTERDAM • PARIS • SYDNEY • HAMBURG
STOCKHOLM • ATHENS • TOKYO • MILAN

To an unsung heroine and hero—
Mary Elizabeth and Richard John Adams,
my parents.
Thanks...words aren't enough.

Harlequin Intrigue edition published August 1987

ISBN 0-373-22072-3

Prologue

Secure in the mottled shadows of the dense woods, he nestled the curved butt of the Savage .303 rifle into the crook of his shoulder.

Beneath damp eyelashes his focused gaze showed concentration. He didn't want to risk killing Lillian Kingsley. He needed Lillian alive—at least for the time being.

But Sara Brennan, her bodyguard, was a different matter.

Entirely different, he thought, a scowl marring his handsome face.

Squinting, he panned the scope through a four-inch arc until he had the two women on the sloping lawn of the ten-acre Kingsley estate centered in the cross-hair grid.

After so many years of waiting, the nine-pound heft in his arms gave him a deadly sense of security. A promise of victory.

Damn those guard dogs. He'd have to wait until they were in the kennels.

He followed Sara's movements through the scope. Smiling, she bent down slightly, saying something to the two tan-colored German shepherds that stood poised on each side of her, their tails wagging appreciatively at the attention.

Her light chestnut hair glistened in the October mist as she shook it off her shoulders.

It's really too bad, he couldn't help thinking. *She's quite stunning.*

But business is business.

Sara was far too canny for her own good. And strong. He'd found that out the hard way. Last time they'd tried to kidnap Lillian, Sara had thwarted the attempt, fighting like a tiger. In the process she'd almost pulled away his disguise.

His dark eyes flickered with remembered anger.

He should never have been there, he knew that now, but the guys he'd hired had bungled it too many times by then. He had to get to Lillian Kingsley and the formula. It was rightfully his.

Sara had become the major stumbling block. With her around, he'd never be able to kidnap the old lady.

Tough, Sara. You're just going to have to be disposed of. And the quicker, the better.

In the rifle's sights, Sara's image waved. He quickened to attention. Now what?

Watching, he saw a silver Mercedes-Benz pull to a stop in the circular driveway and a man get out of it.

Ben Short, the lawyer. Ineffectual wimp, he sneered silently.

As he watched, Ben joined the women, spoke to Sara, then touched Lillian on the arm as if to lead her into the three-story, Tudor-style brick house.

Sara broke away quickly, the dogs following her on command as she headed down a small pathway toward the rear of the house.

He checked his watch in the late-afternoon light. A gray drizzle blurred the dial. Four o'clock. Feeding time for the dogs. Sara would feed the dogs in the kennels, return to the house and then go back to release them after they had finished eating.

He lowered the rifle, resting the solid walnut against the base of a maple tree, its barrel nudging the wet bark. How long did that give him? The dogs would likely be confined for about thirty minutes. That should give him enough time to get across the estate grounds without detection, locate Sara and do what he had come to do.

He glanced back toward Lillian and Ben. They'd disappeared into the house. If he didn't miss his guess, they were heading for the library. He scanned the exterior of the mansion.

A light went on in the east corner.

Right. He knew that house like the back of his hand.

With Ben and Lillian in the library, he had a clear field with Sara. Good. With one down, only two to go.

Noiselessly, he reached for the rifle again, rechecked that the safety was on and slung it over his shoulder.

Stealthily, he edged through the fine mist toward the mansion....

Chapter One

Sara slipped through the white stillness of the country-style kitchen, opting to take the main staircase to her third-floor suite rather than the back stairs.

As she passed the library on the left of the hallway, she could hear voices, raised and agitated, even through the heavy mahogany doors.

Her wide-set hazel eyes twinkled with amusement. Her employer, Lillian Kingsley, and Ben Short, Lillian's lawyer, were likely engaged in another contest of wills.

A woman of whim. And a man of caution.

Occasionally, Sara had been caught in the cross fire between the sixty-two-year-old widow and the conservative lawyer. She'd discovered that when that happened, the only sensible course of action was to duck.

I've become an expert at verbal ducking in the past year, she thought, suppressing a swell of laughter. *Maybe after twenty-seven years, I'm learning some subtlety after all.*

Her camel-colored pantsuit and hiking shoes allowed her to run easily up the staircase. With athletic grace, she briskly reached the first floor in a few seconds, her palm skimming over the highly polished mahogany banister. When she'd first seen the banister it had instantly conjured up the image of a laughing, sliding child, gripping the wooden surface with sheer delight.

But to the best of her knowledge, there'd never been any children in the Kingsley mansion. Lillian and her late husband, Charles, had been childless.

Once though, while she'd been checking the mansion for a suspected burglar, Sara had discovered a bright blue, metal box of toys tucked in the closet of an unused bedroom. Trucks, toy guns and soldiers—a boy's playthings—all neatly stored. The colorful remnants of childhood had seemed tragically new, with few dents and nicks in them.

She'd picked up half a dozen comic books from a pile behind the box, scanning the yellowed covers. The date printed on them read 1958.

Twenty-nine years ago. Whomever they'd been intended for would be in his mid-thirties today.

Recalling that day and the box of toys, Sara thought, as she had before, that it was a shame the Kingsleys had been childless. What better place to grow up than here?

The house was built on acres of rolling hills in the picturesque town of Aurora, approximately twenty miles north of the city of Toronto. Charles Kingsley's ancestors were Americans who had been lured by the offer of free land in exchange for swearing allegiance to the British crown. Originally a farming community, Aurora had, despite its proximity to Toronto, retained its small-town charm.

In the late fifties, Charles had followed the example of Sterling Drug Limited, the town's largest employer, and had built his chemical plant here. At the same time he'd restored the abandoned estate to its current splendor.

Wild, dark woods banked the property to the south. A narrow, meandering stream was constantly stocked with fish, and at one time stables had housed half a dozen horses. Charles had been a passionate horseman, and he and Lillian had both been avid patrons of Aurora's famous annual horse show. The main house itself featured two winding staircases, myriad hallways, a cavernous cellar and Tudor-design window seats. All tempting lures for a child.

Sara gave a quick toss of her shoulder-length hair. *It's a shame to waste all this on adults,* she thought. *The estate ought to be filled with the screams of happy children.*

When she reached the suite Lillian had provided for her, she removed her jacket and tossed it on the back of a chintz-covered chair, absently edging aside the lace curtains of the mullioned windows that overlooked the approach to the estate. A permanent gray mantle seemed to have settled over the horizon from the unremitting rain that had been falling on Southern Ontario for the past few days.

I'll be glad when the depressing drizzle lets up. And when Lillian's safe, she thought, her gaze clouding with concern.

Whenever she thought of Lillian's safety, a question plagued her, as it had from the beginning of the assignment.

Why had Charles Kingsley elected to handle it this way?

At the very least, it was unorthodox. At the very worst—dangerous.

Charles had left instructions that upon his death Lillian was to sell Kingsley Chemicals and keep the proceeds. That was straightforward enough. But one part of the bequest was anything but straightforward—a formula, presumably worth a fortune. What puzzled Sara was the form in which it had been left to Lillian. Charles hadn't simply written down the formula on a piece of paper. Too easy to steal, Sara supposed. Instead, he'd given it to Lillian verbally only a few days before his death.

Even though the existence of the formula was supposedly a secret, within a month of Charles's death, Lillian's possession of it had turned her into a walking target. In protecting the formula from theft, Charles had made Lillian vulnerable.

Sara had been hired by Ben to protect the spirited widow. For a while the attempts to abduct Lillian had fallen off, but throughout the summer and into the fall, the campaign had accelerated.

Sara was convinced it was because the kidnappers were also aware of the extraordinary codicil to Charles's will. Lillian was to retain the formula for two years and then release what the legal profession called her "property interest" in it to another party. The identity of that party was unknown to Ben and Lillian. Further instructions were contained in a letter to be opened November 15.

Almost a month from today, Sara mused.

Once the property interest in the formula had been gifted to someone else, the new owner would likely patent it immediately and go into production, which would make Lillian's knowledge much less valuable. The kidnappers had a deadline and Sara had to assume they knew it.

Sara shuddered at the thought. Only another month.

A light tap at the door interrupted her train of thought. Surprised, she dropped the curtain and strode across the room to see who it was.

"Lillian!" Sara's voice registered her amazement and pleasure as she greeted her bright-eyed employer. "I thought you were with Ben." She held the door open. "You didn't walk," she admonished.

"Nope." Lillian shook her elegant head with its short, silver hair, her blue-fire eyes slanting upward to bridge the seven-inch gap in height between Sara and her. "Took the elevator."

She stretched her delicate five-foot frame proudly. "But my arthritis isn't that bad. I could have walked."

In the background, Sara could hear the soft whir of the elevator as it returned to the main floor.

"Of course," she said, chuckling. Lillian disliked admitting to any weakness. "Come in and sit down." She extended a welcoming gesture, her hands devoid of any adornment.

"Can't stay." Lillian shuffled into the room, her cane tapping on the plush, yellow broadloom. "Just came for a minute. Ben makes me so angry. I just had to work off some steam." Stopping, she faced Sara, planting the cane at straight angles to her body, a familiar flash brightening her eyes.

Sara stifled another grin. "Oh," she managed in a noncommittal voice.

"Well, never mind that," Lillian responded impatiently. Waving the cane around the blue, white and yellow suite, she changed the subject in characteristic rapid-fire fashion. "Pretty rooms, these."

"Aren't they just?" Sara replied, accustomed to Lillian's mercurial nature. Smiling, she walked to the window, brushing aside the curtains with her fingers the way she'd done when she first came in. "Terrific view as well. I often admire it." She surveyed the estate casually.

Below, the grounds were still. Only a few rustling leaves and branches stirred in the autumn breeze. As soon as Lillian was gone, she'd change her clothes and let the dogs out to patrol, she thought.

"Same as mine, but you can see farther from up here," she heard Lillian acknowledge behind her.

Sara turned to face Lillian, wondering what had prompted the widow's visit. The heiress to the Kingsley fortune rarely came to Sara's suite. She waited.

Lillian jiggled her cane. "I really didn't come to talk about Ben," she said. "I came for two reasons. One of them is to thank you."

"Thank me?" Sara gave her a puzzled look.

Lillian sighed with exasperation. "You're as bad as Ben. Always interrupting. Yes, thank you," she repeated. "For risking your life. For being willing to stay in the country with an old woman, when you could be out having fun with some handsome bachelor."

Sara's eyes sparkled with understanding. Romance was a consuming interest with Lillian. "Oh, that."

"Yes, that." Lillian fixed her with a calculating glint. "Don't you *want* to get married again?"

Although accustomed to Lillian's bluntness on the subject of other people's love lives, Sara hadn't seen the question coming. She hesitated.

Her marriage had been a disaster. Her ex-husband had wanted her to be something she wasn't and never could become. As the president of his own electronics company, he'd tried to reshape her into his image of the perfect corporate wife. She'd resisted—and he'd made her pay for it emotionally, piling criticism on top of criticism, until she'd almost lost sight of who she'd been before she married. "Opposites attract" hadn't been true in their case—at least not after marriage. He'd wanted her to change her job, her interests, her whole style. Sophisticated and aggressive, the epitome of success, he'd resorted to every means at his disposal to achieve that end. The strength in him that had attracted her to him in the first place soon deteriorated into emotional bullying. He'd mistaken her directness and lack of guile for a lack of female needs. Consequently, he'd run over her like the proverbial steam roller, never taking the time to treat her like a woman. Shaken by the experience, she'd finally just walked out on him. And she intended to keep walking, for now. She was in no rush to repeat that mistake.

"I've got lots of time," she finally responded to Lillian, a smile playing at the edges of her mouth.

Lillian chortled. "Holding out, eh?"

"I don't follow," Sara answered, perplexed, wondering if she'd missed something while lost in thought.

Lillian gave a delightful, mischievous laugh. "Holding out—for a Charles Kingsley."

Sara's eyes danced with laughter. No matter what her own reservations might be about Charles, to Lillian there had never been a man who could compare to her late husband. Their relationship had apparently been a great love match, and Charles had worshiped her.

"Tell me," she teased the widow. "Have you got any other Kingsley men up your sleeve?" She edged away from the window.

Lillian's merriment immediately vanished, and she took a step forward. "Sara, there's something—"

Lillian never got to finish the sentence. Sara heard the shattering of glass behind her as if in a dream, felt the whistling of a bullet graze her ear, saw Lillian's blanching face and the cane toppling.

' "Lillian," she screamed, diving protectively toward the older woman, but it was too late. Lillian was falling, her pink-and-gray-print dress swirling in a drift of color.

Sara's strong arms reached out for her, catching the small body in her embrace.

"Lillian," she screamed again. "Oh, my God!"

STANDING BESIDE LILLIAN'S BED, Ben was shocked into silence.

"No," he finally managed to whisper.

Lillian lay against the pillows, her pale skin almost translucent in the dim light. He held his breath.

A pair of blue eyes opened and flashed at him. "Sara doesn't need to know I'm not dead, until the very last minute," Lillian was repeating for the tenth time, her voice tinged with irritation.

"You'll end up dead for sure, if you insist on going ahead with this scheme," Ben warned her. "It's preposterous. And it's not fair to Sara. You're endangering her life without her knowledge. I won't allow it. It's too dangerous."

"Fiddlesticks!"

"What am I supposed to tell her? She knows the bullet missed you. She was standing right there!"

"Tell her the shock was too much for me, and I had a heart attack.... Oh, I don't care...make something up...but just do it!"

Ben's fists clenched at his sides. He could barely contain his rage. Of all Lillian's harebrained schemes, this was the most ridiculous one yet. She couldn't be serious! But one look at his old friend told him that that was a vain hope.

Lillian's face was a steely mask of feathery lines, showing her years—and her willfulness. He'd never met a more beautiful woman, or a more outrageous one.

"Is it illegal?" she snapped.

"It certainly is," he retorted. "It's public mischief."

"But why?" she insisted imperiously. "We're not hurting anyone." Her blue eyes narrowed to brilliant sapphire slits.

Ben groaned inwardly. Lillian thought she was a law unto herself.

"It isn't even moral," he countered. "To pretend that you're dead in order not to be a walking target anymore is bad enough, but to propose that Sara be named your beneficiary so that she becomes the target is totally irresponsible in my opinion. And not to tell her... Why—" he suppressed a gasp "—it's downright obscene."

Lillian dismissed his argument airily. "If the criminals think Sara has the formula, they'll come after her. With me out of the way, she'll have a much better chance of catching them."

Ben groaned this time, not bothering to hide his reaction from Lillian. She was so incredibly naive, it took his breath away. "I can't..." he started.

"Oh, for heaven's sake, Ben. Stop being a little old lady. You haven't answered my question. Why is it public mischief?"

Ben sighed audibly, pulling up a chair to sit next to her. He leaned his elbows on the edge of the bed. "The law states, and I quote—" he raised a silver eyebrow at her over his metal-framed glasses "—everyone commits public mischief, who, with intent to mislead, causes a police officer to enter, or continue an investigation, by reporting or, in any other way, making it known or causing it to be made known..." He tapped his fingers on the bed at the irritated look on her face. "Are you listening, Lillian?" She scowled at him, but nodded, and he continued, "...that he or some other person has died, when he or that other person has *not* died."

"So, it's not an offense," she replied in triumph, twisting her patrician head toward him. The blue satin pillowcases accentuated her deceptively soft feminine appeal.

"How do you figure that?" he asked, wondering at his own wisdom in even posing the question.

"Because we're not causing a police investigation. We're only pretending I'm dead so I can have some freedom from all these attempts to kidnap me and so that Sara can catch the criminals."

Ben gritted his teeth. "There will be a police investigation when the whole thing backfires," he warned.

"There won't be," Lillian answered with an emphatic nod of her head. "Sara will be successful...."

"How can you be sure? Your reasoning is ridiculous!" Ben flashed his stubborn client an indignant look. "The whole plan is risky, irresponsible and totally unconventional."

Lillian harrumphed, waving his objection aside with a heavily bejeweled hand. "That doesn't bother me."

"Obviously." He didn't need to be reminded that, where Lillian was concerned, convention was a totally alien concept. "But if I might ask," he continued in a dry voice, "just how were you planning to convince an undertaker to supply an empty casket?"

"Well, I can't very well do it," she retorted. "I'll be dead. You'll have to do it."

"Me?" His eyes widened with incredulity.

"Yes, you," Lillian replied as if talking to a particularly difficult child. "Don't you have friends in the underworld?"

"For God's sake, Lillian," he roared. "I'm a family lawyer, not F. Lee Bailey."

"I can't do it alone, Ben," Lillian persisted, her voice rising. "I need your help."

"Sanction, you mean," he responded with sarcasm.

His mind raced. As the acknowledged heiress to the Kingsley fortune, Sara would be in terrible jeopardy. In the past year or so, he'd grown quite fond of Sara, admiring her independence, her courage and perhaps most of all her loyalty to Lillian. There was a refreshing straightforwardness about her that he found appealing. She deserved better than this charade.

Damn Charles Kingsley, anyway. The eccentric, arrogant millionaire had really done it this time.

Had he really believed that the wall of secrecy surrounding the formula would protect Lillian? If he had, he'd been wrong. Lillian had become a sitting duck. Now Sara would be one. His eyes shadowed over as he considered the risk.

"Sara . . ." he began.

"... will understand," Lillian announced with utmost confidence.

"Then why don't we tell her?"

"Because I don't want to implicate her."

Ben looked at her, astounded. *The woman is impossible,* he thought in exasperation. Sara would be implicated *after* the fact, anyway. Before or after, it was all the same thing. But Ben knew it was useless to argue that fine point with Lillian. She possessed a fuzzy, determined logic that was distinctly her own. She'd been indulged too much, too often, by Charles Kingsley, he thought with a sinking feeling.

He doubted Sara would understand. Would anyone who was put into that position? And what about the coroner's report and the death certificate? He pulled himself up short. He couldn't seriously be considering this, could he?

Lillian drummed her fingers on the sheet in a staccato rhythm, watching him relentlessly. "Well, Ben?" she challenged.

He swallowed hard. Always with Lillian, he had the distinct sensation of being a mouse in the jaws of a proud, playful cat. He supposed that was why he had never proposed to her as a young man.

"I'm thinking..." he answered slowly.

Lillian arched her eyebrows in a seductive curve. "It'll be easy—not difficult at all," she started in a coaxing voice. "All you have to do..."

Chapter Two

Sara's gloved hand rested on the doorknob of the library. She still couldn't believe that Lillian had died of a heart attack in the night following the attempt on her life. Her eyes saddened with the unjustness of it. The bullet had missed both of them, yet still Lillian was gone.

The shock, Ben had told her. It had all happened so quickly. As soon as Ben heard the shot, he'd come running upstairs and taken the shaken Lillian to her room. Then he'd called the family doctor and the York Regional Police, while Sara rushed outside in futile pursuit of the armed intruder. When the police arrived, she'd given them a report, accompanied them on their search and then returned to the house. For a few brief moments, she'd looked in on Lillian, who appeared to be sleeping quietly. The widow had been sedated, Ben told her, and then he'd insisted that Sara rest. Exhausted, she'd fallen into bed, only to awake at her usual 6:00 a.m. Padding down the stairs to check on Lillian, she'd been greeted by a subdued Ben. Lillian had died in the night, he'd said, going on to explain to Sara that her body had already been removed from the estate.

Shock had stunned her, then anger and hurt that Ben hadn't wakened her. Then the grieving had begun, and when Ben told her gently that he'd taken care of everything, she'd nodded, unable to speak.

Later, Ben had said something about an inheritance, but she hadn't paid much attention. What value was money if Lillian was dead? Could she have done anything to prevent what had happened? The question tortured her throughout the sleepless night.

In the morning, Ben wanted to see her. It was half an hour to the funeral. She'd been pacing the house in her black boots and black raincoat for about an hour.

Reluctantly, she turned the knob. Discussions about money rarely interested her, but today she had a real aversion to the topic. Nevertheless, Ben had insisted that they talk.

The lawyer, dressed in a suit, beautifully tailored to his still-trim, tall figure, stood up hastily as she entered the room. She could see he'd been sitting in the plush, burgundy armchair by the fireplace. Behind him, at an angle to the left, the high Tudor windows let in a dull light. A low fire smoldered in the grate.

"Hello, Sara." Lines of anxiety creased around his mouth as he spoke.

"Ben," she acknowledged, drawing closer and attempting a wan smile. Removing one glove, she held out a hand. "How are you?"

"Fine, Sara... Just fine..." His voice sounded odd, his manner distracted, and he seemed to look past her. "Would you mind closing the door for a moment, Sara? There...there's something Lillian wanted me to tell you...."

SARA STOOD BY THE GRAVE, replaying in her mind what Ben had told her in the library. She was participating in a funeral that wasn't a funeral, an heiress to a fortune she hadn't inherited, saying farewell to a woman who was very much alive.

What was she doing here? The situation was ludicrous. Unthinkable. Even for Lillian.

Now, as a light drizzle blurred the background surroundings, the truth of it all hit home.

Lillian had, in effect, forced Sara into exchanging roles with her. Instead of being the protector, she was now the target. It was disturbing, frightening. Sara was not afraid for herself. She was a trained professional and, for a police officer's daughter, danger was part of life, familiar, something to be faced daily. No, her real concern was for Lillian.

The potential for this scheme to blow up in their faces was enormous. Lillian might well have gambled away what little safety she'd had before!

And the legalities! God, she couldn't even think about them. Borderline, Ben had told her. *You bet,* she thought angrily. Don't worry, he'd reassured, once we cross those boundaries, we'll go to the police. *If they don't get to us first,* she thought ruefully.

Ironically though, the situation made a certain bizarre sense.

It wouldn't be the first time in her professional life that she'd been called upon to act as a decoy.

It just might work, she thought.

Beside her, Ben fidgeted, clearing his throat with a nervous cough. The sound brought her sharply back to the scene. She threw him a quick questioning glance. How had Ben, conservative, respectable, upholder of the law, allowed himself to be swayed by Lillian?

In the past two days, grief had shrouded Sara, robbing her of her gift for wary watchfulness. The daze she'd been in had made it possible for Ben to spirit Lillian out of the estate, arrange a mock funeral and let it be known that

Sara was to inherit the entire Kingsley fortune. Had Lillian written a will naming Sara as her beneficiary? She hadn't bothered to ask, but it seemed unlikely. Ben wouldn't want to create any more legal entanglements than were absolutely necessary. He'd said he would tell everyone Sara was to inherit, and the kidnappers, since they were obviously sufficiently aware of the activities of the household to be able to take a shot at Lillian, would get the message, he'd reasoned.

Sara sighed in resignation. She hadn't been the least bit suspicious of Ben's activities in the past couple of days. Lillian's passing had seemed so quick! Now, she knew why. God, she'd been naive.

Damn Lillian and her theatrics. Sara inhaled deeply to control a fresh wave of anger surging through her. She had no choice except to play the scene as written. But at least she could play it as a professional.

Sara looked around at the small group of mourners who had elected to make the trip to the Aurora Cemetery at the southern limits of the town. The secrecy that cloaked Charles's formula convinced Sara that whoever was after it had to be a friend of the family or a colleague. Someone who had had access to Charles.

Her gaze narrowed. Was that person here today? Or deliberately absent?

She surveyed the handful of people standing in respectful silence around her.

Graham Marshall. The middle-aged scientist who had purchased Kingsley Chemicals when Lillian had sold the company. Had he expected to find the formula in Charles's files when he took over, only to discover that Lillian had it?

Tess Bond. Lillian's blowsy-looking friend with the outlandish red-tinted hair. What motive could she possibly have?

Gertrude Cunningham. Ramrod-straight. Charles's secretary for twenty-five years. Privy to most of Charles's confidential business. Lillian had been barely able to tolerate her and the feeling had been mutual.

Three distinguished-looking gentlemen, all of them about Lillian's vintage, stood together. Ex-suitors, Ben had whispered to her in the chapel with a pained expression on his face. *Not bad,* Sara silently complimented the foxy Lillian.

A slim man in his thirties with rumpled clothes. A man she didn't recognize. Features that weren't memorable, except for a pair of penetrating blue eyes that reminded her of Lillian.

Members of Lillian's household staff. A wave of irritation with Lillian swept over Sara. This ruse was totally unfair to them!

And next . . . her gaze moved to a man who stood alone, a distance away from everyone. Why hadn't she seen him before at the chapel? Her gaze froze, locking with his stare, and for a moment, she felt riveted to the wet earth. The fierce, black eyes that bore into her raked her whole body from the tip of her head to her high black boots. The man took his time, making a thorough investigation, lingering at her cinched waist before looking away in outright disdain.

Sara was totally taken aback by the disgust she read on his face before he glanced away. Taken aback and affronted. *How dare he? What was that all about?* she thought, a quick flash of anger heightening her color. Then she recovered. The situation Lillian had put her in left no room for personal feelings.

Who was he? A wild card in a deck of suspects?

She took advantage of the man's shift in attention to give him a going-over of her own. If he could be thorough so could she.

In his mid-thirties, the man was tall, rugged, with massive shoulders stretched taut beneath his navy trench coat. The coat looked disreputable and frayed, its belt jammed tightly into a careless knot. Untamed hair, a mahogany-black, curled on his forehead with the dampness. He conveyed an unbridled anger, emphasized by the square thrust of his jaw, his high proud cheekbones and his arrogant stance. His hands were shoved impatiently into oversize pockets.

The man was dynamite, ready to explode. A sudden warmth rushed through her. *Get too close to him, and you'll get burned for sure,* she warned herself, gulping a deep breath of cool air and forcing herself to look away.

She sensed movement around her. The funeral was over. In seconds, the still tableau of mourners had broken into motion, and people began heading toward her and Ben.

Before anyone had reached them, Ben whispered in her ear, "You won't give us away, will you?"

Sara shook her head. As tempted as she was to call a halt to the charade, she didn't want to let Lillian and Ben down, although privately she felt a growing urge to tear a strip off Lillian—especially now, as she'd have to actively participate in the deception.

"Good," he murmured, a look of relief on his face. His cultured voice then redirected itself toward the woman who planted herself firmly in front of him. "Hello, Gertrude," he acknowledged. "Thank you for coming."

Sara glanced quickly in the direction of the stranger. The area where he'd been standing was deserted. He'd disappeared.

Damn. She compressed her lips. *I hope Ben saw him before he left.*

One of Lillian's ex-suitors materialized in the rain in front of her. "I'm Shane Cameron," he introduced himself with a sad smile. "A friend of Lillian's. I understand you were really close to her. Allow me to express my sympathy.''

"Thank you, Mr. Cameron." She returned his concern with a soft smile of her own. The slim, well-dressed man was courtly and charming, the grace of another era sitting on his shoulders.

"Had you known Lillian a long time?" she asked, thinking the question innocuous enough. The less fabrication she had to get into, the better.

"We grew up together. All of us." He waved toward the other two suitors, who were chatting earnestly by one of the oak trees. Catching his gesture, they broke off their conversation and headed toward the couple. "Mind you," Shane said, twisting to face Sara with gentlemanly grace, "I haven't seen Lillian in years. She was quite the woman," he added with a wistful note in his voice. "Her heart, was it?" he prompted gently.

Sara suppressed a grimace. Lord, she hated lying. "Something like that," she allowed vaguely, inclining her head toward the two men who now stood about three feet away from them.

"What a shame," Shane clucked. "To think that Lillian didn't have a strong heart, after all these years." He broke off to acknowledge the presence of his friends. "Sara, Martin Howard and Graydon Lewis."

"Miss Brennan." Martin, a portly man, taller than Shane, took her hand in a firm grasp. "I'm terribly sorry." His voice booming, he raised bushy silver eyebrows at her.

Sara nodded imperceptibly, turning to glance at the third man. Classically handsome, he reminded her of Douglas Fairbanks.

"Lillian is a loss to all of us," he told her sympathetically.

Sara was about to respond when Gertrude suddenly nudged her way between the men and Sara.

"Well," she said, straightening herself to her full height of six feet, "your time in Lillian's employ paid off handsomely, didn't it, Miss Brennan? It looks like you're going to be a very wealthy woman."

Beside Sara, Shane coughed nervously. Sara's eyes widened at Gertrude's bluntness, then she checked herself. Wasn't this what Lillian and Ben wanted? For people to think she had inherited the Kingsley fortune—and the formula.

She couldn't very well correct Gertrude without undermining the scheme. "It looks that way," she finally answered in a noncommittal voice.

"Good luck to you then," Gertrude sniffed. With a curt nod, she made an abrupt departure. After a few more sympathetic words, so too did Shane, Martin and Graydon.

For about five minutes more, Sara accepted condolences from the other mourners.

Graham Marshall and his wife, Nancy, seemed genuinely upset by Lillian's death. Tess, after monopolizing Ben for some time, managed a few distracted comments. Then at last Sara and Ben were left alone in the cemetery.

"Phew, thank God, that's over." Sara breathed a sigh of relief.

"You can say that again!" Ben whistled uncharacteristically. He gave his watch an anxious twist, checking the time. "I've got to drop in on Lillian. She'll want to know what's happened." His whistle deteriorated into a long sigh. "Patience isn't one of her virtues."

Name me something that is, Sara was tempted to reply, but nodded her head instead. Ben had sequestered Lillian in a condominium he owned in downtown Toronto. "But we'd better talk after that, Ben. Anyone here today could be a suspect." Her hand caught her sleeve. "And I'm not convinced that this plan of Lillian's is the best way to draw that person out."

Ben's brow furrowed into worry lines. "I tend to think you're right. Oh, damn, I should never have agreed with Lillian...." He raised his eyebrows apologetically. "I did try to talk Lillian out of it, believe me, Sara, I did...." His voice trailed with guilt.

Hearing the anxiety in his tone, Sara squeezed his arm for reassurance. "I'm sure you did, Ben."

"Please, Sara. Be careful. From now on, the criminals will be after you."

She forced an optimistic note into her voice. "I'll be fine, Ben. Don't worry about me. I can take care of myself.... By the way," she added, suddenly remembering, "did you happen to see the dark man in the navy trench coat at the funeral?"

Ben gave her a puzzled look, poised in a half turn to leave. "No, I can't say I did. I'll talk to you later, Sara." With a preoccupied look on his face, he disappeared into the mist.

Watching him leave, Sara suddenly felt extremely tired. She'd parked in a different drive, opposite to where Ben was headed. She turned away and walked toward her sports car, lost in thought.

There were so many questions she hadn't had a chance to ask Ben. According to the Vital Statistics Act, every death had to be registered and the certificate signed by a doctor. How had Ben managed that? How could you have a funeral without a body?

As her black-booted feet sloshed through the soft earth and the puddles, Sara shook her head and smiled. Ben's masterminding this event had its humorous side, she had to admit.

The whole plan was insane!

"You might well smile."

Sara jumped, almost losing her balance on the slippery pathway at the sound of the sarcastic voice. She'd had her head down; now she looked up in chilling surprise.

The stranger from the cemetery was leaning insolently against the hood of her blue M.G.

She did a double take. Up close, he was remarkably, if unconventionally, attractive. The strong planes accentuated the square-cut structures of his face. She suspected he might be younger than he looked, but that disillusionment had weathered his features. She'd seen that look before on seasoned cops.

Slouched, his body emitted a coiled energy. As she met his gaze, his eyes bored into hers beneath thick brows. Seeming almost black with smoldering intensity, his eyes were a deep, rich brown.

Recalling his earlier look of disdain, Sara's own gaze turned stormy. Tough men didn't intimidate her. She'd known too many, friends of her father's, from the Toronto police force. But she wasn't stupid, either. She had a wary respect for all powerful creatures—man or beast.

"I don't know what you're talking about," she replied in a haughty voice.

A brow twitched in derision. "Come now, Miss Bodyguard. No need to play coy with me."

Sara eyed him carefully, her instincts sending a message of danger to her brain. *Take it easy,* she cautioned herself. *Whatever this man's game is, he's lethal, and plays to win.*

She dismissed him with an icy glare. "I still don't know what you're talking about."

He gave a rough laugh. It seemed to come from deep inside him. "No? Then why are you smiling? Hardly appropriate after a funeral, is it?" His mouth twisted into a sardonic curve.

"I don't think that's any of your business," she replied, sidestepping the question and daring to give him another scathing once-over.

"I'm making it my business," he retorted, his voice tight with anger. Then his gaze narrowed, fanning lines toward his temples.

"Tell me, Miss Bodyguard, just how easy was it to kill the old lady?"

Chapter Three

Sara gasped. "I didn't kill Lillian Kingsley."

"No?" He hunched his shoulders in disbelief, sending a spray of raindrops off his coat.

"No," she retorted angrily, planting her feet firmly on the ground to face him. He didn't move. He just stared at her. *Who the hell is he?* The question was on the tip of her tongue, when a volley of words came lashing back at her.

"Then how come she left everything to you? Loosen up, Sara Brennan, you can tell me.... A frail little old lady, you're assigned to protect...you wheedle your way into her affections, and then decide to send her on a permanent trip, after she'd written a will in your favor, of course."

"That's ridiculous!"

"Is it?" An ominous laugh rumbled deep in his chest. "For a professional, it must have been child's play. Was it, Sara Brennan? Was it child's play?" Suddenly, the still tension of his body erupted, and he thrust himself from the car, his hands biting into her shoulders in a viselike grip. He began to shake her. "Well, aren't you going to tell me?" he growled.

"Take your hands off me," Sara flashed. The man was either an idiot or fearless. He'd already admitted he knew she was a bodyguard. Did he think she wouldn't defend herself?

"Not until you answer my question." The man pulled her closer, his grasp tightening. "Tell me, Sara."

His breath blew hot against her face. The warmth was almost intoxicating. She struggled again, but managed only to wedge her body more tightly against his. The intimacy seemed to restrain her, the smell of rain on his coat and skin to calm and fascinate her. "Who are you? And how do you know my name?" she challenged, stilled momentarily by the closeness.

A bitter amusement shadowed his eyes, but he retained his grip. He ignored her first question. "Oh, I know a lot about you," he said with a soft mysterious undercurrent. "More than just your name."

All the time he'd been talking, something had been bothering her about his voice. Then she realized what it was. An accent. A slight one, but there nevertheless. Australian? New Zealander? She concentrated on it. So far, it was the only clue she had as to who he might be. He certainly wasn't volunteering any other information about himself.

"How?" she managed, stalling for time.

"I went out to the Kingsley estate," he answered with infuriating nonchalance.

"You spied on us?" she responded, suddenly wary. Was he after the formula?

"Hardly." He grinned, showing even white teeth. The contrast against his tanned skin was startling, but the smile softened him, made him seem younger and less formidable.

Tanned? Why hadn't she noticed that before? The man was deeply bronzed, not like someone who had spent two weeks at an island resort, but like someone who had spent months outdoors, perhaps even years. Intrigued, she stared at him, then her gaze turned icy at his easy dismissal of her accusation. "What would you call it, if not spying?"

"You'd be surprised," he answered cryptically, trailing a finger along the curve of her face.

The man was playing with her. She didn't like that one little bit. "Don't touch me," she warned, pulling back, her shoulders squaring in anticipation of some kind of attack. *If he doesn't tell me who he is, I won't be held accountable for what happens,* she thought angrily. She gave her arm a jerk.

But even his one-hand grasp held her fast. "Not until I get some answers," he threatened, vising his fingers into her arm.

Sara winced, then decided she'd had enough. In a smooth sweep, she raised her arm, leveled her hand into a straight flat line and aimed it at his neck. His eyes flashed and he ducked to the side, just in time. Her hand sliced against empty air.

Straightening up, he laughed, his eyes flashing with admiration. "Not bad, Sara. Not bad at all. You're quite beautiful when you're mad, you know. A real hellcat. So, there's another side to the cold-blooded killer!"

Sara's chest heaved with the frustration of wasted exertion. "I'm not a killer," she protested, her voice rising. She wished he would stop staring at her that way. The cold intensity in his eyes seemed to drain her of the desire to fight. His watchfulness put her in mind of a stronger confident predator.

"You can tell that to the police."

Fear threaded through her. If the police became involved, Lillian and Ben would be charged with public mischief. Not only that, Lillian would be the target again. She couldn't let that happen. Then a chilling thought struck her. Maybe he was the police, and it was already too late.

"Is that what you are?" she asked in a subdued voice. "Are you a cop?"

"No," he answered, his tone brusque. "I'm not a cop, but that doesn't change anything. You're not going to get away with this. I'm going to see that you get everything that's coming to you."

"Please," she attempted, her concern for Lillian overriding her anger and her pride. "You don't understand.... You mustn't go to the police." Her hand reached out to grasp his arm.

He shrugged out of her grip with distaste, the power behind his gesture throwing her off balance. "You're disgusting," he spit.

Sara righted herself with frantic speed, her mind racing. As ridiculous as Lillian's plan was, she couldn't let him jeopardize it—not yet. All they needed was a little time. "You have no evidence to take to the police," she challenged, trying to dissuade him.

He jammed his hands into his coat pockets the way he'd done at the graveside, and straightening his shoulders, towered over her, looking down. "You had opportunity. And motive," he responded.

Sara could feel her composure slipping. How could she tell him there was no motive because there was no crime? Because Lillian was alive. Damn it all. How was she going to stop this raging bull from upsetting Lillian's scheme?

"What kind of motive?" she retorted, thrusting her own hands into her pockets.

He shrugged. "Money. People have been known to kill for greed, quite frequently, I understand."

"I have money of my own," she responded quickly.

A wry smile tugged at the corners of his mouth. "Oh, I know about that. Your father, although he was a deputy police chief, made some pretty tidy investments in his day, and left them to his only daughter."

Sara stared in silence. How much *did* he know about her? Apparently not only his physical appraisal of her in the cemetery had been thorough.

He went on talking. "And I presume you got a hefty settlement from that corporate rich boy you divorced." There was no mistaking the sneer on his face.

Sara was totally nonplussed. Well, he was wrong about one thing. She hadn't taken a cent from her ex-husband. Derek's mindless pursuit of money had been one of the causes of their separation. She was about to tell this man so in no uncertain terms, when his voice cut into her thoughts again.

". . . but your inheritance and divorce settlement could hardly compare to the Kingsley money or the proceeds the formula will bring you. I suspect the money you have only whetted your appetite for more," he finished in the same condemning vein.

Sara barely heard this final insult. Something else he'd said bothered her far more. The formula. He thought she had it. Had Lillian's ruse paid off so soon?

"What formula?" she managed, feigning innocence.

"Forget it, Sara," he snapped. "I know Charles Kingsley bequeathed the formula to Lillian. In all probability, if she left you everything else, she also passed the formula on to you as well."

"And I suppose you want it?" She arched her eyebrows at him in calculation.

"What difference does it make?" He shrugged again. "But as a matter of fact, yes. I'm very interested in the formula."

His attitude surprised her. To her, it made a hell of a lot of difference if he wanted the formula, she thought. But he didn't appear to be preparing to kidnap her. So far all he'd done was challenge her. Her eyes clouded with confusion. If he thought she had the formula and he wanted it, why wasn't he making a move? Just who was he? Only one way to find out. Raising her eyes to his, she asked bluntly, "Who the hell are you?"

For a moment, she thought he wasn't going to respond. Then he met her challenge with piercing eyes. "I'm Nicholas Kingsley."

"Kingsley?" she repeated, giving him a blank stare.

"Yes, Kingsley. As in Charles and Lillian Kingsley."

Sara went rigid. Lillian had never mentioned any living relatives. She struggled to capture an elusive image in her head. Suddenly, it materialized...the picture of a blue box of toys....

Her gaze fastened on his, incredulous. "Their son?"

"Nephew," he corrected.

Confusion bubbled in her brain. "Lillian never..." she began.

"...told you about me, I'll bet," he finished for her, giving a hoarse laugh. "There are reasons for that, but right now, they don't matter."

Sara tensed with suspicion. "How do I know you're telling the truth?"

He heaved his huge shoulders with a shrug of unconcern. "You don't, but I can prove it, if I have to."

Sara's hands clenched inside her pockets. If he was Lillian's nephew, perhaps she should tell him Lillian was alive. But Lillian had never mentioned a Nicholas Kingsley. Suddenly, the importance of Lillian's will struck her with compelling clarity. If there wasn't one, Ben would be under suspicion and the police might suspect a conspiracy. He'd told everyone that Sara was to inherit. If a will written by Lillian, naming Sara as the beneficiary, did exist, Nick would contest it, and it would prove she had motive for killing Lillian. *For God's sake, Sara! Lillian isn't dead, remember?* Sara slanted her gaze at Nick again. Why hadn't Lillian ever mentioned him? Hadn't she once asked Lillian if there were any other Kingsley men? What was it Lillian had said? In the confusion of the moment, the answer eluded her.

A wary light flecked her eyes with gray. "You never came to the estate. Why not, if you're Lillian's nephew?"

"I told you, that doesn't matter right now," he answered with irritation. "*I* don't matter at the moment. In fact, I'm quite irrelevant. You're the one who's important. You're a murderess and I intend to prove it."

So, they'd come full circle. "And how do you plan to do that?" she asked, sounding a lot cockier than she felt. Maybe there was something she could do to head him off...to stall him until she'd had a chance to discuss him with Lillian. Suddenly, she was anxious. The faster she could talk to Lillian, the better.

"I'm sure once I go to the police, the coroner will request an autopsy."

"Autopsy?" The word caught in her throat. Then she cursed her own stupidity. Of course, that was exactly what would happen. But to have an autopsy you had to have a body, and there wasn't one. Her mind raced. How long would it take for the police to contact the coroner? A phone call was all it would take—but if the police didn't act automatically on Nicholas Kingsley's suspicions, she might just have enough time to talk to Lillian and get this whole thing resolved. If she could get to Lillian quickly enough...

Relaxing a fraction, she allowed herself a small smile. "Be my guest. But let me assure you, you're not going to find anything." At least that much was true, she thought.

Nicholas, catching the smile, misinterpreted it. "If you think you're going to have enough time to remove the evidence, don't count on it, Sara." The threat was brisk.

Sara's smile vanished. "Remove...?" What was he talking about?

"Yes, get rid of the body, so we can't check what you used to murder Lillian."

Sara groaned inwardly. Lord, there was no way to win this one. Then her resolve strengthened. It would never come to that, she was sure. Out loud, she said with as much confidence as she could muster, "I somehow don't think I'll be doing that, Mr. Kingsley."

She leveled a direct gaze at him. He returned her stare for a long time, his eyes penetrating as if he were trying to make up his mind about something. They really were incredible, she thought, like a dark sea, flashing and stilling with lightning speed. Then a mask of reserve slid into place.

He stepped away from her and then paused, as though taking final stock of the situation.

"Call me Nick, Sara. I have a feeling we're going to be in some rough waters together."

CALL ME NICK.

That'll be the day, she fumed, marching into the quiet Kingsley mansion with a noisy sweep, the heavy mahogany door slamming behind her.

The arrogance of the man! Did he think he could scare her, push her around? That, too, would be the day, she seethed. Derek had been a crash course on unfeeling, assertive, know-it-all men, and after marriage to him she knew the subject cold. Nicholas Kingsley and Derek had different styles, but underneath, they were the same man. Exactly the same!

As if she would kill Lillian Kingsley. She had been paid to protect Lillian. *Sloppy research, Mr. Kingsley. Inconclusive evidence. You're a real bull of the woods—charge first and ask questions later.*

Why didn't you bother to really check me out? Better yet, maybe you should have interviewed my ex-husband. He thought I was a drudge, wasting my time on lost causes. That would have been an eye-opener for you.

If she hadn't have been so angry with Nick, the absurdity of his accusations compared to Derek's opinion of her might have made her laugh. But right now, her blood was boiling.

"Miss Brennan?" Edie Rohmer, the housekeeper, came bustling down the hallway, her hand outstretched to relieve Sara of the wet raincoat.

Sara shrugged herself out of it, trying to quiet her impatience. "Hi, Edie. Thanks."

She watched the neat, portly, woman toss the coat over her arm. "Would you like a bite to eat?"

Sara thought for a moment. Her encounter with Nick had destroyed any semblance of appetite. "Maybe just some tea," she replied, grateful for Edie's presence. Thank God, people like Edie still came to the door, offered to take your coat and asked if you were hungry. It restored Sara's faith in an ordinary and ordered world. Lillian's charade and Nick's turning up had almost made her forget that normal routines still existed.

"In the library?" Edie asked.

"Great." Sara nodded, thinking ahead to the phone calls she wanted to make. "By the way," she asked before Edie turned to leave. "Do you know a Nicholas Kingsley?"

A guarded expression crossed Edie's face. "Yes, Miss Brennan, I do."

"When was the last time you saw him?" Sara probed, watching Edie's face. The woman looked distinctly uncomfortable.

The housekeeper shrugged. "Eight or nine years ago. I'm not exactly sure."

"Didn't he come for Charles's funeral?"

Edie shook her head, a slight tinge of rose flushing her full cheeks. "No, but..." She stopped, her gaze flickering.

"But...?" Sara prodded gently.

"He was named in Mr. Charles's will."

Sara's eyes glinted with a curious light. "To inherit what?"

"I don't really know," Edie replied, obviously eager to be dismissed. "Perhaps Mr. Short knows," she offered hopefully.

"Yes, of course. He likely does," Sara agreed, not wishing to discomfit Edie any further. "Thanks very much, Edie."

The housekeeper's well-scrubbed face relaxed. "Will that be all?"

Sara nodded, still not accustomed to the deference with which Edie and the rest of the staff now treated her. Had she really inherited this estate, she doubted she'd ever be able to play the lady of the manor. And Nick Kingsley thought she was a gold digger!

"I'll be in the library," she told Edie.

Seconds later, when she reached the paneled room, she realized with pleasure that someone must have anticipated her arrival. A small fire burned in the grate. Sara had always experienced a sense of peace and permanence in this room. Today, she particularly appreciated its calming effect.

Edie served her tea almost immediately, and half an hour later she picked up the phone to dial the number of Ben's condominium.

The faster she could talk to Lillian and resolve what to do about Nicholas Kingsley, the better she'd like it.

Leaning her head against the receiver, Sara stared through the French doors leading to a small concrete courtyard while she counted the rings.

Ten. Eleven. Twelve. She sighed with impatience. *C'mon, Lillian. Where are you?*

Thirteen. Fourteen. She wouldn't be out, would she? Wasn't Ben visiting her?

Seventeen. Eighteen.

I can't believe this.

After twenty rings, she finally hung up and dialed Ben's home number, waiting while it rang four times. His answering machine clicked on. Damn. Her green eyes clouded. Where was everybody?

By NINE O'CLOCK the following morning, Sara was beginning to feel the panic gnaw at her. Nick could have already gone to the police.

She'd kept calling Lillian and Ben until the small hours of the morning. Neither of them had answered their phones. She'd dozed off and on, curled in a big easy chair, but the rest had been fitful and uncomfortable. Rubbing her aching muscles, she tried Lillian's number again. This time, she waited for thirty rings. Still no answer.

Worry creased her forehead. Even if Lillian had gone out, how likely was it she'd stay out all night? Holding her breath, she called Ben's office, impatiently drumming her fingers on the library desk as she successively went through two receptionists and one secretary before Ben's voice finally came on the line.

"Ben, where've you been?" she asked anxiously when the lawyer said hello.

"Sorry, Sara." She could almost see the sheepish expression on his face. "I felt like I needed to unwind, so I went out for a couple of drinks. I'm afraid I tied one on."

"*You*, Ben?" She couldn't mask the incredulity in her tone.

"I'm not totally without my wild side, you know," he answered in defense. "This whole thing is very taxing. I'm afraid I was a bit rattled this morning and hadn't had a chance to return your call."

"It's all right," Sara replied, not unkindly, now that she was over her surprise. Then, remembering the reason for her call, her voice became tense again, "Was Lillian with you? I've been trying to reach her, but there's no answer. Is there a phone by the bedside?"

The flurry of questions made him hesitate. "I visited Lillian for about half an hour, then I left. And yes, there is a phone by the bedside."

"Then why didn't she answer?"

"Probably went out," Ben offered.

"At midnight?"

There was a pause. "No, that doesn't sound likely, although you know how independent she is." He adopted a soothing tone. "I'm sure everything's okay. Do you want me to run over to the condo and check?"

"No, I'd better do it. It's vital that I talk to her."

"Why?" he asked, worry beginning to color his voice. "Has something come up?"

"Not something," Sara corrected. "Someone."

"Someone?"

"Nicholas Kingsley."

"Oh damn." She could hear a whoosh of air blurring the static on the line.

"You know him then?"

"Only too well."

"Well, I hope you're sitting down. He virtually accosted me after the funeral and accused me of murdering Lillian—"

"He what?" Ben roared.

"Accused me of murdering—" Sara began to repeat.

"That's the most insane thing I've ever heard," he cut her off angrily.

"He doesn't think so, and he's going to the police. You know what that means?"

"Oh, my God! Yes, I do. The coroner will be called in."

"And you and Lillian will be charged with public mischief, right? Isn't that what you said?"

"'Fraid so."

"But it's much more serious than that, Ben. Tell me, did Lillian write a will, actually naming me as the beneficiary?"

"Not that I know of."

Sara let out a sigh of relief. "Thank God for small mercies. At least there is no documented motive for my killing Lillian."

"Lillian isn't dead," Ben reminded her tersely.

"No, but Nick doesn't know that. Isn't he likely to call you and ask about the will? Wouldn't you think he'd want to contest it, if one did exist?"

"Yes," Ben admitted in gloomy tones. "To tell you the truth, Sara, neither I nor Lillian counted on Nick showing up. He's been gone for nine years...."

"Look, Ben, why don't we just tell him the truth?" she persuaded urgently.

"I'm not sure we can do that, Sara."

Sara leaned into the curve of the leather desk chair. "Why not?"

"Because Nick has always wanted the formula. He and Charles argued about it years ago, and when Charles wouldn't give it to him, he disappeared."

Sara paused, trying to understand. "But surely, he wouldn't hurt his own aunt to get it, would he? Do you think he's the one who's been after Lillian? He admitted to me that he suspects I have the formula. If he thinks that, why didn't he just go after me? He had a clear field yesterday. There was nobody around to stop him."

Ben hesitated and then said wearily, "I don't really know the answers to those questions, Sara. Anything the Kingsleys get involved in tends to get complicated, I'm afraid."

"Ben, how come I didn't know about Nick? You said he and Charles argued about the formula. I get the feeling I'm missing something here." The exasperation was clear in Sara's voice.

The lawyer sighed. "You're right, Sara. You don't know the whole story. I'd better give you the background. Charles had a twin brother, David, but unlike many twins they never got along. They started Kingsley Chemicals together, but eventually David couldn't stand any more of Charles's impossible arrogance. Charles wasn't a very nice person, you know, no matter what Lillian says."

"So, what happened?" Sara prompted.

"David went to Australia, bought a ranch and married a local woman, Faye. Nick was born, but six years later there was a fire, and David was killed in it. The following year, Faye, who had never been particularly strong, died."

Sara grew thoughtful. One mystery was solved—Nick's accent. "Nick was orphaned?" she posed.

"Yes. His only living relative was Charles, who sent for him. Not that Charles wanted him, but Nick was still a Kingsley. They were like two immovable objects, although I have to admit Charles treated the boy abominably. He was cold and unfeeling toward him. Nick grew up tough and untrusting. He rarely stayed in the mansion except to sleep. He preferred being outdoors, away from Charles."

Sara's eyelashes flickered. The box of toys. Abandoned by an isolated boy. Despite her anger, a wave of compassion for Nick washed over her.

She mentally shook it off, bringing herself back to the present to ask, "How does the formula enter all of this?"

"When David died, it turned out he was still part owner of Kingsley Chemicals. Nick inherited his shares. Against his better judgment, I think, Nick went to work for the company. He didn't really have a flair for the scientific side of the business, but even though he's personally very disorganized, he turned out to be a brilliant business administrator. Profits soared while he was there."

"And the formula?" Sara steered Ben back to the major issue.

"Charles personally invented it in a small lab adjoining his office, but some reason there was a delay in production. Apparently Nick, concerned about the delay, tried to steal it and set up his own company."

"But how could he do that if it was Charles's?"

"Well, actually, it wasn't Charles's, either. In corporations, it's common practice to sign a waver of ownership to anything you invent while working for the company. If companies didn't do that, then employees would be walking away with trade secrets, formulas, software packages, hardware inventions—you name it. And they'd be making fortunes on their own, without any of the investment. Kingsley Chemicals wasn't any different, so not only could Nick not spirit the formula out of the company, but for that matter, neither, legally, could Charles."

Something triggered in Sara's mind. "When Lillian sold the company, was Nick still an owner?"

"No, when the tensions between Charles and Nick reached a peak, Nick sold his shares in Kingsley Chemicals to Charles and moved back to Australia. I wasn't the corporate lawyer, but I understand, all from Charles, mind you, that when Nick sold to Charles, the selling price had something to do with the formula.''

''In what way?''

''I don't know, but there was a terrible screaming match. All Charles said to me, was, 'Well, the son of a bitch got what he wanted.'''

''Does that mean Nick got the formula?'' Sara asked, perplexed.

''I'm sure it doesn't.''

''What makes you so sure?''

''When I called to tell him about his uncle's death, he asked about the formula, and was furious when I told him he hadn't inherited it.''

As Sara tried to make sense of what Ben was telling her, she ran a hand across her brow. ''Let me get this straight. Charles and Nick jointly owned Kingsley Chemicals. Nick tried to steal a formula invented by Charles. Charles stopped him, and Nick sold his ownership in the company to Charles, in exchange for an agreement about the formula.''

''That's right.''

''Then doesn't it seem possible,'' she posed the question uppermost in her mind, ''that the agreement about the formula was that Nick would inherit it on Charles's death? And that Charles didn't keep his promise, but instead left it to Lillian. Nick probably still feels he has a right to it.''

''The scenario's possible,'' Ben admitted.

Things are starting to fall into place, Sara thought. *If Nick believes that Lillian had given the formula to me, wouldn't he feel like he'd been cheated out of what was rightly his twice? No wonder he's been so hostile toward me.* ''Do you really think that all along Nick has been trying to kidnap his own aunt to secure the formula?''

"Depends on how long he's been back in the country, although I suppose he could have hired a couple of thugs to do his dirty work. But, no, to answer your question. Somehow that style isn't consistent with his personality. Not that he isn't tough enough, but he was never underhanded. I also doubt very much that he would hurt Lillian or torment her in any way. Even though she did nothing to ease the tensions between Charles and Nick, he was always quite fond of her—indulgent, even."

"Then we could be dealing with two sets of problems: the people who have been after Lillian, and now, Nicholas Kingsley."

"Yes, but I haven't a clue who else might be mixed up in this."

Sara gave a dry laugh. "Try Gertrude Cunningham on for size. She practically called me an adventuress to my face."

"That's because as Charles's secretary, she'd always expected to receive some kind of bequest on his death, and didn't."

"Tess Bond," Sara offered, recalling Lillian's red-haired friend, who had monopolized Ben at the funeral.

There was silence at the other end. An imperceptible pause. Sara waited. Finally Ben answered. "I don't know what motive she could possibly have. Who else?"

"Shane Cameron, Martin Howard and Graydon Lewis," she replied, naming Lillian's three ex-suitors.

"*Dr.* Graydon Lewis," Ben corrected.

Sara filed away the correction for what it was worth, then questioned, "How about the young man with the blue eyes? I didn't know him."

"Larry Worth," Ben supplied. "He's a chemist who works for Kingsley Chemicals. As a matter of fact, he asked me what had happened to the formula."

"He did?" Sara was surprised that he'd even known about the formula.

"In my mind, that makes him a prime suspect," Ben was saying.

"Or maybe not," Sara replied thoughtfully. "Why would he take a chance alerting anyone's suspicions?" she mused out loud, then came back to a more pressing reality. "Ben , we've go to do something about Nick. I'd better get over to the condo and talk to Lillian."

"I agree." She thought Ben was about to hang up, then she heard him clear his throat with a short cough. "Sara, there's something I haven't told you."

Now what?

She quickened to attention. "Which is?" she prompted.

Ben seemed to be selecting his words with care. "When Charles died, Nick didn't inherit the formula, it's true. But he did inherit something."

Sara suddenly had a chilling certainty that whatever it was would have serious implications for her. Keeping her tone level, she directed, "You'd better tell me what it is."

Ben stumbled over his words. "The Kingsley estate."

"But Lillian—" she protested.

". . . is to be allowed to live there in perpetuity, according to the terms of Charles's will," Ben completed for her.

"I don't understand."

At the other end of the wire, she could hear Ben taking a deep breath. "When Charles died, the only thing he left to Nick was the estate itself—the grounds and the house. Charles was—how shall I put it?—chauvinistic. He believed land and houses should belong to men, so he left them to Nick. But I think he also had an ulterior motive. I think he was concerned about Lillian living alone, without a man, so he probably assumed that if he left the land and house to Nick, his nephew would come back to Canada and look after her. Of course, he was too stubborn to let Nick know in advance, and Lillian was too proud to ask. So, Nick never did come back.''

"Do you suppose he would have?" Sara asked. "Did Lillian ever hint to you that's what she wanted?"

"Oh, no, her highness has too much independence for that, but I suspect if she had, he would have. Nick's a lot of things, but he's not selfish. Anyway, to get back to the inheritance, the actual possessions in the house—the art and the furnishings—Charles left to Lillian. Those he considered fripperies, mere decoration. But now that Nick is here, he has every right to move into the estate, and if I don't miss my guess—" he paused, his voice dropping "—I think he will. God help you."

Chapter Four

Sara's mind raced. Nick Kingsley living here? Her pulse quickened inexplicably.

"If Nick owns the actual estate itself, exactly what am I supposed to have inherited?" Sara asked dryly.

"Everything else," came Ben's prompt reply. "Lillian and I didn't go into any details because there didn't appear to be any need. But she has millions of dollars in investments and other properties—the art collection in the house would be worth millions—and of course, we wanted people to believe you inherited the formula."

Sara's brow furrowed in concentration. "Doesn't it seem strange to you that Nick hasn't contacted you? Wouldn't he want to establish his claim on Lillian's assets? Maybe even contest the will?"

"Yes to all three. It does seem strange. I can only hope, though, that by the time he decides to contest the will, all of this nonsense with the formula and Lillian will be over and he and Lillian can sort it out between them, without either of us having to be involved."

"But if he wants the formula..." Sara mused out loud.

"Then it's a real mess," Ben said.

That's the understatement of the year, Sara thought, biting her lower lip. Then another thought occurred to her. "Why do you suppose Nick happened to come back just when Lillian had died? After all, he's been gone for nine years.''

A grim silence greeted her. ''Ben,'' she prompted.

The lawyer's voice suddenly sounded tired. ''The only reason I can think of is that someone called him and told him.''

Sara gasped. ''Of course, a partner! Whoever's been trying to kidnap Lillian might be in partnership with Nick.''

''I don't know, Sara,'' Ben said, sighing. ''I just don't know.''

That would explain a lot, she thought quickly. Or was she being too suspicious for her own good?

Her mind returned to the more immediate problem of Nick's ownership of the estate. As the rightful resident, so to speak, wouldn't he consider her an intruder? She said as much to Ben. ''Since I have no legal right to be here, won't Nick expect me to leave?''

Ben dismissed her question in a sharp tone. ''He might. But if I were you, I wouldn't. I think it's important that you be in a position to know what he's up to. Anyway, I seriously doubt he'll ask you to go.''

Recalling the animosity Nick had shown toward her, Sara thought Ben was underestimating the lengths to which Nick might go. ''Why not?''

''Well, for one thing, he doesn't know that Lillian didn't leave a will. He'll probably assume that she left specific instructions that you be allowed to stay in the house. Besides, if he suspects you of murder, he'll prefer to have you close at hand. And...''

Sara released the breath she'd been holding. ''Go on.''

''And,'' he repeated, ''if he does finally manage to convince himself that you have the formula, he'll want easy access to you.''

Easy access to torment, she couldn't help thinking. But if she moved out, the other criminals, if there *were* other criminals, she thought ruefully, would become suspicious, and that would defeat the purpose of Lillian's ruse.

"Which is what you want me to have to him—access—right?"

"Right. If Nick is behind these kidnapping attempts, and he thinks you have the formula, then Lillian's scheme is working. It's drawn him out and that's what we wanted—or, I should say, that's what her highness wanted," he corrected, dryly.

"Ben, what will you say if Nick does contact you and asks to see Lillian's will?"

Ben sighed. "Damned if I know. That's why it's better if you stay at the estate with him. You can find out his intentions and warn me ahead of time. He'd be a fool if he didn't ask to see the will and he'd be a bigger fool if he didn't want to contest what he thinks are its contents. Please, Sara. Try and tough it out with him at the estate."

Sara raised her eyes to heaven with a silent prayer that she wouldn't blow up at Nick before she had a chance to discover his guilt. "Okay," she managed.

"Good girl. But, Sara—" Ben paused before issuing a caution "—take it easy. Nick is clear heir to the Kingsley pigheadedness."

Sara didn't need to be reminded of that.

She'd already been treated to a display of Nick's stubborn streak. "All right, Ben. I will."

The lawyer hung up abruptly, and Sara sat immobilized, surprised to find that her hands were trembling.

Nerves, she told herself, standing up. Then a rough-timbred voice echoed in the hallway.

"Hello, Edie. Nice to see you again."

Sara's heart somersaulted. She knew only one person with that accent.

Through the door, she heard, "Mr. Kingsley! What a wonderful surprise! Are you moving back...?"

Edie's effusive greeting, muffled by the library doors, disconcerted Sara. She gave a puzzled frown. Yesterday, Edie had been markedly reserved when they'd talked about Nick. Now, from her tone, it sounded as if she was quite fond of him.

Straightening her shoulders, Sara walked to the doorway just in time to see Edie leading a male servant up the stairs with some suitcases.

Her gaze searched out Nick. He was standing in the huge foyer running a hand through his thick hair to shake out the rain. He stopped at the sound of her footfall and glanced up, untying the belt of his coat as he did so. He looked carelessly rumpled, but his eyes as he regarded her were watchful and penetrating.

Her lips felt dry. This was going to be a real cat-and-mouse game.

Nick's mouth eased into an upward half curve. "Well, aren't you going to ask me what I'm doing here?" he said, releasing the ends of his belt.

Sara jammed her hands into the pockets of her full navy-blue skirt and took a few steps forward. "I don't have to," she said, shrugging her shoulders. "I know why you're here."

"Ah...Ben Short." He nodded his head in understanding. Tendrils of shining black hair fell onto his forehead. His eyebrows raised in speculation. "He told you I own the Kingsley estate, I suppose."

"And more," she couldn't resist adding. "Thanks to Ben, I now know almost as much about you as you do about me. At least now we're on a more equal footing, Mr. Kingsley."

His gaze locked with hers. "I somehow don't think we were ever unevenly matched, Sara," he responded critically, then added in a conversational tone, "I thought you were going to call me Nick." A mocking expression lit his eyes.

"That kind of friendliness doesn't seem appropriate," she retorted, emerald fire flashing in her eyes.

He surprised her by laughing. The rich sound reverberated in the entranceway. "Well. I'll give you one thing, Sara. You're one hell of an opponent." His expression sobered as his eyes met hers. "No wonder you were able to con Lillian. She never did like prissy females. And you're certainly not one of those."

Sara had to physically restrain herself from taking a swing at him. Standing there with his dark hair damp from the rain and his scowling eyes, he was the epitome of self-righteous confidence. *Just like Derek,* she thought. *They're all cut from the same cloth.*

"I didn't con Lillian," she said curtly, wondering at her own sanity for even pursuing the issue.

"Then how do you account for your sudden good fortune in inheriting this rather cushy life-style for yourself?" he replied archly, his eyes narrowing into fierce slits.

"I didn't ask Lillian to make me her heir," Sara snapped. *God knows that's true,* she thought. "What your aunt did was strictly her own decision." *That* was even truer!

A sardonic smile twisted Nick's mouth. "You know, Sara," he drawled, "I think you missed your calling. You should have been on the stage."

"Well, that's a hell of a lot better than being in a pulpit," she retorted.

"I'm not preaching, Sara. I wouldn't waste my breath. With women like you, that's an exercise in futility."

Sara's eyes widened in outrage. "How dare you!" Without thinking she clenched a fist as if to take a well-aimed swipe at him. In seconds, his hand had caught her arm.

"Careful, Sara," he rasped. "I might just swing back."

She wrenched her arm away in fury. Eyes flashing, she planted her feet and leaned into a combative pose. "That'll be the day!" she countered.

"Don't push me, Sara," he warned in a low voice.

Sara drew herself to her full five feet seven inches, her breath coming in quick spurts. "That's just what I would have expected of you," she challenged. "Most men wouldn't even consider hitting a woman, let alone threatening one. I should have guessed." The insult hung in the air between them.

Sara now had the distinct pleasure of seeing that Nick's anger matched her own. Shattering his composure gave her a sense of triumph, but the depth of the anger that showed in his eyes made her thrill seem empty. "Most men, Sara, are fortunate enough not to ever run across a woman like you. But I suspect if they did, they'd feel exactly the same way I do. Killing my aunt is hardly likely to endear you to me."

Sara found her anger dissipating. Nick was right. For a moment, she'd almost forgotten that he didn't know the truth. On the simple basis of the circumstances, he had every reason to suspect her of murder. With an effort, she pulled herself together. She should never have flown off the handle like that. She'd better be more careful. If she angered Nick too much, he might ask her to leave. Damn! She couldn't let that happen.

She searched his face to see how much damage she'd done. His features were still hardened in anger. With a deep breath, she took the bull by the horns.

"Were you expecting me to move out?" she asked bluntly.

He looked surprised at the question, then clenched his jaw irritably, tossing his coat over his arm. "You mean you'd be willing to leave all your newly acquired possessions? Come now, Sara, you could hardly expect me to believe that. Some of Lillian's treasures are quite priceless if I remember correctly."

With an impatient swing, he threw the coat over the banister and faced her. She could see that the tight-fitting jeans he wore were practically molded to his long legs. A black shirt that looked as if it could use a good ironing pulled across his broad chest. It was partially open at the neck, revealing black curling hair. Primitive was the word that flashed into her head. The image was substantiated by the stormy gaze he directed at her.

"Surely," he continued, facing her again, "you're not going to tell me that you don't know one painting alone, in this house, could be worth a million dollars? It's beyond my comprehension that you would be content to entrust everything to my safekeeping." His question dripped with icy disbelief.

She seized on his statement as an indication that he would allow her to remain in the house. Nick already thought she was a mercenary schemer. Why not use that to her advantage?

She tilted her chin in defiance. "No," she replied, "I'm not willing to entrust my inheritance to you. I have no reason to trust you." Her gaze locked with his.

The antagonism she saw mirrored in those depths was palpable. Then it vanished with mercurial speed. A wry smile tugged at the corners of his mouth. "I thought as much," he said. "That's much more consistent with the kind of woman you are."

Sara gritted her teeth with frustration. *Careful, Sara . . . careful. You're losing your cool again.*

"Are you planning to contest Lillian's will?" she asked directly.

"My, my, aren't we the worried little soul. Afraid I might take all these things—" he gestured expansively "—away from you?"

"Maybe." She fought to stay in character and to play the distasteful role he had assigned her. "And the formula?" she pushed. "What about that?"

Nick's body had become suspiciously still. "That depends on whether you have it or not," he replied coolly.

"And if I do?" she said.

"I'm sure I could find some way to get it out of you." His gaze merged with hers.

"Then you *do* want it?"

"As I said before, Sara, what difference does it make?" Their gazes remained locked in silent battle, his velvet-brown eyes as unreadable as her forest-green ones. She looked away first.

"Looks like we've reached an impasse," she said, unnerved by his unflinching stare.

"Appears that way."

Sara raised her head again. They still hadn't resolved whether she was staying or leaving. She inhaled sharply and forced herself to look at Nick again. "I don't want to leave the estate," she said in a bold challenge.

An interested look showed on his face. "Really? Then that gives us at least one thing in common. I don't want you to leave." A half smile she couldn't fathom flirted across his face.

Not quite prepared for his response, she stiffened. "Why not?"

Nick moved closer to her. His big hands came up and rested on her shoulders. Sara's pulse began to beat raggedly. His raw, male energy was devastating at close range. A woman could drown in those eyes, she thought, almost hypnotized. The heat from his fingers seemed to sear her skin through the sheer fabric of her white silk blouse.

"Because," he answered in a slow voice, "I think living with you should prove to be a highly entertaining proposition—a proposition that I'm quite looking forward to."

Arching his eyebrows in a mocking curve, he dropped his hands in a quick motion and without another word, brushed past her, walking with long strides toward the rear of the house.

Sara watched him leave, her heart beating wildly. *Damn him,* she thought, her face flushing furiously, *and all his kind.*

By the time she reached Ben's condominium in downtown Toronto, Sara had almost managed to calm down from her conversation with Nick. Almost, but not quite.

What was there about the man that so unbalanced her? Surely, it wasn't just his accusations. After all, she was innocent, and if she had to she could prove it. Why should his opinion bother her?

Impatiently, she jerked her purse onto her shoulder. Nick obviously enjoyed baiting her. What did he expect to gain? A crack in her composure? A full confession to something she didn't do?

Small chance of that, Nick Kingsley. Think again. Eluding aggressive men is my specialty.

But the way he looked at her! He seemed to be searching for something more than a sign that she was implicated in his aunt's death. But what?

She rang the outside door buzzer, shaking her head to clear the last vestiges of anger.

It was all academic anyway. Lillian would sort it out.

She rang the buzzer again. No reply.

Riffling through her purse, she found the extra key Ben had given her and inserted it into the lock.

Was Lillian getting hard of hearing? Sara wondered. She hadn't noticed that.

Ben's suite was on the fourth floor, and rather than wait for the elevator, she ran up the stairs. Ben had purchased the condominium as an investment, keeping it as an in-town residence and renting it out only on occasion. Fortunately, the suite had been vacant when Lillian had proposed her plan.

Slightly out of breath, Sara knocked on the door of 406 and waited. After a few seconds, she knocked again, louder this time.

Still, no reply.

Caution tensed her body, and gripping the key to the suite, she tested it slowly in the lock. The door clicked and she eased it back.

The first thing she noticed was the quietness, the absence of sound that suggested the place was empty.

That's ridiculous, she thought. *Lillian has to be here.* She stepped into the foyer.

The five-room apartment was furnished the way she would have expected the occasional second home of a professional bachelor to be—efficiently, but sparely. Two love seats in brown leather flanked a glass-topped coffee table with brass legs. A half-filled bookcase hugged one wall. The windows were covered with nondescript beige drapes, tightly drawn, the standard kind often supplied with a condo when you purchased it.

Drawn drapes? Sara stood in the center of the living room, her legs nudging the sharp glass table. Why would the drapes be drawn? Lillian loved daylight and moonlight equally. The curtains at the Kingsley estate were always open.

"Lillian," she called in a soft voice.

Her voice echoed back. Otherwise there was no sound.

Every muscle taut, she felt for the .38 Smith & Wesson revolver she carried in a shoulder holster. Tucked against her chest under her suit jacket, it felt warm from her body heat. Withdrawing it carefully with her right hand, she moved into the narrow kitchen. A red Melitta coffeepot sat on the stove. She reached out and touched it with her other hand. Cold metal greeted her fingers.

Careful not to make any unnecessary sound, she edged toward the bedroom. The door was slightly ajar. Leaning against the wall, she stretched her right foot around and shoved the door open. Holding her breath, she waited. Silence.

Quickly she jerked her head around the opening, scanning the room with a professional eye. It was totally still, undisturbed, the bed neatly made, a beige cover hanging in folds to the taupe broadloomed floor. The night tables on either side of the double bed were clear, devoid of any personal items.

Fear played along her spinal column. Stealthily she stepped into the room, giving it a more thorough investigation. But something was missing. According to Ben, Lillian had brought enough mementos with her to virtually duplicate the cluttered charm of her bedroom at the estate.

Where were they? Where was Lillian?

Her heart beating rapidly, Sara checked the rest of the suite.

The closet was empty and when Sara trailed her finger in the sink of the en suite bathroom, it came away dry. Completely dry.

By now, dread was throbbing at Sara's temples and she'd broken into a cold sweat. There was no question the suite was empty.

Lillian was gone.

She fought back a rising surge of panic and guilt. She should never have let Ben talk her into this scheme. She'd never forgive herself if any harm had come to Lillian!

Just as she was about to leave the bedroom, a tiny glimmer of color under the dresser caught her attention. Bending down, she picked up a faded bluish-green ribbon. A faint aroma drifted in the air. Holding the ribbon to her nose, she sniffed. The fabric smelled of age as if it had been buried away with someone's memories for decades.

A frown furrowed her brow. Something of Lillian's? A treasure from her youth? Sara tucked it into her skirt pocket.

Returning to the living room, she dispiritedly looked around for the phone to call Ben. The police would have to be notified now.

Spying the phone on the bookcase, she crossed the room and was about to pick up the receiver when she saw a piece of paper anchored underneath it. Sliding the white sheet out, she read it.

"Ben—Sara. I'm quite safe. Have gone away for a while. Don't worry. Will call in a few days."

Lillian's signature was scrawled across the bottom.

Sara's tension gave way to relief. Then relief gave way to anger and she swore silently.

"You've gone too far this time, Lillian," she mumbled aloud. "I should have kidnapped you myself. At least I'd be sure you were safe."

Sara's eyes blazed, then narrowed with frustration.

Nick? Just what am I supposed to do about him? Tell him the truth? Or continue this silly game? Thanks, Lillian! Crumpling the letter with quick fingers, she tossed it into the wastebasket.

Now mobilized into action, she dialed Ben's number. On finding he was out of the office, she left a hasty message for him to call her at the estate.

Five minutes later, she stepped outside into the cool air, looking up at the sky in surprise. The day had become ominously overcast. A storm brewed on the horizon as sounds of thunder splintered the air. Checking the dark blanket of clouds, Sara opted to take Yonge Street north rather than one of the 400 highways. When weather was bad, the busier 400 routes could be treacherous.

She wouldn't make as good time, but the drive would be less nerve-racking.

She'd had enough frights for one day.

HE WATCHED SARA LEAVE the ten-story building and make her way to the visitors' parking at the west side.

Without a moment's hesitation, he moved away from the cover of the small alley, walking with purposeful strides along King Street, heading east past a row of small antique stores. He stepped off the sidewalk by a parked car. Circling around, he leaned his hands on the driver's door. The window had been rolled down.

"She's on her way back to the estate," he said in a clipped tone. "Make it count this time."

The driver gave him a surly look. "Why bother? I thought you said the old lady left a note."

"Because, you idiot..." He had to struggle to rein in his temper. "That won't stall her for long. She'll catch on sooner or later—and it'll more likely be sooner."

The driver twisted his mouth. "Couldn't we just scare her off?"

By now, he was breathing raggedly with frustration. "She's a professional. Professionals don't scare easily. And anyway, we already tried that once. She's still on the case—or hadn't you noticed?'' His sarcasm whistled in the air. ''Just do what I tell you,'' he said in a tight voice.

The other man shrugged his shoulders against the car seat. ''You're the boss.''

He flinched at the response, then leaning closer, he leveled a dark, dangerous stare at the driver. ''I want her dead. D-E-A-D. Got that? Dead.''

He struck the side of the car angrily and stalked away for a block before ducking into a break in the stream of traffic to cross the street.

BY THE TIME SARA TURNED off Yonge Street, which had become Highway 11, and onto the country road, a storm was raging. A pitch-black sky was descending like a slow-moving theater curtain.

Torrents of rain lashed across the road, making visibility extremely limited. She'd turned the windshield wipers on high speed, but the blue M.G. sat too low for the action to be effective.

Water washed across the windshield in gushes. She could feel the pull in the steering.

Concentrating fiercely on the winding road, Sara strained her eyes to keep the curves in sight. The road wasn't lit, and her own headlights seemed only to spotlight the sheeting rain.

Maybe this wasn't such a good idea, she thought ruefully. I should have stopped for a while and let this pass.

Suddenly, she saw a car sneak up on her left as if to pass.

''What's the matter with him?'' she muttered with irritation, gripping the wheel tightly as she glanced over through the lashing rain. ''This is only a two-lane road. Doesn't he know that? He could get us both killed in this weather.''

Something wasn't right about the car, she thought. She dared another look through the fogging window, then set her shoulders grimly.

The car's headlights weren't on.

She bit her lip to suppress her anger. The dark-colored car was driving blind.

But before she had a chance to flash her lights as a warning to the driver, the car careened into her.

"Hey!" she yelled, automatically.

The M.G. went into a skid on the slick road, the combined force of the other vehicle and the sweep of water catching it and holding it in an uncontrollable spiral.

Grateful for her professional drivers' training, Sara managed to bring the sports car back on track. Enraged, she leaned on her horn, shouting toward the side window, "You almost ran me over that incline, you jerk!"

Bending her head, she tried to see the other car more clearly. But it was too dark and wet. All she could make out were the identifying features of a four-door sedan. The car was still driving neck-and-neck with hers. She leaned on her horn furiously, and flashed her lights. In answer, the sedan slammed into her with full force.

Sara stifled a scream. It caught in her throat, almost choking her. The sedan was deliberately trying to force her out of control.

Adrenaline shot through her. She swallowed hard to stay calm. There was no one else on the highway and the M.G. was no match for the large, heavy sedan.

Sweat slicked her hands as she gripped the wheel. She'd need more than defensive driving to get her out of this. A miracle might do, she thought ruefully. Then her high beams picked out the road ahead through a moment's gap in the curtain of rain.

A twisting turn loomed in the darkness.

By now her skin was drenched, but her mouth was dry with fear. Taking ragged breaths to control the wild beating of her heart, she tried to gauge the distance of the turn. If she lowered her speed, the sedan might overshoot her, and she'd fall safely behind. Might. It was a long shot but with a quick motion she geared down. The sedan also reduced speed.

Sara cursed her carelessness. She'd misjudged the alignment of his car with hers. Now what? She began to steer into the bend, her breath fogging the inside of the windshield.

Do something, Sara. Do anything . . . outdistance him if you can.

The dark shape beside her edged closer as both cars drew nearer to the turn. Sara made up her mind in an instant. She rammed her foot to the floor. The M.G. bucked and spurted forward.

Then seemingly out of nowhere, a third vehicle appeared, its headlights flashing. But Sara had no time to notice or wonder about it. She was into the curve now. She could hear the frantic drumming of her pulse in her head.

The turn was tighter than she'd estimated. The M.G. was going too fast. Desperately, she tried to gear down, but it was too late. At the same time, the other vehicle slammed into the side door. She felt the right front wheel catch an edge and the whole front end of the car seemed to hover in midair. In a split second, the M.G. jerked violently into a nosedive.

Sara's body snapped forward. A vision of wet, dark dirt rose to meet her.

Her head struck something and she slumped against the leather steering wheel.

Her body shook in convulsive reaction once.

Then she lay absolutely still.

Chapter Five

In the downpour, Nick worked feverishly to pull Sara out of the car, which was angled precariously over the steep incline.

He was afraid that any minute, it would somersault down the earthen cliff, slick with mud.

The compact interior of the small sports car made it difficult to dislodge Sara, but finally he managed to get her free.

Sloshing through mud, he half-carried, half-dragged her body to his car.

Panting with the exertion, he settled her in the passenger seat, then immediately checked her pulse. Still strong. With a piece of cloth he tore from his shirt and dampened with rain, he wiped her facial cuts.

What the hell was going on?

He'd been following Sara ever since she left the estate. On the way home, which he presumed was where she'd been going, another vehicle had cut in front of him at an intersection. By the time they'd reached the country road, the three vehicles were the only ones on the road. He'd kept a discreet distance, then realized that the second car had turned off its lights. On instinct, he'd followed suit, wondering why the driver had chosen to drive blind. It hadn't been long before he realized what was happening.

But he still didn't understand why. There was no doubt in his mind that the driver of the sedan had been trying to kill Sara. As they'd reached the dangerous curve, Nick had had to make a quick decision. Gunning his own engine and flashing the lights, he'd driven into the second lane and tried to ram the other vehicle.

The driver of the second vehicle hadn't wasted any time running scared. He or she had managed to hit Sara's M.G., but with less impact as the driver took advantage of Nick's dropping back to regain control of his car. He'd pulled out quickly and driven off in the darkness.

Nick looked down at Sara's blood-streaked face. Nothing seemed to make sense now. His dark gaze flickered with uncertainty. He'd thought of Sara as a perpetrator of crime, not a victim.

He wasn't convinced she was innocent, but something strange was going on. When he'd received the last phone call in Australia telling him his aunt was dead and Sara might have killed her, he'd immediately caught a plane for Canada. Unknown to anyone, except Edie, he'd slipped into the Kingsley estate, but he hadn't found what he'd expected. Without alerting Edie to his suspicions he'd questioned her about Sara. The housekeeper had been effusive in her praise of Sara. Then he'd met her. He'd painted an image in his head of a cool, sophisticated adventuress with a fondness for the trappings of wealth. But Sara hadn't appeared that way when he confronted her. Wearing little or no makeup, dressed simply, there'd been a total lack of guile in the way she had responded to him. Her eyes had been clear and unflinching. Edie had said she was honest and courageous, and had a warm sense of humor. Was that the profile of a murderess?

He shook the question out of his mind. As he loosened Sara's shoulder holster he noticed a piece of fabric falling out of her pocket. Funny. It felt brittle with age. Without further thought, he shoved it back.

Leaning over Sara's body, he brushed strands of tawny, damp hair away from her eyes. Like a lion's mane, it was thick and shot with blond and brown highlights. An ugly red gash marred her right temple, extending down toward her cheekbone.

Her skin was washed of any color, pale and cool to his touch. But she was still so achingly lovely, his breath caught in his throat.

Just what he needed, he grimaced. To be attracted to his aunt's killer. For a moment he felt a wave of male protectiveness sweep over him. Hurt and quiet, she looked so fragile, so soft... He stifled a groan, hardening himself against Sara's vulnerable beauty. A woman's softness was her deadliest weapon. He'd been taken in by it once too often in his life to fall again. Lillian and his ex-wife had taught him well.

"Sara," he whispered. "Wake up, Sara."

He maneuvered his arm around her to shake her gently. He was rewarded by the flickering of her thick eyelashes. Damp, they seemed to glisten under the interior light.

Relief filled him, although he didn't know why. By all rights, he shouldn't care what happened to her. But right now, for whatever reason, he was glad that she was alive.

"Where...?" He could hardly hear her hoarse question.

"You're in my car. Try to open your eyes," he urged.

Sara felt herself drifting through a veil of pain and semiconsciousness. She tried to move her mouth to answer the soft command, but no sound emerged. Her eyelids felt leaden. Forcing them open seemed to take a supreme effort of will. As they fluttered, a brightness made her eyes flinch. She blinked protectively.

"Sorry," a male voice apologized. "I'll turn the light out."

A peaceful darkness fell. Someone was holding her. Someone strong. She nestled into the curve of the arm, savoring its support, slowly trying to get her bearings. Then she remembered.

The dark earth. Her suspended car. A third vehicle.

Breathing jaggedly, her chest sore, she opened her eyes again, willing them to focus.

"How do you feel?".

Warm breath fanned her left cheek. Whose voice was that? The cadence seemed familiar. Gradually, her thoughts came together to make sense in her throbbing head. Then surprise overtook them.

"Nick?" she questioned, turning her head painfully toward him. Her tone, hardly audible, was incredulous. She could barely make out his features, but the powerful build and those fierce, penetrating eyes were definitely his.

"Yes, Nick," he replied. "Or, as you seem to prefer, Mr. Kingsley," he added in a lighter vein. His hand tightening on her arm, he leaned forward in the darkness. "How do you feel?"

His nearness disoriented her as she struggled to suppress a rising flush.

"Okay, I guess..." With her left hand she felt her ribs and leg. "I don't think..." she began.

"...anything's broken?" he supplied.

She nodded her head, wincing at the bolt of pain that shot to her temple.

"No, nothing's broken. I checked you over before I took you out of the car," he said.

"You did?" She couldn't hide the soft dismay in her voice. The idea of Nick's hands on her body while she was unconscious strangely disturbed her.

Immediately, he stiffened. "I didn't have much choice, Sara. I couldn't very well move you without knowing how badly you'd been hurt." With a weary motion, he released his grip on her arm, moving toward the driver's side. In the dark, his tone sounded distant and cool. "I'm sorry if my touch offends you. It was purely impersonal, I can assure you."

Sara's eyes flickered at his tight-lipped reaction. Had she caught a glimpse of the man who lay beneath the hostile mask? Then her eyes darkened with confusion. Offend? Dear God, she suspected the exact opposite had prompted her dismay. Despite the doubts she harbored about him, and his obvious antagonism toward her, she couldn't ignore the fact that Nick's very presence excited her, made her feel alive....

Unsettled, Sara shook her head distractedly. "I didn't mean to imply anything," she faltered, rubbing her hand across her forehead. "I'm just feeling a bit shaky...that's all."

A noncommittal murmur greeted her response. Then he asked, watching her gingerly touch the cut, "How's your head feel?"

Groaning slightly, she bowed forward. "Like my brain is encased in concrete."

"I don't doubt it," he grunted, but not unkindly, she thought. "You took a nasty blow, but at least you're not concussive. You're a very lucky lady. One more push and your car would have overturned—with you in it."

Sara shuddered as the memory of that nightmare drive came back with unrelenting clarity. "You're right. It was an awful accident."

"Accident, my foot," he growled, suddenly mobilized into action. His big hand jammed the key into the car's ignition. "Somebody was out to get you."

His comment startled her. So, he'd guessed. Had he also deliberately intervened to save her life? Did that mean she could trust him? Uncertainty flared inside her. Without Lillian's say so, how could she be sure?

She adopted a casual tone. "You're exaggerating," she said, "it was just an accident."

Nick whipped around to face her. Scorn edged his words. "I'm not an idiot, Sara. So don't ever play me for one. Something was going on tonight. What was it?"

His angry question jolted her. In the darkness, she could see the flash of his dark eyes. Shrugging as best as she could, she replied, "Likely just some kids trying out a new car."

Nick drew in his breath sharply. It was obvious he was reining in his temper with great difficulty. His left hand gripped the steering wheel as he stared at her. "Don't lie to me, Sara. They weren't kids. For one thing, there was only one driver. And for another—" he turned back to face forward, reaching for the lights with an abrupt motion and twisting the key in the ignition with his other hand "—he was a professional." The car's engine roared to life.

Watching the slick road ahead, Sara waited a few minutes before responding. "Professional?" she stalled.

Nick's jaw clenched in the half-light. "Yes . . . professional killer."

Sara gave a strained laugh. "Why would anyone want to kill me. Other than you, that is?" Her eyebrows arched in bitter amusement.

The car veered sharply to the right. "I don't want to kill you." There was no answering humor in his tone. A slice of light from the dashboard illuminated his straining hands on the wheel. The car came back on course. "I pulled you out of the car . . . remember?"

She forced another laugh. "Oh, yes, I remember. I was going to ask you about that. Why the sudden concern?"

she asked, surprised at the level of her own bitterness. "Why bother to rescue a gold digger and a murderess?"

"You haven't been tried yet," he responded, calmly.

Her eyes widened with mock disbelief. "Why I thought you'd appointed yourself judge and jury and that I'd been found guilty."

"Everyone's entitled to a fair trial, Sara. Even an adventuress."

For some reason this last comment stung her. She knew only too well what he thought of her, but strangely, now, his contempt was wounding. Must be the aftereffects of the accident, she thought, finding it hard to shake a spreading feeling of sadness. "Thanks a lot," she replied brusquely. Then she looked through the window at the pelting rain. "Where are we going?"

"Home. The estate. We'll call the family doctor from there to give you the once-over."

No, we won't, Sara thought making up her mind she wasn't going to see any family doctor. The fewer people who knew about her "accident," the better. Anyway, she hated people fussing over her. But she wasn't going to argue with Nick now. There'd been enough of that already.

Leaning her head back, she closed her eyes with weariness. *God. Let this charade be over soon.* Suddenly, exhaustion and a sense of shock welled up inside her, and she found herself blinking back tears and biting her lip to stop its quivering. *I don't cry, for heaven's sake. What's the matter with me?*

Nick settled the car at a steady pace, then reached across her lap to open the glove compartment. "Tissues are in there," he said, pointing.

"I'm not going to cry," she replied, looking out the passenger window.

"You're too bloody-minded, you know that" was his retort. "Do you good to cry. Get rid of all that pent-up tension. Go ahead. I couldn't care less. Even men need to cry sometimes."

But not you, I'll bet, she thought wryly. Crying in front of Nicholas Kingsley was the last thing in the world she wanted to do, but despite her best efforts to control the tears, a mist blurred her vision, and she reached defensively for a tissue.

He jerked his head toward her. "It's just a delayed reaction, you know. It doesn't mean you're weak."

"Spare me the psychology," she snapped, surreptitiously wiping away the tears from the corners of her eyes. Nevertheless, his perception unsettled her. How had he known she despised weakness in herself?

"Are you always this prickly?" he asked.

"Yes." She gave a dry, self-deprecating laugh. "Just ask my ex-husband."

"Is that why he divorced you?"

His question in the semidarkness took her by surprise. Why would Nick be interested in that part of her life? Was he looking for something else to vindicate his low opinion of her?

"It was only *one* of the things Derek didn't like about me," she replied in all honesty, the ache in her head beginning to pound like a drum. She didn't bother to correct him about who'd divorced whom.

"What else?" His voice sounded low-pitched in the dark.

Sara arched her head to the left to ease the throbbing in her right temple. "You name it, he didn't like it. My job, my casual life-style, the halfway houses I did volunteer work for. He wanted a corporate wife. I'm afraid I didn't measure up. I wanted children; he didn't. Irreconcilable differences, I think you call it." She looked at him pointedly, challengingly. "Should I go on or is that enough?"

"You've made your point. Sounds like he was looking for an accessory, rather than a wife."

Sara gritted her teeth in the dark. "Aren't a lot of men?"

"Some," he admitted, concentrating on the slick road. "But not all. Tell me, why didn't he want children?"

Sara uttered a bitter laugh. "A pregnant woman wasn't Derek's idea of the ideal hostess, and I think he was afraid children would mess up the house."

"Women are their most beautiful when they're pregnant," he answered in a soft voice.

She stole a glance at him. Nicholas Kingsley, you're full of surprises, she thought, then sighed and replied, covering her thoughts with a wry tone. "I'm afraid Derek didn't share your view."

"So now you've sworn off all men," he prodded.

Sara was beginning to feel slightly unsettled by his questions. This was one discussion she would never have expected to be having with Nick Kingsley! "Something like that." She tossed him her reply, hoping to deflect the line of conversation. The subject was disturbing, but not as much as the man who pursued it.

She turned around, determined to shift the focus to him. "What about you?" she asked. "Is there a Mrs. Kingsley somewhere?"

"Was," he corrected.

"What happened?"

He smiled slightly. "Irreconcilable differences."

Despite the pain in her head and overwhelming tiredness, Sara couldn't help sharing his smile in the dark as he repeated her phrase. "The same litany as mine?" she posed.

"Fairly close," he admitted. "My ex-wife liked the so-called 'good life'—parties, socializing, wealth. I discovered too late in our marriage that she loved my potential as a wealthy husband more than she loved me. All along, I'd believed her interest in my background showed genuine concern and a nurturing instinct, the qualities men seek in a woman." He gave a dry laugh.

"So you split up?"

"Charles's death brought it all to a head. She wanted me to return to Canada and claim my inheritance. Except for wanting to see Lillian, it was the last thing in the world I wanted. I couldn't ignore the truth any longer, so we divorced. I didn't want to repeat as an adult the kind of life I'd had as a child. Nor did I want that life for my children."

Nick's candor touched Sara. Knowing what little she did about his upbringing, she could readily understand his aversion to returning to what must have been a cold and lonely life for him in the Kingsley household. Gently, she asked, "Did you have any children?"

"No, I'm glad and sorry to say. Glad because my wife would have used them as a weapon to get what she wanted, and sorry because I always dreamed of having a family of my own some day."

Because you never had one yourself, she thought. *Because you missed all that.* "Would your wife have done that?" she asked. "Used your children."

"You bet!" He laughed. "She was very like Lillian. Underneath soft exteriors, they both hid wills of iron and an armory of manipulative skills."

Nick's criticism of Lillian surprised her. Ben had told her that Nick loved Lillian and would never seek to harm her. Was it possible that Ben was mistaken?

She eyed Nick speculatively. At least one piece of the puzzle fit into place—his belligerence toward her. To him, she must seem like a fortune hunter, just like his wife. He also believed she'd manipulated Lillian into trusting her. Hadn't he implied as much in the cemetery? *But still,* she thought, something doesn't tally. What is it?

To cover her confusion, she commented, "Sounds like you don't trust women very much."

"I don't trust people very much," he corrected in a wry voice. "Especially those who play games."

Like you think I do, she almost replied. At least that was something they agreed on. Out loud, she said, "That's nothing to apologize for."

"I don't," came his terse reply.

After a moment he said in a gruff voice, "Look, why don't you get some rest? We still have a twenty-minute drive ahead of us. Whether you like to admit it or not, what happened tonight is bound to take its toll on you."

Sara was happy to obey. Her ordeal was beginning to catch up with her. Her head ached terribly, her throat was parched, and her body was threatening to stiffen up. Conversation with Nick seemed to demand her total concentration and at the moment she just wasn't alert enough to read him properly.

In the eerie storm-darkness, she glanced over at him, before resting her head back. The strange light exaggerated the strong planes and structure of his face. It was a determined profile, but for the first time she noticed how firm and full his mouth was.

What would he look like if that mouth was curving with pleasure, instead of contempt? If he was smiling, instead of scowling? If he was kissing her, instead of hurling accusations...?

Good Lord, Sara. That blow to your head has unraveled you.

With a sigh of confusion, she allowed her eyelids to drop. The windshield wipers chanted mechanically in her head, and in seconds she was fast asleep.

A MAN'S ARMS WERE WRAPPED around her. Holding her as if she was a precious child. The sense of safety and comfort was overpowering. In her dreamlike state, she moaned, tightening her grip around the man's neck, seeking, and touching, warm, slightly damp skin.

A thrill shot through her with the intimacy of the contact. She buried her fingers under the back of his shirt collar, testing the broad strength of one shoulder. Then she cupped a hand over the curve of a powerful shoulder blade, and sighing, nestled her head against rain-drenched fabric and the thrust of a jawline. The man seemed to inhale jaggedly, which only served to cause her to stretch and burrow like a cat into his encompassing embrace. Wherever she was, being here felt right. She could feel a sense of power, of caring and something else . . . a slow warmth, like a quickening fire. . . . Hers or his? It didn't matter. Being here was good. She snuggled closer.

Suddenly, the sound of footsteps on a hard surface jarred her dazed peace.

"My God, Mr. Kingsley. What happened?"

The man braced her tighter against his chest. "An accident, Edie. I think she's okay, but you'd better call the family doctor just in case."

The words sliced through Sara's sleepy condition like a knife. She didn't want a doctor. Her eyes flew open. She was in Nick Kingsley's arms in the middle of the foyer. Everything came rushing back to her. Now fully awake, she croaked, "No doctor."

"Call the doctor, Edie," Nick growled.

Alarm shot through her. She struggled in his arms. "I don't need a doctor. I'm fine," she protested, her voice gaining strength.

Nick's steel grip arched her into the crook of his arm. "Edie, do what I tell you," he commanded.

Squirming, Sara twisted around. The housekeeper stood uncertainly in front of both of them. Urgently trying to overrule Nick, Sara pleaded. "Edie, nothing's broken. It was a minor accident. It isn't worth bringing a doctor out in this weather."

"Sara!" Nick's breath exploded with fury. The heat fanned her hair.

Pushing against his chest with her hands, Sara tried to break his hold. "Oh, for God's sake, put me down." Nick's wet raincoat and her own damp clothes made his hold tenuous and she began to slide. "Edie, don't you dare call the doctor," she warned.

The beleaguered housekeeper glanced nervously between the two of them. "Miss Brennan...? Mr. Kingsley...?" Her tone and expression begged for a solution to her dilemma.

"There. See, I'm fine!" Sara interrupted triumphantly, landing squarely on her feet, despite Nick's last-ditch effort to restrain her. She smiled winningly at the older woman, her hands outstretched. "Nothing to worry about."

She took a step forward to prove her point. Edie looked dubious. Her lips parted to speak, but all possible conversation and Sara's progress were halted by Nick.

"Sara!" A hand reached out and grabbed her. He whirled her around full circle to face him. A wave of dizziness assaulted her. "You've got to be the most irritating woman I've ever met," he shouted, his eyes blazing.

Out of the corner of her eye, Sara caught a swatch of color as Edie hastily vanished.

Trying to shake the dizziness, she stood her ground. "Why?" she replied archly. "Because I won't do what you want?" Glowering, she tilted her chin. "I don't need a man to tell me what to do."

Nick glared back. "Lady, you already made that point in the car." His brow furrowed in concentration. "Don't you think you're working this tough routine of yours to death? Has it ever occurred to you a man might just be giving you orders for your own good?"

Sara's head snapped up. She wrenched her arm away from his grasp. "No, it has not and it never will."

Nick's jaw was set when he spoke. "Never's a long time, Sara. Some day you'll change your mind. I'd like to be there when you lose that tough exterior of yours. In fact—" his eyes burned into hers "—I'm tempted to knock that chip off your shoulder myself."

He shoved angrily past her, leaving Sara to stare open-mouthed at his disappearing back.

Now, what was he talking about? Was it another reference to her being a heartless opportunist guilty of Lillian's death? Or was it something else—something far more personal?

Chapter Six

Nick's comment still burned in her memory by the time she'd reached her suite, but she had no time to analyze it further before the phone rang. Without taking off her jacket and holster she crossed to the night table and picked up the receiver.

"Yes," she answered in a breathless voice, after pushing the intercom button.

"Ben Short on the line, Miss Brennan," Edie's voice echoed in her ear.

"Thanks," she began, but Edie interrupted.

"You ought to be in bed, Miss Brennan, instead of taking calls," she chastised.

Sara smiled to herself. Any more concern from anybody, and she'd be choking. Still, at least Edie's worry was genuine, even if Nick's was suspect. "I'm just going, Edie. I'll only take this one call," she promised.

"Good." Edie hung up and Sara pushed the flashing button.

"Ben, how are you?"

"Sara, what's happening?" The lawyer sounded tired.

Clearly, but rapidly, Sara told him what she had found at the condominium, but omitted any mention of the attempt on her life during the drive home. If someone had tried to kill her tonight, it meant that the criminals didn't believe she had the formula, but they wanted her out of the way. That seemed to suggest they knew Lillian was alive. The thought chilled her, but she didn't want to worry Ben unnecessarily.

Ben's outrage matched her own when she had found Lillian gone.

"She's hopeless," he sputtered. "You can't trust her for two minutes. Damn her," he cursed. "If someone sees her, she'll blow the whole operation, and it was her idea in the first place!"

He swallowed a few choice expletives, then apologized quickly. "Sorry, Sara. Sometimes Lillian just really gets my back up."

"I know how you feel, Ben," she soothed. "I'm saving a few juicy words for her myself, but I think we should try and find her now. It's too risky our not knowing where she is." Sara tried to keep her tone level, not wanting to alarm Ben. While it was likely that Lillian's disappearance was voluntary, she wanted to be sure.

"Anyway," she added, "we've still got to resolve the Nick question with her. Whether we tell him the truth or not."

"I agree. Have you seen Nick, by the way?"

Yes, and more, she felt like adding. Instead, she restricted herself to what Ben needed to know. "He moved into the estate this morning."

"Did you find out anything?" he asked tersely.

"Well, I think he wants the formula, although he didn't exactly come out and say so...."

"I thought as much." Ben's voice had a triumphant ring to it, then as if remembering Nick's threat, he asked anxiously, "Has he been to the police yet?"

Sara sat down on the bed as her head began to throb. "Not that I know of, but I don't think he's going to wait much longer. I also think he's becoming curious about

Lillian's will. Ben, we haven't got much time. We need to find Lillian before the police start an investigation and before Nick gets tired of playing this cat-and-mouse game," she urged. "I'm sure Nick is going to get bored pretty quickly and start demanding answers. He's a Kingley, and once he moves, people are going to listen to him—especially the police."

"You're right," Ben answered, worry in his voice. "But where do we start?"

"There are only two choices. Either she's with friends or she's been kidnapped."

"God, Sara, you don't really think that's happened?"

"I'm hoping against hope that it hasn't," she replied. "But the only way we'll know for sure is if we eliminate the first option. It's very possible that she is with friends. It's something she'd do. After all, she can't really manage on her own," she reasoned. "If her note is genuine, then she is with someone she trusts enough to take into her confidence. I think we should make a list of her friends and then split the list between us and check them out."

"Sounds good." Ben seemed relieved that a plan was in place. "Can you come to my office first thing in the morning? I'll cancel as many appointments as I can."

"Nine?"

"Fine," he answered in a clipped tone, then exasperation slipped into his voice. "That woman! Honestly... I could just..."

"I know." Although she shared his sentiments, Sara nevertheless found herself defending Lillian in the next breath. "She doesn't like to be alone, and she's been cooped up for a long time, Ben. Maybe we should take that into account." Sara tried to imagine herself in Lillian's position.

"Exercising a little self-denial wouldn't do her any harm," Ben commented dryly. "See you tomorrow, Sara."

The phone clicked in her ear.

After Ben's call, Sara decided to follow Edie's advice and get to bed as quickly as possible, but first, she indulged herself in a much-needed leisurely soak in the tub. The warm water sprinkled with bubblebath eased her screaming muscles and lulled her body into quiet submission. Her head was a different story. No sooner had her body succumbed to the relaxing balm of the bath than her thoughts again began to whirl around Nick's parting remark.

Had she really become too tough, as Nick had implied? All her life, she'd been an open, trusting human being who liked to laugh and enjoy life. Her father had even confessed a concern that she wouldn't be tough enough for the job she'd chosen. He'd often said she was "more fearless, than hardened." Nick's evaluation just didn't seem to fit. If anything, it was her guilelessness that got her into real trouble. *Like now,* she thought, grimacing.

No, Nick. You're wrong. All you're really seeing is me overreacting to being caught in this lie. That, and a natural acquired defense against strong-willed men.

So there, Nicholas Kingsley. Happens to the best of us. Once bitten, twice shy. You admitted that much yourself. Besides, we can't afford to drop our defenses against each other in this ridiculous situation.

The truth of that thought depressed her. Theirs just wasn't a normal relationship. They were trapped by circumstances in an unreal world of distrust and uncertainty about each other. She had to keep her guard up with him. And he with her.

Somehow though, even acknowledging that, Sara knew that her feelings for Nick had changed.

He had saved her life tonight. And, until she had challenged him, had been openly concerned.

Rinsing off, she stepped out of the tub and dried herself, tossing on a fluffy white bathrobe.

Changed, yes, but not to anything simpler.

There was a knock at the door, and she quickly tied the robe and padded over to answer it.

Nick held up a small tray, his eyes dark on her. "If you don't let me in, I'm going to throw this at you," he warned.

Sara looked at the tray. Balanced on the sterling silver surface was an assortment of ointments and bandages and what looked suspiciously like two brandy glasses and a crystal decanter.

For a moment, she felt her old defenses rising, then she stopped herself. What harm could there be in letting Nick in? The cut hurt like hell, and there wasn't any point in being a martyr. She held the door open, "Come on in."

Nick hesitated, giving her a suspicious look. He'd obviously been prepared for a fight. "What, no argument?"

Sara shrugged, feeling vulnerable without the customary wall of antagonism between them. A soft rose tinged her cheeks. "Just tired, I guess." She managed a slight smile. "I . . . I was going to get some bandages myself. . . . Thank you. . . ." She found herself stumbling over the words. "It was thoughtful of you to bring them."

Nick's gaze softened with uncertainty, then recovering, he offered, "Well, I guess if you're not going to see a doctor, this will have to do." He stepped into the room. "Where . . . ?" Glancing around, he continued to hold the tray. It looked like a sliver of metal in his huge hands.

"Over there." Sara indicated a small round table nestled between two chintz-covered chairs, beside the white Georgian fireplace.

She watched as he nodded and slid the tray onto the table. He must have just showered and changed. Silver-wet moisture clung to his thick black hair, making the strands glisten in the soft glow cast by the table lamps.

A strange unsteadiness seized her, and joining him at the table, she sat down on one of the chairs, thankful for its support. Standing, he poured brandy into the two glasses from the decanter and handed her one.

"Here, drink this," he commanded. "It'll make you feel better."

"Or knock me out," she managed in a slightly teasing voice.

Nick gave her a quick look before sitting down opposite her. "That wouldn't do you any harm," he replied, watching her across the table. "You could do with a good night's sleep after what happened today."

Sara forced herself to raise her head to meet his dark gaze directly. "Are you usually this solicitous with women?" she asked.

He settled himself in the chair, raising one long jean-clad leg to balance on the other. "Depends on the circumstances," he replied, "and . . . on the woman."

Sara edged her fingers nervously around the glass. They were only a few feet apart, but she found herself inordinately grateful for even that distance. Still, he was so near that she couldn't seem to catch her breath.

His drawl seemed to reach out and stroke her. Stifling a shiver, she said, "I see. So why do I rate a rescue?"

"You're far too vitally alive and beautiful for me to have just abandoned you, Sara. No matter what else I might think of you, you show courage and independence and I have to respect and admire that."

Sara turned clear green eyes darkened with confusion on him. Vital? Alive? Beautiful? Derek had never used words like that to describe her. Foolhardy and stubborn had been his stock phrases.

"Beautiful . . . ?" she stammered.

Hearing the questioning note in her voice, it was his turn to be surprised. "Surely you know that?"

Unable to answer, Sara shook her head.

"Your husband must have told you that, Sara," he said with disbelief.

Sara was beginning to unravel under Nick's scrutiny. She had longed to be told, not that she was beautiful, but that she was attractive to Derek. But he had saved his charm for the boardroom. She shook her head again.

"I'm afraid that, to Derek, beauty was synonymous with elegance. And I never possessed much of that." She smiled tentatively. "No patience, I guess." She stopped to catch her breath, trying to control the quiver that seemed to have slipped into her voice. "As for the rest, well, courage and independence weren't high on his list of must-haves for the corporate helpmate. He didn't see those qualities as virtues."

She stopped when she realized what she was doing, rambling on to a man she didn't trust, confessing her innermost feelings. What had come over her? One compliment and she'd fallen to pieces! She waited for him to laugh.

He didn't. An inscrutable expression crossed his face, and he slowly returned his glass to the table. "Then Derek was a fool," he replied, his voice strangely husky. "Now—" he stood up quickly "—I'm going to dress that cut."

Sara's eyes fastened on him in fascination as he drew near. Suddenly she didn't want him to touch her. "I can do it myself," she protested, his body heat already warming the gap between them.

He reached for a small jar on the tray and worked the lid open. A strong whiff of antiseptic tickled her nostrils. Ignoring her protestations, he towered over her.

"Lean your head back," he ordered, nudging her shoulder with his free hand.

Her eyes grew large in alarm at his disturbing closeness. The lingering scent of soap on his skin captured her attention. She felt weak, off balance, the brandy contributing to the effect. Her skin seemed flushed. "You don't have to do that," she tried again. "I can—"

"Damn it, Sara," he cut her off, hesitating in mid-motion. "I'm only going to put on a bandage." He dipped his fingers into the jar. "You must be feeling better. You're getting testy again."

Sara gave up her protest. Despite herself, his comment made her smile. And she saw in the twitch he seemed to be trying to conceal at the edges of his mouth, that he was fighting his own smile.

"Guess you're right." She sighed, then flinched as his fingers spread the cool ointment on her cut.

"Sorry," he apologized, lightening his touch. "I haven't had much experience ministering to a woman."

The feathery stroking of his fingers began to have a strange effect on her. She struggled to feign a clinical interest. "I would have thought you'd had more than your fair share of women."

His finger lingered on her skin for a moment. "I didn't say I hadn't been to bed with women. I just said I haven't had much experience tending to any of their other needs," he replied in a rough voice.

Sara blushed. Well, she'd asked for that.

He reached behind him for a piece of gauze, pulling it out of the open box. "Now, hold still," he commanded, placing the gauze on her forehead. "Keep it in place while I cut the bandage."

Sara's hand reached up to anchor the gauze, her fingers grazing his. That brief contact seemed to send all coherent thought to flight, and watching him unroll the bandage, she was at a loss for words.

Seeing a tear in one of his sleeves, she seized on it as a safe topic of conversation. Fingering the fabric, she asked, "Have you always been careless about your clothes?"

He stopped what he was doing for a minute, his eyes widening fractionally. "Believe it or not, I've improved a lot in the past couple of years," he replied at last, cutting the bandage and holding it between his hands. "Lillian used to despair of my carelessness, then she gave up. We were both happier then." He laughed, poising the bandage in front of her. "Why? Do you think it's important?"

"No, not at all," she rushed to explain, not wanting him to misunderstand. Derek had been obsessed with appearances, including his own, and it was startling to her to realize that Nick's maleness had nothing to do with surfaces.

He leaned over her, ready to position the bandage. "I've never cared much about how I looked. I think there are other, better ways for a man to express his masculinity." He gave the dressing a final pat. "There, you're all done."

Sara felt helpless in the power of his nearness. His warm breath fanned a spark inside her and she knew she should change the conversation, that she was fuelling a fire she would not be able to control.

"Other ways?" she repeated in a hushed tone.

Nick had been about to shift to a standing position, but he stopped in midmotion. His arms were anchored on either side of her on the armrest. He stared at her, his eyes darkening to embers.

"Other..." His gaze strayed to her mouth and then back to her eyes.

Helpless, Sara stared at the fire in those eyes, willing it to catch and consume them both.

"Such as . . ." she prompted dangerously.

Something flashed, then dimmed in his gaze. "You ought to know better than to ask a question like that, Sara," he growled, then lowered his mouth to hers.

Yes, I should, she thought dreamily, anticipating the touch of his lips. When his mouth came down on hers with tenderness and passion, heat flared inside her. She groaned as the sweetness spread through her. Her arms strained to wrap around his neck and she could feel the taut muscles leading to his jaw.

With light fingers, she caressed the bronzed skin. A low moan escaped him, and his kiss deepened. Forcing her lips open, his tongue searched her mouth to savor and touch the inner recesses. Dizzying heat seemed to strike every part of her body.

Nick slid to his knees, his large, callused hands stroking their way up her bare arms. One hand reached the top of her robe and eased aside the soft white fabric. With infinite gentleness, his palm cupped her full, rising breast.

A gasp of pleasure caught in her throat, and then another as his finger circled her nipple, teasing it to a tender peak. Waves of sweet sensation began to wash over her, as she welcomed the rising trail of fire. He slid his mouth away from her lips, trailing down the curve of her neck toward her breast.

"Sara." He groaned her name before closing his full moist lips on her nipple and taking it in primitive possession. His breath when he spoke her name warmed her nipple in a rolling caress. She felt herself sinking. Then he returned his mouth to the hollow in her neck. "My God, Sara," he whispered in a raw voice against her sensitized skin, "how can anyone as lovely as you be so devious?"

Nick's words trickled the cold fingers of sanity down her spine. "Devious?" she cried in a voice as ragged as his.

"Me—devious?" Reality warred with sensual need as she opened her luminous eyes to gaze at him.

Nick's mouth stopped its exquisite torment as he tilted his head to return her look. A flicker of sadness lightened his rich brandy-colored eyes. "Admit it, Sara. There's enough suspicion surrounding you to bury you with my aunt." He seemed to have to struggle to get the sentence out.

Sara visibly flinched. Suddenly her skin felt cold...very cold. "You don't know what you're talking about," she whispered.

"Sara—" a tortured sigh escaped Nick's lips "—don't you think I wish those suspicions weren't there? But they are and as much as I'd like to, I can't ignore them."

Sara's eyes flashed with pain. "Don't do me any favors."

"Sara, what am I supposed to think?" The agonized plea seemed torn from his chest.

Sara tightened her grip on her robe. "Think what you like. You're going to anyway, no matter what I say," she retorted, her throat parched.

Nick grasped her arms and forced her to face him. "Sara, be reasonable. You may have killed my aunt. But I want you and you want me. Surely, you can see the conflict."

"The conflict is only because you don't trust me," she interrupted, her voice rising. "Because you don't know me...really know me. I'm not anything at all like you think." A strangled sob caught in her throat. "I don't want possessions or wealth. I've never been interested in any of those things, and I certainly wouldn't kill anyone for them. I'm just a woman. Don't you understand?" Her eyes blazed dark on his. "Just an ordinary woman. Oh God, what's the use?" She twisted out of his grasp and looked away, tears slipping through her lashes onto her face.

"And I'm just a man, Sara," he began in a halting voice, "as you must now realize only too well." He grimaced painfully. "Sara, look at me." With his fingers, he forced her chin up. Reluctantly, her eyes opened. "You say you didn't kill Lillian, but how can I be sure?"

Suddenly, Sara had had enough. Anger, not just at Nick, but at the insane situation they'd been put in rose in her. Behind the veil of tears, her eyes turned stormy-green.

"Well, what about you, Nick?"

"Me?" He looked startled.

"Yes, you." In desperation, she searched for a way to hurt him in retaliation for his hurting her. "You'll do anything to get the formula, won't you, Nick? Including seducing me." As soon as she'd said the words, she realized how much sense they made. How could she have been so stupid? He'd come to her room—called her beautiful, made her feel special—and for one reason. When she'd asked him whether he'd contest her possession of the formula he'd said, "I'm sure I could find some way to get it out of you." Now, it hit her with chilling clarity. This seduction had been a setup!

Her words hung like a barrier of ice between them. Nick didn't move and his features had hardened into an impassive mask. His hands fell from her arms but she could still feel their warm imprint on her skin.

He stood up slowly, rising to tower over her. "Sara, you don't know what you're saying," he said in a restrained voice.

Sara took a deep breath, then looked up at him. "Don't I?" she challenged, clutching the robe tightly around her throat. "Suddenly, it all falls into place, Nick. I don't know how I could have been so blind...."

"Sara..." he protested.

"Go ahead, Nick. Tell me once and for all that you don't want the formula."

Nick stared at her for a long time. Then with cold fury in his voice, he spoke. "All right, Sara. I admit it. I do want the formula."

Sara had harbored a foolish hope that he would deny it all, but now the sickening truth was spoken between them and that hope was gone.

"Enough to lure me to your bed?" she accused between tight lips.

Nick's eyes flashed with anger. "Correction," he countered. "I wasn't doing the luring, but even if I had been, I don't need a motive to make love to you. I want you, Sara . . . more than any formula." As he turned away, he added in a low voice, "God help me."

Without another word, he stalked from the room, slamming the door behind him.

SARA SAT IMMOBILIZED, stunned by the cutting truth of Nick's statement.

What had come over her? What kind of wanton yearnings had welled up inside her to maneuver a man into making a pass at her? Nick was right. *She* had done the luring. A slow flush crept up her neck.

How could she? Nick was exactly the kind of man she'd promised herself she'd stay away from—aggressive, opinionated, strong. How could she be attracted to someone like him, a man she didn't trust, a man who thought the worst of her?

For a moment, she'd seen another side of him. Holding and caressing her, he'd been gentle, caring, giving—the kind of man she'd dreamed of, when she allowed herself to.

Dreams are games for children, she told herself angrily. The only game now was a matter of life and death.

But she couldn't ignore the reality. The formula.

She took a cloud of depression with her to bed, and found that it made an uncomfortable companion. Tossing and turning, she bunched the sheets into endless different configurations before she was able to drift off. Even then, she found herself wide awake an hour later, roused by vivid dreams.

She lay there, her body slick from the exertion of chasing sleep, images of Lillian in danger and erotic visions of Nick still fresh in her memory. It seemed she could not find peace anywhere, even in sleep.

She closed her eyes again and Nick's face and body flashed before her, stirring memories she'd just as soon forget—the sweet grazing of his lips on hers, the heat of his hands on her body...

For God's sake, Sara. Get a drink of water or something. Take a cold shower. Inching her way out of the bed, she padded to the bathroom, filled a glass with water and shuffled back to bed, glass in hand.

Impatiently, she propped up the pillows and then positioned herself against them, half closing her eyes.

The house was quiet. Silver light from the moon slanted through her open curtains, adding to the dream-haunted quality of the night. Then she heard a sound.

Like someone pacing.

Nick's room was directly beneath her suite, Edie had told her. Then...the grating noise of a window being opened. Silence. More steps. Then silence again.

Nick? Couldn't he sleep either? That prospect strangely consoled her.

WHEN THE ALARM WENT OFF, Sara groaned. Every muscle screamed for more rest. Her eyes opened reluctantly to see dawn nudging the day in a pale glow. Grimacing, she forced herself from under the bed covers.

Five minutes later, splashing cold water on her face, she winced as the water seeped under the bandage. Gingerly, she checked the cut on her face. The skin was blue and bruised, vivid against the snow-white bandage.

Makeup, she'd discovered as a teenager, was one of those feminine rituals she wasn't particularly adept at. The lack of patience she'd mentioned to Nick was nowhere more evident than in her haphazard approach to primping. The concentration it required was totally beyond her.

Not much choice, though, this morning, she thought ruefully.

With quick fingers, she added a light dusting of powder to her skin to hide the blue-black bruise and give color to the rest of her face. The skin above the right eye was significantly darker than that over her left so she applied a deep green-gray shadow to even out the effect.

The person staring back at her in the mirror possessed a feminine vulnerability that Sara barely recognized. A slight tracing of lipstick and a hint of tawny blush accentuated the image. Sara felt as if she was looking at a stranger.

A softer stranger. Where had she come from?

Unnerved by it, she shook her head as if to dispel it.

Today, she needed to be as tough as nails.

The first thing she had to do was try to get out of the house *and* to Ben's office, without risking another confrontation with Nick. *That won't be easy,* she mused. *Judging by the pacing that I heard last night, he's probably lying in wait for me, ready to pounce.*

A flush crept up her neck as she recalled the previous night's events. What had she been thinking of to practically fall into his arms that way? She hadn't been thinking—that was the problem. *From here on in, Sara Brennan, keep your wits about you.*

The self-admonition strengthened her resolve. Ten minutes later, dressed in a navy-blue pantsuit, the jacket concealing the gun nestled against her white turtleneck sweater, she slipped quietly down the back stairs toward the kitchen.

Taking a deep breath, she swung the door open, and looked around the always gleaming white kitchen. At first glance, she was sure the room was empty, and was about to let out a sigh of relief when a movement at the window caught her attention.

A shaft of rising sunlight blinded her for a moment, then the person came into focus. Nick. She bit her lower lip nervously, then gasped as she realized she'd bitten into a cut.

Nick's eyebrows raised sardonically at the sound. "Rough night?" he queried.

"No rougher than any other," she snapped obliquely, forcing herself toward the stove where a fresh pot of coffee simmered. The delicious aroma filled the air. Sara breathed in deeply convincing herself the rich smell prompted the action, and not Nick's presence.

With a less than steady hand, she pulled open a cupboard and took down a coffee mug. Out of the corner of her eye, she saw Nick move toward the table. "Cream and sugar are already on the table," he offered. She heard the scraping of a chair.

"No thanks," she replied in a stiff voice, turning. "I take mine black." She steeled herself to look at him. He was leaning his elbows on the table, watching her. Damn. Did the man have to be so blatantly male? Her gaze traveled to the open V of his shirt. Dark hair nudged the fabric.

He caught her look, then her eye. "Edie ironed some of my shirts," he said in explanation. Sara flushed, realizing he'd misinterpreted her look. But the comment brought home their encounter of the previous night, and she blushed anew.

"So I see," she managed, allowing herself a second look. The shirt did look somewhat more presentable than what Nick usually wore. "Well, if you'll excuse me..." she attempted, planning to leave, taking her coffee mug with her, "I'll just be on my way." She took a step forward and went to brush past him, but his hand snaked out and caught her arm.

"What's the rush? Now that Lillian's dead and you've inherited all her money, you hardly have to work for a living." Sarcasm edged his tone.

Hurt and anger flared in Sara. God, did the man never let up? "There are other clients I can offer my services to, Nick, and anyway, strange as it might seem to you, I actually *like* to work." She jerked her arm out of his grasp, and shot him a defiant look. So much for avoiding a confrontation, she thought.

A slow, taunting smile twisted his mouth. "I can see why. Your last assignment certainly paid off."

Sara's determination not to be drawn into an argument with Nick disintegrated in a flash. Her eyes narrowed into green-fire slits. "You're a real son of a bitch, you know that?"

Nick shrugged, a mirthless sparkle in his gaze. "That's at least ten rungs above murderess."

"For the hundreth time, I am not a murderess. You have no right to accuse me!" Her husky voice rose in agitation.

"On the contrary, I have every right."

"Rights beyond those of a loving nephew, it seems," she retaliated.

"What are you talking about?" Nick went dangerously still.

"I'm talking about you thinking you have the right to make love to me to get the formula," she lashed out, then would have bitten back the words, had it been possible. The expression on Nick's face was one of outraged fury.

She hadn't wanted to remember that part of last night—hadn't wanted *him* to remember. Why had she brought it up?

His tanned fist clenched on the table. "If memory serves me correctly, Sara, we've already had this discussion. Anyway, I think you've got it all wrong."

"Oh, I don't think so," she replied, shaking her head with more conviction than she felt. Tawny hair bounced on her shoulders in a cascade. "You want the formula. You think I might have it. And you're willing to go to any lengths to get it."

"That's enough, Sara!" In an instant, Nick was on his feet, towering over her. His fingers seized her upper arms in a steel grip. "I think it's the other way around. I think *you* would go to any lengths to keep me from getting it."

Again his nearness seemed to rob her of reason. Even though Nick's hands were bruising fabric rather than caressing her skin, the woman inside remembered their touch only too well. Fighting to regain her advantage, she tilted her head defiantly and said, "By what twisted logic do you come to that conclusion?"

"By this twisted logic, as you call it—" his mouth set into a hard line "—I want the formula. Actually, I'm entitled to it. But you don't want me to have it. So, you used your body, a beautiful one at that, I might add, to ensure that I wouldn't press charges against you . . . take my suspicions to the police. You flaunted—"

"Flaunted!" A look of shock registered on her face.

"Yes, dammit—" his grip tightened and he stepped closer "—*flaunted* your oh-so-obvious charms at me. And I, in all innocence, fell for it, right into your arms."

"Innocent?" Sara's tone of incredulity matched the sheer disbelief in her eyes. "You?"

"Well, I wasn't the heavy," he said archly. "I didn't come to your room with seduction in mind."

"I didn't know you were going to pay me a visit," she protested. He couldn't believe *she* deliberately tried to seduce *him*, could he? She might be ingenuous, but a seductress? She was no more that than a murderess. That was no defense to him, she realized with a sinking heart.

"No? But you certainly took full advantage of the situation once I did," he retorted.

"How dare you!" she whispered, the affront leaving her breathless.

"Come now, Sara. Surely you don't expect me to believe you were just carried away by the moment."

She looked up and was swallowed by his stormy-dark eyes. "Was I what?" she murmured in confusion.

"Dammit it, Sara." He shook her. "Were you just carried away by the moment or were you pretending?"

"Pretending?" Sara heard herself speak as though from a long way away. "Pretending what?" She was drowning in those eyes and her lips parted as if to yield to the experience.

"This, dammit... This." His mouth found hers, and in a sweet-savage assault his tongue invaded the moist cavern of her mouth. Without thinking, she welcomed the tender, tormented invasion. While her mind rejected Nick's lovemaking, her body welcomed him, urged him on.

A moan issued from his lips and he wrapped his arms around her as if to weld her body to the contours of his. She felt his need against her and her own answering response within.

A tortured groan sounded in the room and she realized it was her own. "Nick, no..." The words were torn from her woman's heart, from a body that betrayed her.

He pulled back reluctantly, his eyes glazed with desire, his mouth ripe with moisture. Breathlessly, he whispered,

"Well, Sara, were you pretending? Are you even now pretending?"

Sara did not answer.

His eyes fired dark. "I asked you a question. Answer me."

Lies. Lies. Sara had had enough lies, innuendo and veiled threats to last her a lifetime. Maybe once, just once, in this ridiculous ground swell of fabrication, she could tell the truth. She inhaled deeply, replying with every breath of honesty in her. "No, Nick. As God is my witness, I wasn't pretending."

Nick's deep-set eyes searched hers for what seemed a suspended moment in time. Then his hands dropped to his sides. With a hoarse whisper that wrenched her heart, he rasped, "I hope you believe in God, Sara." In seconds, he'd twisted his body away from hers and left the kitchen, abandoning her to face a confusion of emotions.

Oh my God. What have I done? What have I admitted?

Her hand flew to her flushed face. Five minutes with Nick, and she'd not only let him provoke her anger, but also allowed him to trigger a raging sexual need inside her.

With shaking hands, and on trembling legs that yesterday had seemed so sturdy, she vacated the kitchen. Car? Car? What had she done with her car? Then she remembered. The accident. She'd have to make arrangements to have it towed to a garage.

Mason, the chauffeur, met her at the back of the house.

"Morning, Miss Brennan." He smiled at her.

She returned his smile. "Morning, Mason. My car's out of commission. I left it on the side road on the way to the estate, about twenty minutes from here. Could you make arrangements with the garage to fix it?"

"Sure thing."

Sara looked past him toward the six-car estate garage. "Is there another car I could use today?"

The husky fifty-year-old raised a speculative eyebrow. "Just the Rolls. How about that?"

Sara grimaced. As beautiful as the classic car was, she felt uncomfortable and conspicuous in it. Whatever Nick might think, ostentation was not her style. But if it was that or nothing... "Okay." She nodded to the waiting Mason. "If I have to."

The uniformed man guffawed good-naturedly. "Most people wouldn't mind, Miss Brennan."

Her mouth twitched softly. "I guess not."

"Do you want me to drive?"

"No, I'll be fine. I just feel like puddling around. Thanks anyway, Mason. I appreciate the offer."

"All right, I'll get it for you." While Sara waited, she thought of Nick, wondering what he would be doing today. The idea that he might go to the police station to report his suspicions was a chilling one. *Get a move on, Sara.*

AN HOUR LATER, Sara found herself staring openmouthed at Ben Short's secretary.

"You're absolutely sure?" she queried Esther Reynolds.

Sitting at her desk, Ben's secretary fussed and clucked in sympathy while Sara stood over her, every muscle tense.

"Quite unlike him, isn't it? He said he just had to get away for a few days. Just like that." She snapped her fingers in the air. "Told me to cancel all his appointments and to convey his apologies to you."

First, Lillian had disappeared. Now, Ben. Sara's green eyes darkened. Surely this couldn't be coincidental? Why would they flee and leave her to hold the bag? That Lillian might, she could almost accept, if not forgive. Lillian would be too caught up in the idea of an escapade to consider the consequences. But Ben?

Sara struggled to keep the worry out of her voice as she asked, ''Did he see any clients before he told you he was leaving, or take any calls?''

Esther tapped her pencil on the edge of the typewriter, shaking her head first sideways, and then up and down. ''Saw no one, but took a call.''

Sara quickened to attention. ''Anyone you know.''

Esther considered the question with maddening efficiency. ''I do and I don't. She didn't give her name, but she's called Ben before and I remembered the voice, so I put her through.''

Sara's mind seized on one word. She. ''Did the voice sound at all like the late Mrs. Kingsley?'' she asked, trying to make the question seem casual.

''No, not at all. A lot earthier than that.''

''Could you remember the name if you thought about it?'' Sara pushed.

''Maybe. She hasn't called for a year or so. All I can recall is that it's a nickname of some sort. She's one of Ben's friends, not a client, so I wouldn't have a file on her. I don't tend to remember personal calls, which I've discovered is an asset.'' Esther raised her eyebrows meaningfully at Sara.

''Yes, of course,'' Sara answered distractedly, not paying much attention to Esther's response. ''Could you call me if you remember the name?''

''Sure.''

''Thanks.'' Sara mumbled her reply, then left Ben's office. Something had happened to both Lillian and Ben. She could sense it.

Sara sat in the car, mulling over her options. There were very few, and the only sensible one sent a trickle of sweat down her back under the sweater.

The police.

What choice did she have now? She couldn't handle this alone. There was no one she could turn to.

Except . . . Nick.

Life would be so much simpler if she could share this with him. But she couldn't . . . could she?

No, that's not an option.

But there is one thing I can do, she thought resolutely. *Before I go to the police, I can check out some of these names. Lillian, and maybe Ben, might be with one of them.*

It's worth a shot.

She flinched at her own choice of words, then turned the key in the ignition.

Chapter Seven

"Mr. Kingsley?"

Nick glanced up from his position in the visitor's chair of a small office in the York Regional Police detachment in Aurora. "Yes."

A dark-haired, classically good-looking officer in his early forties came up behind him, extending his hand. He was wearing a navy pin-striped suit. Well cut, it hugged a trim, fit body. "I'm Detective Sergeant John Adams." Rather than moving to the other side of the desk, he perched himself casually on its edge, facing Nick, one long leg stretched in front of him. He leaned forward to complete the handshake. Under his open jacket, Nick caught sight of a shoulder holster and snub-nosed .38 revolver. The image inadvertently reminded him of Sara, and he shoved the thought impatiently out of his mind.

"Pleased to meet you," Nick acknowledged, then he noticed the detective had a folder in his hand. The officer opened it and pulled out a few sheets of paper.

"This is your statement, I understand." He held the sheets toward Nick for verification.

Checking the signature, Nick nodded.

Detective Adams continued to hold the folder open, and stared thoughtfully at Nick. "You think your aunt's been murdered, Mr. Kingsley?" he asked in a quiet voice.

Nick's response was firm. "I do."

"And you'd like an autopsy?" Adams continued, still looking directly at Nick.

Nick nodded again.

The officer laid a hand across his thigh. "You realize, of course, that before we can exhume your aunt's body, we need reasonable and probable grounds to do so."

"I was under the impression it was my duty to report a suspicious death to the police," Nick replied tartly. Now that he'd brought his suspicions to the police, he wasn't feeling very comfortable with his decision. Sara's passion in his arms last night and this morning had unnerved him. Her avowal that she wasn't faking her response to him had unsettled him even more. If she was telling the truth about that, then maybe, just maybe, her consistent affirmations of innocence were also true. Dammit, what the hell was he supposed to do? His aunt was dead. He couldn't let his feelings for Sara override that glaring fact.

The officer's words propelled Nick sharply back to the conversation. "Oh, it is, Mr. Kingsley," the detective was reassuring. "Don't get me wrong. Your aunt died 'suddenly and unexpectedly,' as the term goes. That in itself is cause for suspicion. I was just giving you the opportunity to reconsider your statement. I assume then that you're satisfied with it as it now reads?" He raised a brow inquisitively.

Satisfied? Anything but, Nick thought gloomily. Aloud, he replied, "I wouldn't have signed it if I wasn't." He sounded testier than he'd intended.

The detective's gaze fixed on his. Nick felt as if he was being appraised under a microscope. "I'm sure this is quite difficult for you, Mr. Kingsley, coming back and finding your aunt dead. It must have been quite a shock."

Nick's response was tight-lipped. "It was."

After an eloquent moment of silence Detective Adams broke the deadlock of their gazes and looked down absently at the folder again. "Tell me, Mr. Kingsley, do you know the person you claim is the prime suspect—Sara Brennan?"

"I do."

"I see. You've met her then?"

"Yes, once or twice."

A flash of perception shone in the officer's hazel eyes. "That in itself can be disturbing." he commented offhandedly. "People often find themselves upset by the fact that they might actually know a killer."

Nick watched the detective with grudging respect. The man seemed capable of finding the most sensitive nerve in the shortest possible time. *You don't know how right you are this time,* Nick thought.

"I guess we're not as seasoned as the police," Nick remarked in a strained voice.

The detective laughed. "We're not that seasoned either, Mr. Kingsley. We're just better trained at not showing it." His gaze strayed to the folder again. "Now, let's see. Have you by any chance talked to the doctor who treated Mrs. Kingsley the night she died?"

Nick shook his head. "No, I'm afraid I don't know who he was."

Detective Adams nodded, seemingly absently. "Who was with her when she died? Sara Brennan?"

"I don't know whether Sara was there or not. According to the housekeeper, though, Ben Short, Lillian's lawyer, was with her. I don't know if he was alone or not."

"The lawyer—really?" Detective Adams's inflection showed interest. "Have you talked to Mr. Short?"

"No."

"Oh. That's a bit unusual, isn't it?"

Nick gave the detective a sharp glance. "Why?"

"It was no secret that your aunt was an incredibly wealthy woman," he replied in a quiet voice. "I would have thought you'd be named in her will. It wouldn't be considered unnatural for you to contact her lawyer and make inquiries to that effect."

"Well, I didn't and I haven't," Nick responded. "I intended to, but I'm afraid I haven't gotten around to it yet."

"I see."

Nick wasn't sure that *he* saw at all. There was always the possibility, of course, that Lillian had bequeathed him the formula in her will, but he seriously doubted it. According to Gertrude, Charles had passed the formula to Lillian verbally. He suspected that Lillian had then given it to Sara. Once Sara had it, she had probably convinced Lillian to write a will naming her as beneficiary to everything else she owned. Then she'd killed his aunt. Lillian's will didn't really interest him. His only concern was the formula and avenging Lillian's death.

It was time to get to the point, Nick thought. "Detective Adams, if Lillian named Sara as her beneficiary, would that not provide a motive for Sara to have killed my aunt?"

The detective shifted his position on the desk. "It would establish a motive, but it wouldn't prove that Sara had acted on it. Has the will been probated?"

"I don't know."

A detached expression masked the officer's face. "Seems to me, Mr. Kingsley, that both of us should be contacting Mr. Short."

Nick was finding that the conversation was making him tense. What he had to do was distasteful enough, without talking endlessly about it. He took a deep breath. "Detective, are you or are you not going to order an autopsy?"

"The coroner does that," Adams corrected. "But yes, I can take steps. If you'll just bear with me for a few more moments."

Impatience flared in Nick. "Okay, but let's get on with it."

The detective's eyes grew large for a second at Nick's tone, then he resumed the conversation. "Were you aware, Mr. Kingsley, that the day of your aunt's death, there was an attempt on her life?"

"Yes. I heard about it shortly after I arrived back in Canada."

The officer pulled another batch of papers from the file. "I have the police report on that incident. It says here that Sara was with her at the time. Someone apparently took a shot at your aunt with a high-powered rifle."

Nick sat forward. "There. Doesn't that prove something?" he asked in a harsh voice.

"I don't follow."

"If she was with Sara, Sara could have set it up."

The officer shrugged. "Maybe. But the shot was fired through Sara's window."

"So?" Nick asked irritably, not sure what he was getting at.

"So..." Detective Adams stood up slowly, tossing the folder on the desk. "There's always the possibility Sara was the intended victim."

Nick frowned. "How likely is that?"

"Hard to tell." Detective Adams moved to the other side of the desk and reached for the telephone. "Just one more thing, Mr. Kingsley—" his fingers rested on the black phone "—someone has tried to kidnap your aunt a number of times, and on each occasion, Ms Brennan thwarted the attempts, rather successfully, I might add."

"Are you saying you think she's innocent?" Nick asked through clenched jaws.

"I'm saying she's innocent until proved guilty," the officer reminded cautiously. "But what I'm also trying to point out is there are some other aspects to this case you might not be aware of." He picked up the receiver.

Nick interjected, "I think that Sara set up the last attempt on my aunt's life, and when her accomplice with the gun wasn't successful, she took matters into her own hands, and tried to kill my aunt again the same night. Except—" his voice dropped "—this time she was successful."

"Interesting theory," the detective allowed as he dialed. Nick waited impatiently, then the officer spoke into the phone. "Dr. Hess, please. Detective Sergeant Adams, York Regional Police, Aurora. Yes . . . yes . . . I'll wait." Covering the mouthpiece, he made an aside to Nick. "We have a new chief coroner," he explained, then he broke off to speak into the phone again.

"Hello, Doctor. How are you liking the job? Good. I wonder if you could do me a favor. Could you check your records for me? I want to confirm the cause of death for a Lillian Kingsley and the name of the doctor who signed the death certificate. Hang on—" He cupped the mouthpiece again, addressing Nick. "What was the exact date?"

"October fifteenth," Nick replied.

"October fifteenth," Detective Adams repeated. "Fine . . . okay . . ." He paused as if waiting for a response, his gaze directed at a far blank wall, then he turned to face Nick again. "Yes, Doctor, I'm here. . . ." Watching him, Nick saw a frown suddenly deepen the fine lines on his forehead. "You're sure?"

"What is it?" Nick stood up impatiently and came to stand next to the officer.

The detective's eyes flickered upward. His hands rested on the mouthpiece. "The coroner can't find a death certificate for your aunt."

"He what?"

The officer edged away from Nick for a moment. "Doctor, could you please double-check...."

"Here, give me that." Nick grabbed the phone from Detective Adams and rasped into it. "Doctor, this is Nick Kingsley, Lillian Kingsley's nephew. Are you sure there's no death certificate?" A film of perspiration broke out along his top lip. In some obscure corner of Nick's mind a slim hope had remained that something would be discovered to remove any possibility of Sara's guilt. This discovery removed that hope. The absence of a death certificate meant that whoever had killed Lillian hadn't wanted to risk either a doctor's or a coroner's examination.

"I see," he replied as the doctor's clipped voice reiterated what he'd told Detective Adams.

"Please, Mr. Kingsley. Let me speak to him," the detective urged beside him.

Woodenly, Nick returned the phone to the officer and, seconds later, slumped in the chair he'd only recently vacated. The detective's voice droned in his ears.

"Yes, I agree. You'll issue the exhumation order right away then? Good. I'll send Constable Canfield to pick you up and I'll meet you at the cemetery. Yes. Thanks. Good-bye, Doctor."

Nick heard the click of the receiver in the cradle, and raised his head to face the detective. There was nothing to say. He had come here to prove Sara's guilt and it looked as though he'd succeeded. Why was it all so depressing?

The detective's voice broke the silence. "Well, Mr. Kingsley. You got what you wanted, but you don't appear pleased."

Nick ran his fingers distractedly through his thick dark hair. "I guess when push comes to shove, I really didn't want to believe it."

"We all prefer that our suspicions not be confirmed," Detective Adams offered politely.

Nick looked up to acknowledge the comment. This was one suspicion he'd have given a king's ransom to dispel. "I'll come with you to the cemetery," he said in a quiet voice.

The officer stopped shuffling the papers on his desk, and glanced up in surprise. "You don't have to, Mr. Kingsley. It might be unpleasant for you."

"I'd rather come."

Detective Adams shrugged. "As you wish. Now, if you don't mind, I'll tell Constable Canfield to pick up the coroner and the warrant. We'll meet them at the grave site."

Nick nodded, unable to say anything more.

HALF AN HOUR LATER, Nick and Detective Adams were on the way south on Yonge Street to the cemetery. The officer slanted a look at Nick. "Did you know that Sara Brennan is a deputy chief's daughter?"

Nick knew. "Do you think that makes a difference in terms of her innocence or of her guilt?" he asked cryptically.

"Neither." The officer deftly changed lanes in the busy traffic. "She isn't above the law, regardless of whose daughter she is. I was just making conversation. I knew her father—Jack Brennan. He was a superb officer—incorruptible."

"That doesn't mean his daughter is," Nick replied bitterly.

"No—" Detective Adams adjusted his sunglasses "—but it does mean that if she's guilty, it's a double tragedy." The regret in the officer's voice made Nick sorry that he had been so abrupt.

"Yes, I see what you mean. Sorry. I didn't mean to sound so abrasive."

The detective gave a half smile. "No problem."

Both fell into silence for the balance of the trip, and by the time they had pulled into the cemetery grounds Nick could see the grave digger was already there with Constable Canfield and another man, who Nick assumed was the coroner. The trio stood waiting in the distance, while Detective Adams parked the car.

"Not much of a walk. Come on, Mr. Kingsley," Detective Adams directed conversationally. Nick got out of his side of the car and followed the officer.

"Tom. Henry. Dr. Hess." He acknowledged the three waiting figures. "This is Nick Kingsley. Did you want to start, Doctor?" Nick inclined his head to the three figures without actually focusing on any of them. Then as he heard the doctor give the order to commence, he looked away. He heard the first load of soil being tossed aside, then fixed his gaze on a huge tree, almost stripped of its foliage by the ravages of autumn.

God, what did he want them to find? What didn't he want them to find? Confusion roared inside him ebbing and flowing like an erratic ocean tide. Although Lillian had been offhanded and selfish at times, Nick had loved her. The idea that she'd been murdered had filled him with rage when he'd first encountered it. Now that he faced the idea that Sara had been responsible for Lillian's death, that rage was slowly turning to despair. Behind him, he could hear the rhythmic chug of the small mechanical steam shovel. Then the sound stopped, and he braced himself.

"Okay, let's get it out," he heard Detective Adams say. Nick felt a sudden chill and pulled his coat tighter around him. The sound of a heavy object being moved sliced through him like a jagged razor. Then...a click, a lid being lifted.

Then, a gasp. "I don't believe it." Detective Adams's incredulity shattered the stillness that had settled over

Nick. With a start, he turned around, and saw the open casket....

It was empty. The white satin interior shimmered in the gray light of day. "There's no body," he managed, his mind rejecting what he saw.

"You can say that again!" someone quipped, but Detective Adams interrupted.

"I hadn't expected this," he said quietly.

Nick continued to stare. "But what does it mean?" he rasped. "Is it possible...?" His thoughts spun in circles. "Is it possible my aunt is still alive?" He looked around distractedly at the other three men, seeking confirmation or denial.

Detective Adams met his stare. A perplexed frown creased his forehead. Then he shook his head.

"Somehow that doesn't make sense. I suspect the body's missing because an examination of it could prove foul play. That's probably why there was no death certificate. I think the body's been moved—"

"But the earth..." Nick interjected.

"...is still freshly turned from the burial, so it would be difficult to prove it had been disturbed," the detective finished for him. "I think the body could have been moved, and that whoever did it guessed that sooner or later we'd order an autopsy. Either guessed or knew..." His words trailed off as his gaze narrowed on Nick. "Any ideas, Mr. Kingsley, as to which it is?"

Nick's blood ran cold. He knew where the detective's question was leading. *I tipped off the killer myself,* he thought. *I told her myself....*

NICK STORMED INTO THE MAIN HOUSE bent on vengeance. What a fool he'd been to even think of trusting Sara! He slammed the door behind him.

When he got his hands on her, he was going to get the truth out of her, if it took all night.

He could postpone the inevitable no longer. If Sara had killed Lillian, she had to be brought to justice, regardless of how painful it would be for him.

"Mr. Kingsley!" The housekeeper stared in shock as he stomped through the vestibule, his muddy boots streaking the pristine white tiles.

"Where is she?" he barked, without stopping.

"She?" Edie twisted a corner of her apron in her hand, confused by Nick's behavior, and suddenly wary of the elemental force emanating from him. "Sara?" she posed, her manner hesitant.

"Yes, Sara. The supposed bodyguard," he spit out.

"The—the library," she sputtered.

"Is there any booze in there?" he asked angrily.

"Yes..." she faltered. "Sara wouldn't..." she attempted, totally misunderstanding.

He scowled, equally perplexed. "Wouldn't what? You'd be surprised at what she would do—has done, in fact." Then seeing the confusion and fear on Edie's face, he forced himself to calm down. Contrite, he muttered, "Sorry, Edie. I need a good stiff drink."

Edie shook her head in wonderment. Lord. Since Lillian Kingsley had passed away, this house had been in a turmoil and its two prime occupants, Nick and Sara, had been as jittery as thoroughbreds at the gate. Edie couldn't fathom the tension and longed for the old-world elegance that Lillian had filled the house with, foolish as she had sometimes been.

Nick sat on the bottom step of the spiral staircase, removing his boots with jerky, impatient motions. Edie hurriedly retrieved his shoes from the foyer's walk-in closet. In seconds, he'd rammed his feet into them.

"Thanks," he murmured. "I'll be in the library." He turned sharply on his heel, heading past the staircase toward the back of the house, his body tensed for battle, his trench coat flapping.

Edie stared, shocked into silence by the angry thrust of his shoulders, then hurriedly withdrew to the kitchen.

Nick threw open the double doors of the library with one energetic sweep.

Sara had only just arrived home. Slumped in exhaustion on one of the love seats, she looked up in surprise at the noisy intrusion. Nick slammed the door behind him, his anger unmistakable. His dark eyes flashed as he crossed the room.

Oh no, she thought. *Not now.*

He strode over to her, looming, his mouth set in a hard line.

Sara drew in a deep breath and waited for the onslaught. The day had already been a disaster. She'd systematically gone through the list of friends with whom Lillian could be staying. But a house-to-house search had turned up no trace of Lillian. She'd needed an excuse for the visits, so she'd used the explanation that she wanted to thank them personally for their notes of sympathy. Everyone had been gracious and conciliatory, but that was it. Not one single clue she could follow up on! And now this.

Sara stared resignedly at Nick. "Well, what do you want?"

The coffee table separated them, but she could almost feel this hot breath as he snarled, "Where's the body?"

Her stomach lurched. He'd been to the police! So much for thinking she'd beat him to it! If only she'd gone straight there instead of stopping here to marshal her thoughts. Angry with herself for the time she'd lost, she answered in defiance, "I don't know."

"Don't know?" he repeated in disbelief, falling into the love seat opposite her. "Don't know or don't care? What's the matter? Didn't your accomplices tell you where they put the body?"

"Accomplices?" The man had gone off the deep end. What accomplices? Ben? If she hadn't have been so distraught, she'd have almost laughed at the image of Ben as a criminal accomplice. "I haven't a clue what you're talking about."

He thrust his body backward impatiently. The cushions sank against his weight.

You could hardly wait to come in here, and accuse me. Is that it, Nick? You didn't even stop to take your coat off, she thought sadly.

He leveled a scornful look at her. "You really push a man too far, Sara. Give me credit for some intelligence. You couldn't move the body alone. Admit it. You're a first-class fraud."

The last remark was the final torturous blow for Sara. This crazy scheme of Lillian's had brought them to this. Might she and Nick have had a chance together if it hadn't been for this ruse? Maybe. But now all they had was suspicion and deception.... Regret formed a hollow ache inside her.

"Nick, maybe if you'd given me a chance..." she started.

He didn't let her finish. "A chance? A chance to do what?"

"To explain. A chance to give us time to trust each other."

"Trust! That's a fine word coming from you, Sara. Lillian trusted you with her life."

Sara fought back the tears that welled up in her. "I didn't betray that trust, Nick."

"No?" he asked, in a scandalized tone. "Then how come she's dead, Sara?"

"I—" What could she say and still keep her promise to Ben? Nothing. Nick would never know what kind of a person she really was—what kind of a woman. If she could have grieved for that lost chance, she would have...but the grieving would have to come later.

"What, no snappy answer?" He raised a dark brow at her.

"Please," she pleaded, raising misty eyes to his, "I've had enough. Can't you see that? Have you no heart?"

The question startled Nick, and forced him to take a long, hard look at Sara. He could see something different—yes—but what was it? A golden rose stained her cheeks, but it was a feverish blush. Her green eyes, usually so vibrant and flashing, seemed sad and dulled. He hesitated before responding. Finally, he repeated, "No heart," testing the phase as if it was unfamiliar to him. Then his voice dropped to a murmur as if he was talking to himself. "No heart, you say? You forget, Sara, I'm not the one who killed Lillian. And you talk to me about no heart." He gave her a pained look.

His expression mirrored the deep anguish she was feeling. For a fleeting moment, the realization that this charade had cheated them both knifed through her. Then she sagged on the love seat, tired and beaten.

She took a deep breath to reanimate herself, but found it didn't help. "I'm only going to say this once, Nick. I love your aunt very much. I enjoyed the time we spent together. I would no more have killed Lillian than my own father. And especially not for money. Nothing would please me more than to see Lillian walk through that door." She inclined her head toward the other end of the library, the tears almost spilling. "I miss Lillian a great deal." She straightened her shoulders, tension knotting her neck muscles. "Now, if you don't mind, I've had a tiring day... and it isn't over yet. You'll have to excuse me."

With that, she stood awkwardly, every moment costing her a supreme effort of will, and walked through the open doors.

Seeing her leave, Nick wanted to say something to stop her, but he didn't know what he could say. For some reason, he didn't think he'd won anything by challenging her. Watching her begin to crack had been a hollow victory at best. As Sara had turned to go, the table lamp had illuminated her face. Exhaustion had been etched deep on her usually animated features. Her drawn skin was so pale, it had been almost translucent. What was happening here? What was happening to Sara?

Sitting alone, still in his coat, Nick frowned. Something Sara had said still bothered him. Something he couldn't put his finger on.

Then it dawned on him.

Love. I love your aunt very much.

Sara had used the present tense.

With a start, he jumped up and walked quickly to the foyer. "Sara," he called.

But the entrance was empty, a shimmering light dancing a soft gold pattern on the tiled white floor.

"And it isn't over yet..." she'd said.

What isn't, Sara? He stared up at the empty staircase.

SARA TURNED ON THE WATER for her shower dispiritedly. Fear for Ben's and Lillian's safety throbbed inside her head like a relentless drumbeat. Nick's continued contempt disturbed her. Her head felt as if it was going to burst.

If she could just trust Nick... if he didn't despise her so much! If... if...

Sighing, she began to strip off her clothes, then stopped. She'd almost told him the truth tonight. There was strength in his persistence, even if it was misdirected. His pain over Lillian's supposed death had moved her, and for a few seconds, she'd caught a glimpse of that other man beneath the aggressive surface—a man with sensitivity and depth.

When he touched her, there'd been an openness to his passion. Remembering, she shuddered. Heat rose inside her. Could a man's touch lie? *You bet. Happens all the time.* She could feel her ardor cooling at that thought.

So where did he fit in the scheme of things.

Should she add him to the flimsy list of suspects? Graham Marshall, owner of Kingsley Chemicals, the three suitors, the chemist and Tess Bond?

Questions. No answers. Damn it all. Who was behind all this? How had they known that Lillian was still alive? That Ben was involved?

Defeated, she went back to undressing. *Let the police sort it out. Just get over there and give them a statement. If you wait much longer, it could be too late for Lillian and Ben.*

Mobilized out of her musings, she pulled the rest of her clothes off and stepped under the water.

Five minutes later, she stood on the fluffy yellow bathmat and reached for a towel on the rack.

As her fingers made contact with the towel, the light went out in the bathroom.

"Damn," she cursed, under her breath. A blown bulb.

Hurriedly drying herself as best as she could in the dark, she felt for her robe on the back of the door and threw it on, wrapping the belt firmly around her waist.

Reaching for the door handle, she turned the knob.

She stepped into darkness. All the lights in the suite were out.

A power failure? She frowned. If so, it would affect the security system.

Groping along the wall, she used her fingers as sensors, testing where the wall would stop. She should almost be at the end of the corridor now. Her outstretched fingers found the edge.

Good, she murmured to herself, relaxing. There it was.

More confident now that she had her bearings, she walked purposefully into the bedroom, turning left toward the night table. She kept a flashlight in the top drawer.

She took a few steps forward, then suddenly, out of nowhere, a body hurtled into her. She gasped as the wind was knocked from her lungs.

She tried to scream, but the loss of air had taken away her voice. A rough hand moved in from the right to clamp over her mouth. Two more hands seized her arms, twisting them fiercely behind her.

As she struggled, her mind clicked into neutral, then began to make a professional evaluation of the situation. There were two of them, moving in on her from each side. From the size and angle of the hand over her mouth, at least one of them was big.

Squirming with every ounce of energy she could muster, she found herself immobilized against a male body. The hold was skillfully executed.

These men were professionals.

Fearing for her life, she placed a kick and found a vulnerable spot.

A constricted male voice rasped, "Get that needle in her...fast."

A needle! They were going to tranquilize her.

To kidnap her? Or make her easier to kill?

An extra surge of adrenaline shot through her at the thought, and she wrenched with all her strength. She fought furiously, using the only weapon she had—her body weight. The two men were struggling now to maintain a hold on the suddenly fierce bundle of angry energy she'd become.

Jerking with all her might, Sara pulled her head away from the hand and bit down on it as hard as she could. The man on the right yelped, but before she could open her mouth to scream, his hand slapped across her jaw, trapping air and sound in her throat. The brutal blow almost stunned her.

And then she felt it…a needle prick grazing the skin of her left arm. Yanking wildly to stop the penetration of the needle, she hurled her body and the opponent to the left of her against the wall. He hit with a heavy thud. In the confusion, the other man loosened his hold.

It was a slim advantage, but she took it. Using her left hand like a hammer, the thrust her right elbow into the man's midsection, breaking his clawlike grip on her upper arm. Her right hand now free, she brought it sweeping down on the hand clamped over her mouth.

The karate blow infuriated the man. "You bitch!" he snarled, lunging for her. Sara didn't wait to hear the rest.

"Nick!" she screamed, breaking free and darting across the room to where she'd hung her gun on the back of a chair. Before she could reach it, one of the men tackled her.

A cry escaped her lips as her leg smashed into the dresser. She twisted her body around, her arm flying in a wild curve, searching for a handhold, a brace from which she could fight.

Then her eyes widened, as the man made a quick motion with his hand, reaching inside his jacket.

She gasped as she saw what he held.

A silver glint. Sleek and eerie in the dark.

A knife, poised and glittering, aimed at her heart.

Chapter Eight

Nick paced the bedroom, his shirt already half-open, pulled askew by agitated fingers.

He scowled. The last thing in the world he needed now was to feel sympathy for Sara. It was bad enough that his loins seared with heat whenever she was around. Passion was one thing. You could always take a cold shower for that. But tenderness was quite another.

He'd sworn he would never let another woman turn him inside out as his ex-wife had done. Her emotional games had jaundiced him for life. As had Lillian's.

Still...

He paused in the middle of the room. Maybe Sara wasn't playing games. Maybe...

Maybe what?

Maybe her affection for Lillian was real. *Maybe the intense loyalty and conviction you saw tonight in her wasn't play-acting....*

Maybe, just maybe... you're as wrong about her as she is about you. If she is wrong...

Lord knows he didn't have much patience or polish. Living with Charles Kingsley had taught him aggression, but not much else. In Charles's world, tender emotions were scoffed at, not admired.

When Nick had finally married hoping to find the gentleness he'd missed in his early years, he'd discovered another side to the coin. Tenderness, as his wife had practiced it, could be as exploitive as any of Charles's more obvious ploys. Was it any wonder he didn't trust people easily?

And how different from him was Sara? Not much, he guessed. She could jump the gun pretty fast as well.

He swore, slumped on the bed and jerked his shoes off. He and Sara were two of a kind. Which was probably why sparks flared whenever they were in range of each other.

That...and this ridiculous formula business...and a certain chemistry between them that was becoming increasingly impossible to ignore. The force of that attraction seemed to be with him always now. He gritted his teeth as desire for her flashed in him like a firebrand.

With difficulty, he set it aside, concentrating instead on the other Sara, the one he'd seen tonight. He sensed somehow that she was in trouble—on the brink of exhaustion. Why? What was going on? Had she killed Lillian, or loved her as she said? Why had she used the present tense? Where was Lillian's body?

And, the big question. Why had someone tried to kill Sara?

Suddenly, he couldn't stand the confusion any longer. Purposefully, he rammed his feet back into his shoes. *One of us is going to have to let the guard down, and for once in my life, it might as well be me.*

Standing up, he headed toward the landing, leading to Sara's suite.

The sound of running water made him hesitate. He swallowed a curse and returned to his room. *Better give her a chance to finish her shower before you go barging in.*

Pacing impatiently, he heard another sound echoing on the grounds. The dogs, Cloud and Storm, were barking.

He walked over to the window. The barking was becoming increasingly high-pitched and excited. Then the noise suddenly stopped. Standing to the side of the windows, he strained his eyes to scan the grounds.

Everything seemed normal. Discreetly placed lanterns illuminated the formal gardens, but the woods were dark, shrouding the extensive fencing that totally surrounded the estate.

He hadn't checked how sophisticated the estate's alarm system was, although he knew an intercom system operated the entry gates.

Why had the dogs barked, then stopped?

A sense of foreboding crept up his spine, and without reaching for a jacket, he moved to the landing and ran down the back stairs, through the kitchen and out into the night.

An evening mist caressed his bare arms and throat. He took a few seconds to adjust to the darkness, then unerringly picked his way through the courtyard banked by shrubbery, glancing around for the dogs.

At night, the German shepherds were turned loose to patrol. They could be anywhere.

He decided to start at the kennels to the rear of the estate. A pathway led to open grassy ground, and as he followed it his eyes became accustomed to the darkness. As he drew near the kennel enclosure, he spied two dark shapes lying on the ground. Racing toward them, he recognized Cloud and Storm.

Both dogs growled low in their throats, each raising its head. Storm went to stand up, but fell back, unable to make it. Wary, Nick approached Cloud first. The dog's lower lids were red and the eyes glassy.

Tranquilized, he thought. Not hurt. Just tranquilized.

Quickly, he scanned the ground, his suspicions confirmed. A syringe lay on the cement near Storm. Then he noticed another syringe still lodged in Cloud's leg muscle. With deft fingers, he removed it.

The significance of the situation hit him quick and hard. The threat of two prowling dogs had been removed. Someone was trying to get into the house, or—he broke into a clammy sweat—was already in the house.

Sara!

He jumped to his feet quickly. Taking a shortcut to the front of the house, he raced, heart pounding, along a narrow cobblestoned pathway.

Stopping, he looked up, searching for Sara's windows.

They were completely dark.

His lungs constricted as if banded with steel. Sara had been taking a shower. Since when did people take showers in the dark?

"Sara!" he bellowed. At the same time, he tore up the front steps and reached out to shove the door open.

It was locked.

"Damn it to hell," he roared, banging on the massive wooden panel. "Edie! Open the door!"

AT THE DISTANT SOUND of Nick's voice, the second man stopped in his tracks halfway across the bedroom. "I'm getting the hell out of here," he said nervously.

Sara also heard the muffled voice. Scrambling against the dresser, she opened her mouth to scream, but the man with the knife saw her.

"Oh, no, you don't," he rasped, and with a fast vicious swipe, struck her.

She fell back, a swell of darkness sweeping over her like the crest of a warm wave. But even as she fought to keep from sinking into its cavernous blackness, she heard the man answer his companion.

"One thrust of the knife, and it's over.... You hear me! We don't get paid if we don't finish her off. And that's exactly what I'm going to do...."

In a haze, she saw the deadly flash of silver. Forcing open her mouth, she concentrated every fiber of her body into forming one word, one name....

"Nick!" Her deep-throated cry echoed through the house.

NICK HAD JUST TURNED AWAY to head for the back of the house when Edie yanked open the front door.

"Mr. Kingsley! What on earth..." she questioned in a breathless voice, feverishly tying the belt of her housecoat. "Why..." Before Edie could finish, Sara's scream filled the mansion.

Her eyes widened in horror as she stood riveted to the spot. Her head swiveled backward toward the stairs.

Hearing the bloodcurdling sound, Nick wheeled around in midmotion and stormed past Edie. "Someone's in the house. Activate the alarm. Sara!" he yelled, taking the stairs two at a time.

Recovering, Edie ran toward the rear of the house.

When Nick reached the third floor, he sprinted down the long hallway past the elevator to Sara's suite, just in time to see a dark shadow dart down the back stairs.

"Stop!" he shouted. He didn't expect the command to be obeyed, but the man might hesitate. He did, for a fraction, glancing furtively back at Nick on the landing. The unlit passageway hid his features. Nick crouched, preparing to spring, just as the man pulled a gun. The dull gray shadow alerted him and he ducked back a second before a bullet whistled past his ear. Then he heard the man running.

What the hell happened to the alarm system? he thought.

Sara. What was happening to Sara?

With rapid steps, he raced to her darkened suite. At first he couldn't focus. Then, when he could see, he emitted a gasp of rage.

Sara was fighting for her life.

When Nick had yelled her name the second time, her attacker had hesitated, and Sara had mobilized herself into action. With lightning speed, she'd thrust her body upward, lashing out with her hand to knock the knife out of his grip. Gleaming, it had spun in the air, and both the attacker and Sara had dived for it.

Her fingers had reached it first, but her opponent's bearlike hand anchored over hers, trying to wrest it from her grasp.

Seeing the pair struggling for the knife, Nick sprang in the air, the full force of his weight sending the man sprawling. But in the split second before that, the assailant had managed to wrench the knife away from Sara, and dragged her with him, twisting her around so that the knife was at her throat.

Panting for breath, Sara fought against the man's grip, but he jerked her to her feet, one arm wrapped around her. The knife grazed the skin of her neck.

"One more step, and she's a dead woman," he snarled at Nick, breathing hard.

Sara squirmed against his hold. "Nick..." she began, her gaze searching for him in the darkness, but the man flashed the knife in front of her face. Inhaling sharply, she fell silent, swallowing hard to control the wild beating of her heart. The edge of the knife pressed against her throat.

Nick stood up slowly, his hands clenched in angry fists by his sides. "You harm one hair of her head...and *you're* a dead man," he growled. He stood poised like a snake, silent, still and watchful.

Sara held her breath. She could sense her attacker's caution. His whole body had tensed. Nick's stance and voice possessed a deadly, dangerous calm.

At last he responded, but his voice now had a nervous edge. "Yeah? Maybe...but I'll still take her down first."

"Don't even try it." Nick's answer was ice, brittle and cold. His body inched forward. The man panicked. He thrust out with the knife in Nick's direction and Sara broke free, just in time to see the knife sideswipe Nick's arm as he tried to avoid the man's lunge.

Blood spurted, staining his white shirt.

"Nick!" Sara gasped in shock. But he couldn't hear. He hurled himself at the man, and before Sara could do anything, the two men became a blur of rolling bodies. She heard the crack of fists against bone and muscle. She was about to go for her gun, when she saw Nick knock the knife out of the man's hand.

She dived for it, but the man was too fast for her and reached it first. Grasping the handle, he swung it in an erratic curve toward her, and she ducked. Seeing what was happening to Sara, Nick loosened his hold on the man, and the assailant, chest heaving, struggled to his feet. Nick tried to stop him, but the man shoved him aside. Nick fell heavily against the coffee table, crashing to the floor, and the man made a run for it.

Sara, recovering, raced after him, tackling him around the knees just as he reached the entrance. With an angry thrust and a throaty curse, he jerked his foot, hitting her in the shoulder and throwing her body against the wooden doorframe.

She cried out as pain seared her temples in a blinding flash.

Then she slumped, unconsciousness pulling her into its dark embrace.

SARA DREAMED. Nick was holding her, his strong arms cradling her, his firm mouth warm and caressing against her temple. Occasionally, his hand stroked her hair tenderly, and all the time, words echoed that she couldn't understand, except for one phrase, "Wake up, Sara."

She struggled to obey, to break through the haze, drifting for a few minutes longer, then finally, reluctantly, her eyes fluttered open.

She groaned as she tried to focus. She was in her own bed in the third-floor suite, still wrapped in her terry-cloth robe.

"Welcome back," a voice said. Squinting, her vision clearing, she saw Nick sitting on the side of the bed. Rumpled and tired looking, he watched her, his face bruised.

An ironic smile played at the corners of his mouth. "Considering how often you hit that head of yours, it's a good thing you're so damn hardheaded."

"Yes, I suppose it is." She tried to return his smile, but it was a weak effort. As she attempted to sit up, Nick leaned forward, anchoring his right arm around her to help. The intimate gesture reminded her of an earlier one and a spark glimmered somewhere in her. Ignoring it as best as she could, she asked weakly, "Did they get away?"

He plumped the pillows behind her with one hand, then braced her against the curve of his chest. She bent forward slightly. His body felt warm and inviting.

"'Fraid so," he admitted.

"Damn." She swore under her breath, settling against the welcome support of the two pillows. His good arm dropped to the bed.

Nick suppressed a smile. "How, I'm not exactly sure...because you certainly gave them a run for their money."

Despite her throbbing head, Sara was pleased with the compliment. "Thanks. You were no slouch either... John

Wayne would have been proud of you.'' But remembering caused Sara to frown. Her gaze immediately searched out his arm. It was bandaged. Concern showed in her eyes. "How is it?"

"What? This?" He brandished his left arm for her to see. "Just surface. Nothing serious. We were more worried about you. That's the second blow to the head you've taken in the past twenty-four hours. This time, though, we sent for a doctor, but she said you'd be all right. The phones were out of order so Mason drove into Aurora to get her."

Understanding flashed through Sara. "So that's how they did it."

"Did it?"

"Got through the security system. They probably disconnected the main phone line to which it's wired." Then her brow furrowed. "But how did they get past the dogs?"

"I can answer that," Nick said. "They were tranquilized."

"Are they okay?" she asked, concerned.

"Fine. Dr. Sellers was a good sport. She agreed to look at them as well, even though she isn't a vet. She said they'd sleep it off." A wry smile flickered across his face.

Sara looked at his arm again. "And did she do that, too?" she asked, indicating the bandage.

"Yes."

Sara stared at the stark white bandage wrapped around Nick's upper arm. Tonight Nick had jeopardized his own life for hers. She said in a hoarse voice, "You could have been killed."

He shrugged, his dark eyes boring into hers. "So could you, Sara." He hesitated, then still staring at her, planted his palm flat on the sheet. "Now, don't you think it's about time you leveled with me?"

"I don't know what you mean," she answered, her voice unsteady.

"Come on, Sara," Nick said quietly. "I let you get away with that answer once, but not again. Let's quit playing games with each other. My aunt is dead. Someone is definitely trying to kill you—" he exaggerated the *definitely* "—surely you don't expect me to believe nothing's going on."

"Nothing's going on," she replied, her mouth trembling as she realized she was dangerously close to breaking down.

A flash of fury lit Nick's eyes. "I told you once before, Sara. Don't ever play me for a fool. If you don't tell me what's going on, then I'll have to make my own assumptions."

Sara bit her lip to stem the tide that was eroding her strength. "Go ahead then," she said.

"Damn it, Sara!" He pounded the bed with his hand, then winced as he realized he'd used his wounded side.

"Is that what you really want? Do you want me to believe you killed my aunt, removed the body, and that now you're in danger because you double-crossed your accomplices?"

"Double-crossed?" Sara repeated, her voice rising. "That's the most ridiculous thing I ever heard."

"Is it?" he cut her off brusquely. "Well, unless you tell me the truth, it's what I'm going to believe."

"I can't tell you the truth, and I won't." She clamped her mouth in determination.

Nick exploded. "For heaven's sake, Sara. Why not?"

"Because," she lashed back, "I don't trust you."

She'd never expected to see Nick silenced. But he was now, his eyes wide. "You don't trust *me*?"

"That's right." She leaned her head heavily against the pillows.

"Then why did you call my name?"

She'd been hoping he wouldn't ask that question. She'd been wondering exactly the same thing herself. It was part of her confusion. She suspected his motives, yet when threatened, she had called out to him. "I don't know," she managed, in a halting voice.

"Well, I do," he responded. "Or at least I'm beginning to think I do. You're so ambivalent about me as I am about you, and it's tearing both of us apart. I don't know about you, but *I've* had enough. Now, for the last time, why don't you trust me?"

There was something oddly familiar about the rawness in his voice, as if she felt it herself and it was cutting into her. "You want the formula," she challenged.

"Damn right I do," he practically roared.

"Well, then." Her insinuation hung in the air between them.

"Hang on, Sara," he retaliated. "Before you judge me, maybe you should hear my side of the story. You were pretty quick, a few hours ago, to accuse me of having no heart and not giving you a chance to explain. Now, here you are, doing exactly the same thing."

"But you've admitted wanting the formula," she protested.

"Yes." Impatiently, he stood up and stalked to the end of the bed. Then he stopped, and looking down, stared at her intently.

"I do want the formula. I've never denied that. But I also saved your life. Twice." He held up two fingers for emphasis. "Tell me, Sara. Just how many times does a man have to prove himself to you?"

Chapter Nine

Sara's eyes grew larger, her fingers clutching the edge of the floral sheet in a tight grip.

"You don't have to prove yourself to me," she said in a shaky voice.

But she knew that wasn't true. Desperately, she wished for some sign that would prove Nick's innocence. She surveyed him warily as he stared down at her. His smoky-brown eyes smudged with exhaustion, he didn't look like a dangerous man. That is, if she discounted the treacherous ache his presence seemed to arouse in her.

"It's more likely the other way around," she mustered defensively.

He gave her a smoldering look. "Well, you can hardly blame me for that, Sara. Every time I ask you a direct question, you evade it."

"And I'm going to keep doing it," she snapped back.

"You can't evade the police, Sara," he reminded her, his voice flat.

His comment pulled her up short. She'd been hoping to see the police alone, without Nick.

"You've called them?" she asked in a quiet voice.

He ran his fingers through his already disheveled hair. "I had to."

Suddenly, Nick felt incredibly tired. "After they discovered Lillian's body was missing, they started an investigation. The attack on your life had to be reported.
They're on their way over now."

His gaze fixed on her intently. Earlier in the evening,
he'd decided to get to the bottom of whatever was going on
with Sara. Was it worth another shot? He wanted to hear
what was happening from her, not from an impersonal
police report. He wasn't sure why, but it was important.

Taking a ragged breath, he came back and sat again on
the edge of the bed. "Sara, before the police get here, I'd
like to hear your side of the story from you. I'd like to trust
you. But you're going to have to tell me the truth."

Her eyes widened automatically in protest, but he held
up a hand, determined not to be swayed.

"Let me finish." He picked his words with care, watching her all the time. "I get the feeling that something terrible is going on. I also get the feeling you're in over your
head and that you could use a friend."

"But . . ." Sara voiced a quick objection.

"No, Sara," he said in a firm tone, shaking his head and
reaching for her hand. "No more evasions. I think we'd
better start trusting each other. Whether you like it or not,
I'm involved in whatever is happening to you. Don't forget I almost got myself killed tonight as well as you."

Sara's troubled gaze locked with his.

For a split second, he was stricken with a moment of
stark need. What was there about this woman that
wrenched his heart?

"Sara, please," he urged.

"I . . ." Sara faltered. He had risked his life for her. She'd
been terrified when she saw the blood spurting out of his
arm. Suddenly, she understood that she cared deeply for
this man. "I don't . . ." She couldn't finish.

Seeing her pain and sensing her disorientation, Nick pressed the advantage. He leaned closer. "Sara, trust me." With that, he reached out and pulled her into his arms.

At first, the movement startled her, and her body tensed in resistance. Then slowly, she found herself relaxing. There was something so reassuring and safe about being in his arms.

She allowed herself to cave in against his chest. He breathed against her hair. "Sara, we've got to stop fighting each other."

She didn't want to fight Nick. She wanted... God, she wished she could just share this with him... stay in his embrace....

There were so many questions about Lillian, about Ben; about Nick. How could she expect him to understand. Yet, she knew the moment had arrived. The suspicion and fear—not knowing about Lillian, about Ben, about Nick—that had warred within her for so long, now joined forces to defeat her. A sob escaped her lips. She'd had enough.

She shook convulsively in his arms. Tightening his embrace, he held her close, repeating, "Please, Sara. Talk to me. Tell me what's going on."

Sara knew she could no longer resist. What was the point? The police would be there soon. Nick was right. It would be better if he heard the truth from her.

With reluctance, she composed herself and pulled back from his embrace. She answered the unspoken question in his eyes with a tired sigh. "All right, Nick. I'll tell you everything."

In a halting voice, she began her story.

Nick listened quietly, not interrupting. Every once in a while his gaze flickered as she spilled out the sequence of events. He continued to hold her hand.

Sara found it was a relief to finally share her burden with him. She couldn't help thinking that, if nothing else, Nick would no longer think so badly of her. That was important to her and she didn't fight it.

At last she was finished, drained. Fatigue showed in her eyes. "That's it." She sighed huskily, preparing herself for his reaction.

Nick sat in silence. Lillian was alive. Sara was innocent. Not only innocent, but she'd demonstrated incredible courage and loyalty.

"Well," she prodded, unable to read his silence.

He shook his head disbelievingly. "That's the most outrageous thing Lillian has ever done."

Then he gave her a harsh look. "Also risky. You should have refused to let her jeopardize your safety and gone to the police immediately."

Sara allowed herself a wan smile.

"The thought had crossed my mind...."

"Well, you should have acted on it," Nick responded roughly. He shook his head again, dark strands of hair brushing his forehead. "No wonder someone's been trying to kill you," he said gruffly. "You're a walking target."

Sara studied him with amazement. It almost sounded as though her life mattered to him. The prospect made her heart jump, but the elation was shortlived. She had leveled with him. Now it was his turn.

"Well?" she asked pointedly. "Don't you have something to tell me?"

He looked surprised at her inflection, not answering immediately. Then recovering, he played with her fingers thoughtfully. "Yes, I do," he replied at last.

He released her hand and shifted position, leaning forward and appearing to concentrate. "I'm just not sure where to begin."

Sara settled against the pillows, watching him. Nick always exuded such aggressive confidence. This more reflective side offered her a glimpse of yet another dimension of his nature.

"Why not start with the formula?" she proposed. "Do you know what it's for?"

He nodded. "Yes, it's a miracle drug, or rather, a near-miracle drug for cardiovascular disease. A heart drug."

Sara hadn't known what she expected. But the implications were obvious. "Then it could bring relief to a lot of people," she stated, thinking out loud.

Nick's mouth was set in a grim line. "Not just relief, life." He looked at her darkly. "And you'd better make that millions of people, worldwide."

He glanced away from her to stare at a fixed spot on the wall, as if retreating into his private thoughts.

She prompted in a low voice, "You wanted to bring it onto the market?"

His attention returned to her. "Yes and no," he replied.

Puzzlement made her blink. "I don't understand," she began.

He interrupted quickly to explain. "Yes, because it could make a major medical impact, but no, because as the drug stands now, it has serious side effects."

Her interest piqued, Sara tossed her hair away from her face so she could see him better. "Such as?"

Nick abruptly pulled away from his position beside her and stood up. He began to pace the room, his leg muscles taut under his jeans. "For one—irretrievable loss of memory. For another—interference with some basic motor functions of the body." He stopped by the window, his massive frame blocking the image of a half-moon in the night sky. For a moment, she thought he wasn't going to continue, then he turned around to face her. "Actually, the side effects are too numerous to list. Some are quite minor, no more upsetting than what you would expect with aspirin. But others, I'm afraid, are far more dangerous." There was a brittle edge to his voice.

"Ben said that you and Charles argued about the formula," she inserted quietly.

He laughed sardonically, running his fingers through his hair. Its ebony sheen caught the light. "We did—bitterly."

"Why?"

Staring at her, he paused before answering as if trying to order his thoughts. He hooked his thumbs tightly into the belt cinching his jeans. Watching him flatten his palms against his lean body, a warm flush began to creep up her neck.

His voice brought her back to earth. "Charles and another young chemist developed the formula in a private lab that Charles maintained in his office. I was unaware of what they were doing until the chemist came to me, very concerned. Charles and he had been experimenting for a number of years, then all of a sudden Charles told him he would continue alone. The formula was at the point where it could have significant impact on heart disease, but still risky in terms of side effects. The chemist suspected that Charles was going to bring the product onto the market without the appropriate testing."

"But how could he do that? Surely, the Federal Drug Administration in the U.S. and Health and Welfare in Canada would have stopped it," she said.

Nick nodded. "You're right. That's exactly what would have happened...in North America. They'd have demanded specific tests before the drug could be sold."

Sara's tone indicated her bafflement. "So...how?"

Nick stopped pacing and stood at the bottom of the bed. He looked down at her, an angry expression accentuating the square thrust of his jaw. "Unfortunately, not all countries operate the same way. There are a number of countries in which Charles could have easily brought the product onto the market without much interference. All he would have had to do was set up a subsidiary company in the country in which he hoped to market it."

Engrossed, Sara asked, "Did he?"

"He tried, but I stopped him. Our shareholder agreement had what you call a deadlock provision. In essence, he needed my consent."

Sara scrutinized him carefully. Bitterness was etched into his face as if a sculptor had used grooves to show pain. It was obvious that Nick strongly disapproved of Charles marketing an untested drug. But why did he want it himself? Another question was first in her mind—a question of ethics. "Why would Charles take that kind of a chance with people's lives?" she asked in a hushed tone. "Was he that unscrupulous?"

He emitted a dry laugh. "You can say that again. The answer is money." He sat heavily on the bed, twisting so he was facing her. "Money was a god to Charles. That and power. He could never have too much of either."

"How much money?"

Nick cocked his head sideways. "Well, if you could market the drug in Canada, for instance, your profits would likely be around forty million dollars annually. But remember, Canada has a small population. In other countries, the profits would be phenomenal."

Sara smothered a gasp. "So the stakes are high," she whispered with awe.

"Yes." He stared at her intently, his gaze pitch-black and serious. "High enough that whoever now wants it isn't going to let the presence of one bodyguard stand in their way."

Sara shuddered, realizing anew how deadly a game she and Lillian had been playing and were still playing. She had known the formula was valuable, but she'd had no idea how valuable. No wonder, as Nick said, someone was more than willing to kill for it.

"How did you stop Charles?"

"At first he had hoped to keep the formula a secret and was going to set up subsidiary companies without telling anyone. The chemist coming to me stalled that, because I challenged Charles. I could have slapped him with an injunction or a lawsuit."

"Because the formula belonged to the company, even though he invented it," she supplied, remembering what Ben had told her.

He nodded. "Right."

"So what did he do?"

"He tried to get me to agree to the separate companies. Because of the way Kingsley Chemicals was set up, he needed my compliance. I refused. I also had an ace up my sleeve. I threatened to tell Lillian what he was up to. Charles was furious. He would never have wanted Lillian to think he was anything less than perfect. Lillian was his Achilles' heel—his weakness."

"That's when you left the company?"

"Shortly afterward. Following the confrontation, our relationship became so tense it was affecting everyone there. I made a deal with Charles. He could buy me out as a partner for very little money, but there was a proviso— he had to sign a document stating he would not produce the drug and that on his death the formula would revert to me."

A remembered phrase flashed in her memory. "So that's what Ben meant," she said quickly. " 'The son of a bitch got what he wanted,' he said." Slowly it was falling into place.

Nick looked startled. "Is that what Ben said?"

She nodded. "Yes."

"Unfortunately, Ben doesn't know all the details. For one thing, he only knew what Charles chose to tell him, and there's some doubt as to how accurate that might have been. Secondly, Charles and I used another lawyer to handle our agreement. Ben has always been very loyal to Lillian and has always loved her. Ben might have told her the truth and Charles couldn't risk that."

If Nick was telling her the truth, Sara thought, then the formula was rightfully his and he wasn't a thief. Relief welled up, then ebbed. Why did he want the formula so desperately? The money? That didn't make him much different from Charles.

She asked reluctantly, "Why do you want the formula? For the money?"

Nick flinched, as if wounded. "No," he answered in a slow, tired voice. "The money doesn't interest me. And in any event, I wouldn't keep the formula."

"You wouldn't?" Sara was confused.

Nick seemed surprised she didn't understand. "What would I do with it? The costs of bringing a drug onto the market are beyond my financial capability. By the time all the required testing was complete, it could cost approximately a hundred and ten million dollars and take up to ten years of research. I no longer own a chemical company."

"Then why?"

Nick seemed to drift as if he wasn't going to reply. Then a veiled mist swelled in his eyes, vanishing as quickly as it had appeared.

"My mother died a horrible death because of severe heart disease," he answered haltingly. "She was young and vital. A drug such as this might have spared not only her life, but all the pain and her lost dreams. I felt so helpless, watching her try to do things that she couldn't...especially toward the end." A ragged breath caught in his throat, then he composed himself. "That's why I wanted the drug. To give it to another chemical company. To ensure its testing."

"Oh, Nick, I'm so sorry," she said, her own voice raw with emotion. Suddenly, it all fit together, his story and Ben's. Sad images flashed in her head. A young boy robbed of his parents, teenage years filled with cold confrontation, Charles's vilification, Lillian's preoccupation with her own pursuits. So little love, so little to believe in.

The image of a child's abandoned toy box flashed through her mind. "How awful it must have been for you," she whispered, clasping her hands over his in a comforting gesture.

Nick knew a moment of surprised gratitude at her concern, then realized that her touch was beginning to have an effect that she hadn't intended.

Needing a distraction, he shrugged away her comment. "Thank you." His voice sounded brusque even to his own ears. He softened his tone. "But right now, I think there are more immediate concerns. The police for one. Do you feel up to going downstairs and talking to them?"

She nodded quickly. "I was on my way to see them anyway, before our uninvited guests arrived."

"Good." He gave her a slow smile of encouragement.

Sara's hand on his arm stopped him from standing up. "I have a couple of other questions, Nick. Why did Charles so readily agree to sign over the formula to you if he wanted the enormous profits?"

"That's easy." He grinned wryly. "I practically gave him my shares in Kingsley Chemicals. That was money in his pocket right away, with no effort at all. With the formula, he always ran the risk that I might bring action against him. Buying me out also gave him total control over the company. Charles liked to be the only king on the block.''

Sara eased herself into a sitting position at the edge of the bed.

''The other questions?''

Sara swung her legs over the side. ''With you out of the way in Australia, couldn't he have tried to market the formula anyway?''

Nick moved closer. ''I have enough contacts in other countries to maybe have headed him off in advance. That probably discouraged him. Also, in the past ten years, his health deteriorated and he lost a lot of his spunk.''

''Couldn't you have just produced the document that Charles signed to get the formula back?''

''Sure.'' Nick shrugged. ''But that would have meant telling Lillian how unscrupulous Charles was. I wanted to spare her that. Here, I'll help you up.''

Before she could protest, his arm had swung around her and he eased her off the bed with infinite tenderness. She knew she was perfectly capable of moving under her own steam, but she surrendered to the delicious sensation of being cared for.

''All right?'' he asked, watching her stand with an anxious look.

She nodded, blushing at his closeness. He steadied her with his unbandaged arm, the motion causing the full length of her body to press lightly against his. An immediate heat surged through her.

''You'll feel better after a good night's sleep,'' he said to reassure her, misinterpreting her silence.

''Yes,'' she responded in a self-conscious murmur. His thigh nudged hers, and she felt silent again. His hand in the middle of her back seemed to sear her, and she stared up at him with wide eyes.

As Sara's gaze locked with his, her green eyes flecked with gray shadows, her mouth moist and parted, Nick's pulse skipped a beat. He wouldn't be getting a good night's sleep, if she kept looking at him like that. The soft body beneath the robe made his hand ache. He dropped it quickly. "Shall we go then?" he asked, his voice hoarse.

Distracted, Sara nodded and he went to move away, but something made her stop him. "Nick," she ventured.

He half turned, an expectant look on his face.

Suddenly, she felt shy. "I—I'm glad we were wrong about each other."

He hesitated, then taking a step back, he reached for her hand slowly. Intense brown eyes locked with hers. Sara found she could hardly breathe.

Finally, he spoke. "So am I, Sara." Tenderly, his mouth grazed her forehead, and Sara knew a moment of such pure joy that her pulse seemed to skip in happy counterpoint to the thumping of her heart.

"Can you believe it?" Constable Canfield whistled, hooking his hands into a belt that covered a well-toned girth.

The night air wrapped around him and Detective Adams as they paused in the circular driveway fronting the Kingsley mansion.

"Can or do? I'm not really sure," the detective answered almost to himself. The call to the estate hadn't really surprised him, but what had been odd was the changed relationship between Nick Kingsley and Sara Brennan. Both had looked strained when he'd interviewed them, but he hadn't missed the obvious tender glances the pair exchanged. Sara's retelling of the events leading to tonight's incident had prompted the constable's incredulity. Now, the detective heard him whistle again.

"You've got to admit it's quite a story," the constable was saying.

His superior officer gave him a distant look. "It certainly is that."

"So, what do we do now? Let it ride or bring her in?" the constable pressed.

Detective Adams didn't answer directly. Instead, he posed a question of his own. "When you checked on Ben Short, exactly what did his secretary say again?"

"Just that he was out of town and wouldn't be back for a few days."

"Interesting." The detective bit his lower lip as he stared out over the magnificent, night-shrouded expanse of the Kingsley estate. In the distance, he could see two other officers combing the grounds.

"How's that?" The constable's voice returned him to the conversation.

He took a good whiff of the damp air into his lungs. "Sara has one corroborating witness and he's out of town. I find that *very* interesting. Highly convenient for the other criminals, if there are other criminals, as she intimates, because she'll take the fall. It's neat, but a bit too neat for my liking, and it doesn't explain why someone tried to kill her tonight."

"You believe that part?"

Detective Adams nodded. "Yes, but mostly because of Nick Kingsley. I suspect *he* isn't lying, but that he's the only one who isn't."

"But if you don't believe Sara's innocent, what..."

"...do I think happened?" Adams interrupted.

Constable Canfield nodded.

Detective Adams expelled a tired sigh. "Try this on for size. Ben Short and Sara are partners in crime. They kill Lillian Kingsley so that Sara can inherit the Kingsley fortune and the formula. Nick returns, warns Sara he'll get an autopsy. The partners panic and move the body. Ben panics even more. He disappears, willing to forgo his share—I'm assuming Sara agreed to pay him off—but before he disappears, he wants to make sure there are no witnesses to his role in the murder...."

"Sara?"

"Right. So he hires a couple of thugs to bump her off."

"But if they murdered Lillian, why have a funeral? Why not just bury the body and say she disappeared?"

"To legitimize Lillian's death. We would investigate Lillian's disappearance, maybe even find the body—but unless we suspected foul play, we'd have no reason to start an investigation just because she died of a heart attack. Dr. Hess hadn't been coroner long, so it was easy to cover up the absence of a death certificate, and that also meant they didn't need to have a doctor in on the scam. Unfortunately, they hadn't counted on Nick returning."

"Clever," Constable Canfield clucked.

"Sloppy," Detective Adams corrected. "Anyway, it's only a theory."

"It's going to be tough coming down on a deputy police chief's daughter," the constable volunteered.

"Even tougher not to," Adams replied tersely. "We can't run the risk of being accused of 'protecting our own.'..." He broke off as the other officers crossed the grass toward him. "Find anything?"

The slimmer officer answered. "Just some prints. Not much else."

"Okay. Check again tomorrow in daylight." Turning, Adams addressed Constable Canfield. "Get over to Short's office in the morning and see if his secretary has a will on file for Lillian Kingsley."

"Right."

"Okay, guys." His strained gaze took in all the officers. "Let's call it a night." With heavy steps, he moved toward his own unmarked vehicle parked partway into the driveway, but Constable Canfield's voice stopped him.

"Detective, there's something been bothering me...."

"Yes," he prompted, his hand on the door handle of the car.

The younger officer approached him. "Why's Kingsley suddenly changed his tune? This afternoon, he didn't believe Sara Brennan was innocent."

The seasoned detective gave a hoarse laugh. "Some women have a way with men, Constable...or hadn't you noticed?"

Chapter Ten

Lillian regarded the elegant den room with disdain, swallowing the fear that kept threatening to choke her.

A gilded cage, she sniffed to herself. *That's what it is.* Then her eyes narrowed in self-reproach. *There's no fool like an old fool.*

She sat rigidly in the small wing chair, waiting. She'd run out of time. Today it would be over. A shiver ran down her spine, and she straightened her already erect back as if to dispel it. Glancing over at the high second-floor windows, she could see a golden-purple sunrise nudge the day.

The door opened, unlocked from the outside. The click was sharp. She clenched her teeth together to fight back her terror. Turning with a regal twist of her head, she faced the man walking through the door.

So sophisticated, she thought. So evil.

"Good morning, Lillian." He smiled, a practised almost mechanical smile. "I see you're up bright and early."

Her gaze flashed like bright sapphires. "I won't sleep properly until I'm in my own bed," she snapped.

"Ahh..." He shook his head knowingly, then bent to pull a chair next to hers. Lounging with unaffected grace, he leaned forward, coiling his well-manicured fingers around the armrest of her chair.

"You'll be able to do that really soon, Lillian," he said in a deceptively nonchalant tone. He studied her. After all these years, he had to admit, she was still a beautiful woman. Her skin had become more textured with age, but had retained its soft glow, and her eyes had lost none of their electric brilliance. Yes, still beautiful. Still arrogant. Still appealing. For a split second, he almost regretted what he had to do. Then he remembered Charles.

His face hardened and his fingers tightened on the chair, grazing the fabric of her dress. "Well, have you decided what you're going to do?" His tone was clipped, cool, impersonal.

Hearing his voice, Lillian knew that any hope she'd been harboring of a last-minute reprieve was just that—a hope. It withered inside her, but still she managed to fire back, "I don't know why you had to drag Ben into this."

He sighed with bitter amusement. "Insurance, Lillian. Just extra insurance. I could hardly kill you when you know the formula, but Ben..." His voice trailed and he deliberately paused to gauge her reaction.

She didn't disappoint him. A flash of fear sparked in her eyes. To finally see her cowed gave its own pleasure, he discovered. "But Ben," he repeated, "is...how shall I put it? Expendable? Yes, that's it." He gave a hoarse laugh. "Expendable."

"You're despicable." Anger gave her voice a throaty energy.

His eyes narrowed into slits. "No, Lillian. Just a good negotiator. Ben's life for the formula. A simple deal."

"A deal made in hell," she spit.

He shrugged. "Nevertheless, a deal."

"How do I know you've really kidnapped him?" she said mutinously.

Irritation creased his high forehead. He was getting bored now. "Take my word for it. We have him."

Lillian saw a chance to buy some time and took it. Adopting her haughtiest air, she tossed her patrician head backward in defiance. "I want proof... or no deal."

He went completely still, staring at her, his eyes widening with growing anger. Their gazes locked in mutual antagonism. Lillian held her breath but struggled not to let him see. Then a glimmer of careless arrogance darkened his gaze and he laughed mirthlessly. "Why not? I'll get you proof."

He stood up slowly, feeling tired. Dealing with Lillian had always been a taxing experience.

"But then..." He turned, facing her, already halfway across the room. "The formula, Lillian. No more games. I mean business."

The threat was all the more deadly because of the icy grace with which he delivered it. Lillian shuddered, knowing he meant what he said. He'd always been different—dispassionate, detached. A boy with little conscience who'd become a man with no conscience at all.

She nodded painfully. "For Ben," she said in a quiet voice. "I'll do it for Ben."

His mouth twisted into a smile of ridicule. "I knew you would, Lillian. You've always had a soft spot in your heart for the men in your life."

Lillian bit back the retort rising in her throat. What was the point of disagreeing with him? His assessment was accurate. How well he'd known just which emotional buttons to push. First to get her here, and second to get the formula. A lover's tryst, he'd called it—"let's get away together and recapture our romantic youth"—and she'd fallen for it.

Oh yes, he'd preyed on her weakness. A weakness that could now be fatal, not just for her, but for her old friend, Ben.

Her cobalt eyes shadowed to a dull-metal blue.

How could she have been so vain?

A silent, agonized plea whispered in her heart.

Sara, where are you? Help me....

SARA HARDLY NOTICED the golden-purple sunrise as she approached the kennels.

"Storm? Cloud?" Both dogs bounded out of their enclosures barking a greeting. They appeared normal as she fed them. In all probability the assailants had inserted acepromazene into syringes and fired them over the fence, using a dart pistol, she thought. Acepromazene was a common tranquilizer used by vets and its effects lasted only six hours. Well past six hours now since the drug had been administered, the dogs were bouncy and as exuberant as ever.

Reassured, she returned to the house via the front, checking the grounds for clues as she went, even though the police had already done so the night before.

The session with Detective Adams had been draining, his questions incisive and thorough. A true professional who had likely seen and heard it all, he'd expressed no visible reaction to her and Nick's stories. Whether she'd be charged with public mischief hadn't been mentioned, and she'd breathed a small sigh of relief for that mercy.

But had they really believed her? That prospect had crossed her mind a dozen times during a restless night.

Thank God, Lillian hadn't gone so far as to make a will, she grimaced ruefully, *or I'd be a prime suspect.* Her thoughts strayed to Lillian and Ben. Lillian's safety and Ben's whereabouts were now in the hands of the police. The thought, although reassuring, still depressed her, making her feel helpless.

Somehow, it didn't seem right to just wait and do nothing.

How would Nick feel about waiting?

Thinking about Nick's reaction propelled her to assess his other qualities as well. She knew he possessed the same kind of impatience that she did, but last night she'd also seen other traits—compassion, gentleness, integrity, the stuff of which dreams are made.

She tossed her hair back, a surge of heat fanning her. All she'd wanted to do, when she'd felt his body against hers, was to press into his chest, to mold her body to his.

To hold him, exploring every aspect of him.

But reality had intruded. Just as it was going to have to now, she told herself as she slipped down the hallway toward the kitchen.

She pushed the swinging doors open.

"Miss Brennan!" Edie looked up from the stove, consternation written all over her face. The compelling aroma of bacon and eggs filled the room. "You're as bad as Mr. Kingsley!" She waved her spatula in the direction of the kitchen table.

Nick glanced up with a sheepish look on his tanned face. His dark eyes smiled in mischief. Sara hadn't noticed him when she came in, and now she tried to steady the lurch of her heart.

"In Edie's orderly world, *we* do not belong in the kitchen," he explained, grinning.

Reaching for the back of a chair, Sara eased herself into it, sitting across from him. "Oh," she managed, smiling.

"It isn't right," Edie chastised, before Sara could comment. The housekeeper plunked a steaming plate of food in front of Nick. It perched dangerously on the edge of the table, and Nick had to rescue it with a quick hand.

Spatula still in motion, Edie turned toward Sara. "Even as a boy, I couldn't keep him out of here, but then—" she took a rushed breath "—he had an excuse." Her mouth hardened. "You, Miss Brennan, you have none. You belong in the dining room." Her disapproval now firmly vented, she asked in resigned reproach, swinging the spatula toward Nick's plate, "The same thing?"

The breakfast smell was tantalizing, and Sara was famished. She gave Edie a wide grin to pacify her. "If you don't mind." Then she raised a speculative brow at Nick. "An excuse?"

Nick's hand poised in midair as he went to spear a piece of bacon. "I was always trying to avoid Charles. This was a good place to do it."

"Oh, I see." Sara flashed a quick look at Edie. So she'd been his conspirator as a young boy. Sara suddenly felt glad that there'd been someone in the Kingsley household to show him affection and friendship. "When I was a kid, the kitchen was my favorite place as well. I guess it is for most children. Thanks, Edie." She glanced up as the housekeeper deposited a mug of freshly brewed coffee in front of her.

Still standing by the table, Edie asked abruptly, "How are you feeling, Miss Brennan?"

Sara gratefully breathed in the aromatic steam of the coffee. "Fine, Edie." Tentatively, she cupped her fingers around the mug. "Are the phones working yet?"

Edie shook her gray head. "No. When Mason went to get the doctor and call the police last night, he also advised the phone company. Bell said they'd have to send someone out," she replied.

Sara's eyes clouded. As long as the phone system was down, so was the alarm system.

"How does the alarm system work, Sara?" Nick asked.

She explained. "If someone pushes any one of the 'panic buttons' placed inside the house, the phone automatically dials a twenty-four-hour monitoring station. We have a code assigned to us. The operators check the code, then call the police to alert them. To break the system, you have to disconnect the telephone lines. But the fact that the siren didn't go off means that whoever broke in here last night also cut the line of the security system.''

Nick's mouth set in a thoughtful line. He toyed with his coffee mug. ''Not exactly foolproof, is it?''

Sara sighed, leaning backward as Edie placed a plate of bacon and eggs in front of her. ''No, you're right, it isn't. But Lillian didn't want anything more sophisticated such as magnetic door devices, cameras or fence sensors. The intercom at the gates, the dogs and the 'panic buttons' were all she'd let us have. She just didn't want to feel barricaded in her own home.''

A mound of toast materialized on the table, and Edie hovered over them, removing her apron.

''I don't know what you two are up to, but I'm glad to see you both still have your appetites.'' She sniffed. ''Coffee's on the stove. Help yourselves. I'll be upstairs if you need me,'' she told them.

They both shared a glance, and murmured simultaneous thanks before she swung her way through the doors to the hallway.

''Nick—''

''Sara—''

They both spoke at once.

Nick broke off, laughing. ''Ladies first.''

A sudden shyness seized her. Now that she could relax about Nick, a new wave of emotion, just as intense, washed over her. She'd forgotten what she was going to say. ''Did you sleep well?'' she finally managed.

''Fine,'' Nick lied valiantly. Images of Sara had kept him awake most of the night, but at least they hadn't been shadowed by doubts about Sara's motives. ''And you?'' he posed.

''Okay,'' she replied, grateful that the first hurdle of conversation was over with. ''Although,'' she said with a grimace, ''I could have used more of it.''

He smiled, knowing what she meant. He'd had to fight his own body that morning to get it into motion.

"Nick . . ." A worried expression marred her lovely features. He saw the change. "It bothers me to just sit and wait while the police are looking for Ben and Lillian."

He crossed his knife and fork on the plate, then stared pointedly at her. "Maybe we don't have to."

A grateful light flashed in her eyes. "Oh, I was hoping you'd say that."

"Have you got a list of suspects?" he asked, not wasting any time.

"In my pocket." Rummaging, she quickly pulled out the piece of paper she'd jammed into her camel slacks when she was getting dressed.

"How did you compile it?" he asked, watching her unfold the paper and open it in front of them on the table.

Sara shoved aside her breakfast plate, smoothing out the edges of the list. "Not very scientifically, I'm afraid. There isn't much to go on. I think someone has discovered the hoax and has kidnapped Lillian and Ben. Lillian for the formula, and Ben . . ." Her voice trailed off as her eyes darkened with concentration. "I'm not sure why they've taken him. I also think that the reason they've been trying to kill me is because I'm the third part of the circle and therefore a threat."

"And the list?" he prompted.

"Is primarily of friends or people at the funeral," she continued. "Although I think Lillian and Ben have been kidnapped, it's apparent that each of them went willingly with someone. There was no sign of any struggle in the condominium, and Ben told his secretary he was leaving."

"So you figure that whoever lured each of them away is someone they know—a friend, or friends?"

"Exactly."

Nick's eyes were trained on her, but she could tell he wasn't seeing her. There was a distant shadow in his gaze. Finally, he picked up the list, righted it in his hands and scanned the contents.

For what seemed like a long time to Sara, he sat in mute deliberation. She bit her lower lip, watching him, then unable to stand the suspense any longer, prodded, "Well, am I off base? Do any of them look likely to you?"

Nick took his time looking up. When he finally did, his eyes were pensive. "None of them," he told her conclusively.

Sara's heart sank. The list was all they had to go on. If no one on it was a possible suspect, she had no idea where to begin.

Seeing her disappointment, he interjected, "That's just on first glance, Sara. Let's go through it. Maybe I'm missing something." He glanced at the sheet again. "You've got Graham Marshall at the top of the list. I doubt that he's a candidate."

Sara might have expected him to discount any of the other suspects, but certainly not Graham Marshall. "I thought he was the most probable," she protested.

Nick raised his eyebrows at her in speculation. "Because he bought Kingsley Chemicals? Did you think he expected to find the formula?"

"Why, yes." She gave him a startled look.

Nick leaned back heavily in his chair. "He knew the formula wasn't still with the company. He bought the company knowing full well that the formula wasn't one of the assets. He knows that legally I own it."

"But how?" She was puzzled, remembering the secrecy that surrounded the formula.

"I told him," he said bluntly, standing up to go to the stove. Coming back, he carried the coffeepot with him. "More?" he asked, holding it up.

"Please," she replied. "When did you tell him?"

Refilling each mug, he answered, "When Graham decided to buy the company he called me in Australia to ask a few questions about the operations of Kingsley Chemicals. Although it had been ten years since I'd had any active involvement with the company, I was still able to remove some of his concerns."

He planted the pot firmly on the table, sitting down again. "Graham is a very ethical man. I have a lot of respect for him. When I realized he was planning to buy the company, I told him about the formula. I wouldn't have wanted him to be misled. In addition, I promised to sell him the formula for a minimal price if I could find it."

Sara blinked, distracted. That eliminated one suspect. A prime one, in her mind. She searched out the second name.

"Gertrude?" she questioned.

Again he shook his head.

"But Ben said she had expected an inheritance from Charles and was upset when she didn't get one. As his secretary, wouldn't she have known about the formula? Couldn't she have thought she was entitled to something?" she argued.

"Maybe," he answered slowly, as if weighing her arguments. "But I doubt it. I think what she was looking for from Charles was recognition. A small bequest from Charles would have given her that. The formula wouldn't." He paused, taking a sip of coffee. "Anyway, I trust Gertrude. She's the one who called me in Australia to tell me that Lillian's life was in danger."

"She did?" Sara couldn't suppress her astonishment.

"Yes, and I didn't act on it soon enough—or so, I thought." His mouth set into a grim line. "That's another of the reasons I exploded so vehemently at you. I was feeling some guilt at having waited so long. I thought I was partially to blame for my aunt's death."

Sara's eyes widened. Lillian had, in all probability loved Nick, as she wasn't a cold woman. But there was no getting around the fact that she'd done little to smooth the relationship between Charles and Nick, or so it seemed to Sara. Yet Nick felt guilt at not protecting her. He was a lot more forgiving and accepting than she might have been under the circumstances.

Sidetracked by her thoughts, Sara couldn't remember who the third suspect was. "Who's next?" she asked.

"Larry—and it definitely isn't him," Nick replied with a shake of his head. A dark thatch of hair fell in disarray over his forehead. He impatiently pushed it back. For a man with big hands, she couldn't help thinking how beautifully shaped they were. Just tapered enough to offset their male bluntness. Remembering the feel of those fingers at her breast sent a shiver through her, and she had to force herself to remember who Larry was. Then Ben's comments came back to her.

The chemist from Kingsley Chemicals. He'd asked Ben about the whereabouts of the formula at the cemetery.

"Whyever not?" she asked, tearing her gaze away from the distraction of Nick's hands.

"He's the chemist who worked with Charles originally on the formula."

Sara seized on his response. "Then maybe he thinks he's entitled to it?"

"He's the one who warned me about Charles—remember?" he reminded. "Larry's a dedicated scientist. He developed a lot of salts for Kingsley Chemicals. There are other formulas he could have stolen with a lot less effort."

"But the money..."

"No way." He shook his head determinedly. "All he cares about is experimentation."

The seeds of dejection were beginning to take root in Sara. If none of these, who? Despondently, she turned the paper around so that it was facing her. "That hardly leaves anyone." She couldn't keep defeat from coloring her voice.

Nick steepled his hands together. "Read off the other names," he told her.

Sara concentrated on the list. "The three suitors—Shane Cameron, Graydon Lewis, sorry, make that *Dr.* Graydon Lewis, Martin Howard—and Tess Bond." She raised her eyebrows. "Not much, is it?"

"Unless we can think of a good motive, no, it isn't," he admitted, then repeated the names slowly. "Shane, Graydon, Martin, Torchy..." But he didn't get a chance to finish.

Sara bolted upright, interrupting him. "What did you say?"

Nick looked startled at her interjection. "I just repeated the names."

"No—no—" she said excitedly. "What was the last name?"

Nick thought for a moment. "Torchy? Tess Bond?" There was a question in his voice when he said the names again. Seeing her excitement, he asked, "Sara, what is it?"

Her eyes sparkled. "Torchy is a nickname. Right?"

"Yes. For Tess's red hair. But Lillian never used it. She thought it was an affectation."

That was why she hadn't picked up the clue earlier, Sara thought. When Lillian referred to Tess, it was always as just that—Tess.

"That's it, Nick. The clue we've been looking for." Her voice rose in triumph, and she stood up quickly.

Nick rose from his chair, stalling her with his hand as she prepared to cross the kitchen. "But what difference does it make that Tess's nickname is Torchy?"

"Remember what I told you Ben's secretary said? Before Ben disappeared a woman using a nickname called him."

Nick inhaled sharply. "I'm with you," he replied. "Come on, what are we waiting for?"

Chapter Eleven

Ben had never felt so cold and groggy.

Judging from the dampness in the air, he was some-where near a lake. Occasionally he thought he could hear the tight lapping of water as if the building he was in sat on a wharf inlet.

He'd been blindfolded when he lost consciousness. Now the musty smell of a dock drifted over him a haze.

When he woke up, he'd found he was in an elevator cab, an industrial style similar to those found in factories. He'd only been awake a few minutes, although awake was an exaggeration, he thought.

He huddled in the elevator. Why they'd put him in here, he had no idea. But he was grateful for one mercy. At least the hatch on the cab had been removed. He was terrified of confined places. The open space above him relieved the pressure.

He looked up at the cables. They didn't look any too secure, and he shuddered as much from fear as from the rank dampness and the smell of disuse that surrounded him. The cab appeared to have been stopped between levels. Why? he wondered.

They'd taken him to another location initially. Some-where in the country, he thought, but he'd been drugged then as well and when he woke up, he'd been blindfolded, and lying on an old cot. Fortunately, he hadn't been tied, and by inching his fingers along the walls, he'd found a small washroom. The walls had been concrete like those of a cellar. Then they'd come for him again—the following morning, he guessed. A few hours ago.

Depression seeped through him. When Lillian had explained her plan, as resistant as he'd been, it had still sounded simple.

But now, how had these people known that Lillian was still alive? He knew they had kidnapped her as well. Before losing consciousness the second time, the captors had discussed her.

These people. Who were they? He recognized none of them. They just sounded like thugs.

Suddenly, the sound of a large metal door opening jarred him alert.

Now what?

He struggled to sit up straighter. The cables squeaked.

The burly figure of one of his captors stood at the top of the shaft. "How ya doing, lawyer?" he called down sarcastically.

Ben tried to focus on the huge shape. He hadn't eaten since he'd been kidnapped and he was beginning to feel nauseated and dizzy.

"None of your damn business," he managed to croak.

The blurry figure gave a cruel laugh. "Here, lawyer..." He seemed to be tying a rope around an envelope. With a swing, the rope landed near Ben. "Put something of yours in the envelope," he instructed. "A ring or something if you've got one."

Ben surveyed the brown manila envelope near him with confusion. "Don't have a ring," he muttered.

"Then, anything, lawyer," the man snapped, jiggling the envelope from his position above the shaft. "A watch.

Your wallet. Just as long as it's something that will iden-
tify you. But make it fast.''

Were they going to ransom him for money? Ben hurriedly unhooked his gold watch. It had been a present from
Charles and Lillian on his fiftieth birthday and was in-
scribed. He jammed it into the envelope, then looked up.

''Tighten the rope around the envelope, you idiot,'' the
man ordered. ''Lord, I wouldn't want you defending me.''

Fat chance of that, Ben thought mutinously. He tightened the rope with trembling fingers.

No sooner had he secured the rope, then the envelope
was whisked up into the air. The man discarded the rope,
opened the envelope, and as if satisfied, threw away the
paper and pocketed the watch.

''Thanks, lawyer. See ya.'' With that, he went to turn.

''But wait.'' Ben tried to stretch his aching limbs.
''What's going on?'' God, were they going to leave him
here again? For how long?

The man stopped and laughed. ''We're just making a
trade, lawyer. Your life for the formula. As soon as the old
lady gives us the formula, why...you're just as safe as can
be.'' His laugh turned evil then, as he looked at the cables. ''That is, as safe as this elevator can be.'' Bursting
into a savage guffaw that trailed behind him into hollow
emptiness, he disappeared.

Panicking, Ben glanced above his head again, and
wincing, forced himself into an upright position.

The elevator screeched with a threatening lurch.

Ben's feet felt like cement, rooted to the spot in terror.

Now he knew why they'd hidden him in the elevator cab.
Any attempt to escape, any sudden movement, would
break the cable, and the cab would crash with him in it.

He broke into a clammy sweat.

With or without help, there was no way out of the elevator—alive!

"I WAS RIGHT!" Sara announced in an excited voice, scrambling into Nick's car. "Torchy did call Ben before he disappeared. I think we should pay Tess a visit."

Nick watched while she settled herself, strapping the seat belt around her. With the phones down at the Kingsley estate, he'd had to drive Sara to a pay phone in Aurora so she could call Esther, Ben's secretary. He waited for Sara to look up, and when she did, a frown was creasing her brow.

"Esther said something else though as well. She said the police were at Ben's office this morning inquiring about the whereabouts of Lillian's will."

Nick turned the ignition on. "But it doesn't exist, does it?"

"Not one naming me as a beneficiary. At least, according to Ben." Sara bit her lower lip nervously. Too many things had gone wrong with Lillian's charade already for her to trust anything to chance. What if a will did exist?

Noticing her thoughtfulness, Nick squeezed her hand. "Relax, Sara. It's going to be okay."

Sara let out a soft sigh. Nick's touch felt like the most natural gesture in the world to her. She gave him a half smile. "All right."

"Good girl." He smiled back. "Now do you know where Tess lives?"

She nodded, as he adjusted the rearview mirror. "I was there once with Lillian," she responded. "The High Park area in Toronto."

"We're on our way. What's the best route?" he asked, merging with the heavy traffic from his position in the parking lot.

"It's rush hour, and everything will be bad," she replied, looking at her watch. The time read 8:00 a.m. "Why not just go down Yonge Street?"

Nick shook his head in agreement, at the same time indulging himself in a lingering warm glance at her, before returning his attention to the rush-hour traffic.

Last night had been a revelation to him. He was still recovering from the pleasant shock that Sara was innocent. Now that his mind was free to indulge in fantasies about her, he was finding it was tempted to run wild. But he held himself in check. This terrifying situation with Ben and Lillian had to take priority.

Sara interrupted his reverie. "I don't know what confirmation that Tess called Ben will produce, but I'm hoping it's worthwhile. I'm so worried about Ben and Lillian."

Nick recognized uncertainty in her tone. He felt it himself. But Torchy was all they had to go on. "It's a start," he attempted, in an effort to reassure her.

Sara sighed. "I can't help thinking this is partly my fault," she commented, raising her arm to brush away thick strands of hair from her forehead.

Nick's gaze strayed from the road again. Sara's motion had forced her loosely buttoned beige tweed jacket to open and he caught a glimpse of her shoulder holster nestled against her left side. The gun and her question painfully brought home to him what Sara's occupation was—and how dangerous.

The notion disturbed him, but he forced himself to keep his voice level. "Why? Because you're a professional bodyguard?"

"I was hired to protect her," Sara reminded in a soft voice.

"Lillian needs protection from herself more than she needs protection from anyone else," he replied gruffly. "Believe me, what's happened is not your fault. Nobody can stop Lillian once she's made up her mind." Softening his tone, he squeezed her hand. "Don't do a number on yourself, Sara. You're not to blame."

Sara gave him a sideways glance of gratitude. She appreciated his efforts to reassure her, even if she didn't totally accept them. Until Lillian and Ben were found, safe and unharmed, she knew she'd feel guilty. But he was right about one thing—Lillian's headstrong nature was a force to be reckoned with.

Recalling Nick's other criticisms of Lillian when he'd compared her to his ex-wife made her ask, "Didn't you like Lillian, Nick?"

He gave her a startled look at the question that seemed to have come from left field. "Why, yes. I liked her very much—*do* like her very much," he corrected. "I admire her strength a great deal, but I never had any illusions about her. She lives in a fantasy world—always has."

"Fantasy? What do you mean?"

A smile twitched at the corners of his mouth. Sara noticed that today the lines feathering his mouth were less pronounced. It was a good strong mouth. Designed for laughter. *Too bad he doesn't smile more,* she couldn't help thinking.

"Charles treated Lillian like she was royalty. As you've probably noticed, she has a tendency to be quite regal, like an unchallenged queen. He set her up that way, and the whole household just fell in with the conspiracy. To the best of my knowledge, no one ever brought an ordinary household problem to Lillian. So consequently, that included . . ."

"You." She finished for him in a soft voice. She could see it all now. Lillian, imperious and spoiled, playing the role of moneyed chatelaine, while Nick grew up unnoticed.

"Right." A low laugh reverberated in the car. "So like the rest of the household, I came to accept Lillian as a distant reigning monarch whom you didn't bother with mundane problems. In Lillian's defense, I just don't think she realized a child might need more than an occasional pat on the head.''

"Did she never wonder why you left the Kingsley estate?''

"I suspect she did. Lillian is a very intelligent woman, but old habits die hard. Her loyalty to Charles was indomitable. We exchanged letters occasionally, but they were superficial, and neither one of us discussed the rift between Charles and me."

"She never asked you to come back?''

"After Charles's death—she alluded to my return, but I wasn't sure how I felt about that. I'd just gone through a divorce, and there was still the issue of where the formula was. Remember, until Gertrude called me, I didn't know that Lillian had it."

"Gertrude knew?''

"Yes. How, I don't know.''

Once again, Sara felt a wave of compassion for Nick's early life. "Growing up with the Kingsleys sounds like a lonely experience.''

"It was,'' he admitted matter-of-factly. "But—'' his eyes twinkled as he turned to look at her ''—things are looking up all the time.''

Sara laughed. "Glad you think so.''

"I do,'' he replied warmly. "What was your family like, Sara?''

"Great.'' Her response was enthusiastic.

"Your mother died quite young,'' he prompted with a slight trace of hesitation.

A shadow crossed her face. "Yes, but mercifully, it was quick.'' Then she brightened. "After that, it was just Dad and I. I think he would have preferred a boy, but I don't think I disappointed him. I was quite a tomboy.''

"Which is probably why you're in this profession," he teased, surprised at his own ability to hide the reservations he had about her job.

"Yes." She joined in his laughter. "For a while, because of Dad, I flirted with the idea of being a police officer. Growing up with him, I was no stranger to what the profession entails, but Dad gave me the idea of becoming a bodyguard. During his years on the force, he discovered that wealthy women and women constantly in the spotlight resented having male bodyguards. That prompted me to open a small agency offering that kind of service to women. Most of the assignments are short-term, following threats...that kind of thing. I studied law enforcement and self-defense, applied for an agency license, put up a bond...and here I am."

"When did your father die?"

Sara's throat constricted for a moment. "Just four years ago, in a fluke car accident. Imagine. All those years on the force and he was killed in an accident. I miss him terribly. I respected and loved him a great deal."

"I'm sorry, Sara." Taking his right hand from the wheel, he stretched over, folding her fingers into a warm grip.

"Thanks." She shot him a warm look.

"I know it's small consolation," he said in response. "But at least it gives us something in common—a loss we can both understand. Neither one of us has anybody."

"Unless you count Lillian." She raised her brows in mock resignation.

He couldn't resist a quick laugh. "That's right. I almost forgot about Lillian."

Sharing his laughter and their past experiences, Sara could have almost believed she and Nick were on their first date. Lillian hadn't given them a normal context in which to get to know each other. And even now, there was nothing normal about their being together. They were desperately in search of two people they both cared for, people whose lives were in danger.

The thought was sobering. Lillian was no joking matter.

"I'm afraid that forgetting Lillian could be a fatal mistake," she responded quickly.

Nick immediately understood what she was saying. The mood in the car had changed and its grimness dulled his eyes.

HE TURNED THE WATCH OVER in his hand, reading the inscription.

Engraved into the fourteen karat back were the words, "To Ben, on his fiftieth birthday, Love, Lillian and Charles."

A warm glow crawled through his veins.

Soon, the formula would be his. He could hardly contain his pleasure, but years of deception made it easy.

He gave the man a cool glance. "This is fine," he said with dry understatement. "Now go back and cut those cables. I don't want Ben Short as a witness."

The husky man nodded and left the room.

He stood, once again feeling the rush of victory race through him.

Charles wasn't the only one who could find power and wealth in his lifetime.

He cradled the watch in his palm one more time, then handed it to the second man.

"Give this to her highness, with my regards," he ordered in a caustic tone. "And tell her—" his words stopped the man at the door "—tell her, it's time to deliver the goods."

NICK TURNED OFF High Park Avenue onto a quiet tree-lined crescent.

"Number twenty-six," Sara told him. "It should be about there." Waving with her right hand, she indicated a small red-brick house with dark-stained shutters partway up the block.

Through the windshield, Nick's gaze followed the direction of Sara's hand. A woman carrying a suitcase was walking with a brisk gait down the three cement steps that led to the sidewalk. A Volkswagen sat in front of the house. Tess's telltale, bright red hair was unmistakable.

Simultaneously, Sara spotted her. Before Nick could say anything, she blurted, "My God! She's leaving."

Almost as if she'd heard Sara, Tess stopped and looked their way. Her eyes widened as she recognized them, and without a moment's hesitation, she broke into a run toward the driver's side of the Volkswagen.

"We have to stop her," Sara urged in a desperate voice as Tess yanked open her car door.

"Hang on." Nick gunned the motor, bringing the car to a screeching halt alongside Tess's. The car had barely come to a stop when Sara jumped out. Nick raced from the driver's side.

Seeing them, Tess became frantic, scrambling to lock the door, but Sara was too fast for her. She jerked the door open, just as Tess pushed her foot down on the accelerator.

The car shot forward, the swinging door throwing Sara onto the road.

Nick had better luck. He'd managed to secure a foothold inside the passenger side. Pushing himself forward he fell across the seat and with a savage jerk shoved the car into neutral, reaching for the keys.

The car lurched to an abrupt standstill. As Tess tried to clamber out, Nick's massive left hand caught her arm.

"Leave me alone," she screamed, trying to wrench free, her flame-colored hair tossing in a tangle around her face.

Nick tightened his grip. "Take it easy, Tess. We just want to talk to you," he soothed, trying to still her.

But Tess wasn't listening. Her voice rose in hysteria. "Let me go, let me go," she wailed, her struggles to break away wild and disjointed.

Nick didn't want to hurt her, but he couldn't allow her to get away. Anxiously, he looked over his shoulder. Sara had struggled to her feet and was rushing over to them.

"You all right?" he asked over Tess's head.

"Fine." Sara gave a brisk nod, a concerned expression crossing her face as Tess continued to squirm. The woman was crying, her whole body seized by a spasm of shaking. Sara bent over, touching Tess's shoulder in a reassuring gesture.

"Tess, please relax. Whatever's wrong, we can help. Let's go—" She was about to suggest they go into Tess's house, when Tess began to scream again.

Sara's eyes flashed with worry. "Tess, please..."

Sara took a deep breath. They couldn't very well stay here on the street struggling with a hysterical woman. Tess could be a major link to Ben and Lillian. They had to calm her down. Gritting her teeth, she flashed Nick a resigned look and slapped Tess across the face.

The slap wasn't hard, but was delivered with enough force to shock Tess into reason. She stared, wide-eyed, at Sara for a few seconds and then she seemed to cave. With a plaintive cry, she slumped against the steering wheel.

Sara instantly threw her arms around the woman to console her. "Tess, I'm so sorry. I had to do it. Can we go inside and talk?"

Tess didn't move for a moment. Sara wasn't sure Tess had heard her and was about to repeat the question, when Tess slowly, almost painfully, nodded her head.

"Good." Sara put warm reassurance into her voice, and with the help of Nick she guided Tess out of her car and into the house.

The front door was unlocked. Tess had obviously planned to come back to the house at some point. A small overnight bag sat inside the entrance hall.

The house was quiet, the mature trees shading and silencing the interior. Sara recalled that the kitchen was located at the back of the house. Gently, she led Tess toward the rear, guiding her to one of the kitchen chairs.

"You'll feel better once we've talked," she soothed. Unprotesting, Tess slid onto the seat and, bowing her head, cradled it between her hands.

Sara pulled up a chair beside Tess and placed a comforting arm around her shoulders. "Tell us what's going on." She spoke in a low, quiet voice.

"Nothing...nothing...going on." Tess's response was muffled. To Sara's ears, the denial sounded halfhearted.

Encouraged, Sara leaned closer. "We know you called Ben before he disappeared," she continued in an unhurried tone. "Where did they take him, Tess?"

Standing on the other side of Tess, Nick shot Sara a quizzical glance. Looking up, she shrugged dramatically.

So, he thought, *a shot in the dark. Good for you, Sara.* He almost applauded when Tess dropped her hands and faced Sara directly.

"What will happen to me?" Tess's voice was no more than a pitiful whisper.

Sara was quick to answer. "It depends on what you've done," she replied honestly. "But if you tell us the truth, we'll do everything we can to help you."

Tess spun her head around to Nick, her frantic gaze seeking confirmation. He nodded in agreement. "Sara's right, Tess. Help us, and we'll help you."

A jerky sob escaped her as she bowed her head again. "I didn't mean any harm," she cried.

"Of course you didn't," Nick interrupted. Then he crouched on the floor, so that he was eye to eye with Tess. "But you've always loved Ben, haven't you, Tess?" he questioned gently.

Sara suppressed a double take. So that was what all those looks directed at Ben were about at the funeral. She should have guessed. Nick, growing up in the Kingsley estate would have seen more evidence of Tess's true feelings.

Tess's hand fell to the table and she gave him a sad look, then glanced again at Sara. Her eyes were shadowed with pain. "Always," she breathed.

Then she directed her attention to Nick again, as if seeking approval.

Nick's gaze was understanding, compassionate. "It's all right, Tess. Ben is a wonderful man."

Sara sat very still, impressed with Nick's sensitive handling of Tess. She had calmed down considerably.

"Yes, he is, isn't he?" Tess replied, as if lost in thought.

Nick reached for her hand. "Then why not tell us what's going on?"

"Please," Sara pleaded.

Tess took a deep breath, staring at the wall. Then she started to talk, dreamily, as if to herself.

"I turned down other men, waiting for Ben. But he always loved Lillian. When she died, I finally thought I'd have a chance. I invited him here the night of the funeral. I literally threw myself at him—but he turned me down." Bitterness edged her voice.

Snatches of memory surfaced in Sara's brain. Ben had been missing that night. She'd tried to reach him to tell him about Nick's appearance. When she talked to him the next day, he'd admitted to her that he'd tied one on. Tess had probably upset him, but Ben was obviously every inch the gentleman he appeared to be. He'd kept that part to himself.

"Go on..." Sara prodded, sympathy in her voice.

"I was so angry. I'd waited all those years. After he left, there was a knock at the door. A man I didn't know asked if he could speak to me about Ben. I invited him in."

Sara and Nick both held their breath.

"The man told me that Ben wasn't the kind of person I thought he was," Tess continued. "That he'd duped his boss, a client of Ben's, out of millions of dollars. That Ben had used the money to buy gifts for Lillian."

Sara recognized the old con. Take one upset woman. Build on her jealousy. Then set her up to do what you want. But how had they known that Tess would be susceptible?

"This man's boss wanted to talk to Ben alone. To scare him a little, the man said. He didn't want to go to the authorities because the client didn't want any publicity. He said he was sure that I didn't want Ben to get into any...real trouble. He said his boss was convinced he and Ben could just talk it out."

Tess stopped to catch her breath. After a few moments, she started again. "At first I couldn't believe it, but Ben's always catered to Lillian. When I thought that he loved her enough to steal that kind of money, I became very angry and hurt. I wanted to get back at Ben for rejecting me, but I really didn't want anything terrible to happen to him." She swallowed hard, looking at each of them in turn. "So, I agreed to help Ben's client," she finally said.

Nick pressed her hand. "Then, what happened?"

Tess clamped her lips together, her eyes dark, then she spoke again. "I didn't know how to get him away for a few days. That's how long his boss said they needed since the deal was complicated. I mean, he'd just rejected me, why would he go away with me?'' A bitter laugh was torn from her throat. ''But the man told me what to say.''

''What was that?'' Sara interrupted.

''I was to say, 'Lillian is alive. She needs to see you for a few days. I'm to take you there.'''

Her voice trailed off as she looked at them in wonder. ''You know, Ben never even asked me anything. All he said was, 'Where shall I meet you?' Isn't that strange? Why would Ben believe that Lillian was alive?'' The question hung in the air between them.

Sara and Nick shared a glance, but neither of them answered.

Not noticing their exchanged looks, Tess went on talking. ''I followed this man's instructions completely. I met him and two other men in a limousine in an abandoned scrap yard in the west end of the city. When Ben arrived, I was just to get out of my car, take him over to the limousine and leave.''

''Did you do that?'' Sara asked in a hushed voice.

Tess nodded sadly. ''Yes. I did exactly what I had been told to. I wanted to get out of there as quickly as possible. When I looked back, the men seemed to shuffle him into the car. Ben didn't look very happy. In fact, they seemed quite rough with him. I began to have doubts about what was going to happen, but I was scared to do anything. I thought I'd be considered an accessory. I decided to go away for a few days and think my way through everything, then I saw you, and I panicked.'' A look of shame crossed her face.

Sara interrupted quickly. ''It's all right, Tess. But I want you to think really hard. It's very important. Do you have any idea...any idea at all as to where they might have taken Ben?''

Tess hesitated, then responded. ''I thought I heard one of them say, 'Edwards Metals.''' Her tone sounded dubious. "I'm not sure what that means." *I know,* Sara almost shouted. She'd been holding her breath. Now she let it out with an audible whoosh. At last, something to go on. Edwards Metals was an abandoned landmark on the Lake Ontario waterfront.

"Thanks, Tess. Thanks for telling us everything." Her reply was filled with heartfelt gratitude.

Nick tried to make a connection, but he didn't know Toronto as well as Sara did. From the expression on Sara's face he gathered that Tess's information was valuable.

"Important?" he asked.

"You bet."

Tess glanced between the two of them, her eyes anxious. "Does that help?" she asked, her words halting.

They both stood up. Sara pressed her palm on Tess's shoulders, giving her a kind smile.

"More than you know," she answered. "You just might have saved Ben's life."

THE MAN STARED DOWN at the lawyer with disgust. As soon as he pulled out the wire cutters to slice the cables, Ben had passed out.

Soft, he thought disparagingly, then began to work on the already frayed wires. A creaking door sounded in the cavernous background and he hesitated.

He'd deliberately parked in the empty lot next to the warehouse so as to avert suspicion. Still, he wasn't going to take any chances. Standing motionless, he waited, then heard two voices—one male, one female.

Dammit. He jammed the wire cutters into the back pocket of his jeans. The voices seemed to be coming from near the doorway. Whoever was coming in, was being cautious.

Good, that worked to his advantage. He could slip down the stairs and out through the back before they saw him.

Quietly, he began making his way down the old wooden steps, staying in the shadows. The sounds, although still in the distance, drew closer.

Recklessly, he jumped the last three steps and darted toward the back. Then he heard a cry of surprise and bolted for the door with all his strength, slamming the metal door open. His heart pounding, he turned along the waterfront toward the lot.

There was no way he was going to take the rap for this one, or any way he was going to tell that coldhearted bastard who'd hired him that he'd failed!

He was heading across the border into the States as fast as he could!

Chapter Twelve

As soon as Sara had seen the shadow move, she'd cried out and broken into a run. Nick followed. They reached the back door almost at the same time. Sara raced toward the wharf. A speeding car, its tires screeching, spun out of the empty lot next to the warehouse. Sara went to chase it on foot, but Nick's hand stalled her.

Out of breath, he swore. "It's too late, Sara. We've lost him."

Sara clenched her hands into fists. "Every time we get close..."

"I know," he answered soothingly. "Did you see where he came from?"

Sara turned, her features taut. "The stairs."

Nick elbowed her back into the warehouse. Without wasting any time, they climbed the set of stairs, avoiding the splintered, broken wooden handrail. An elevator cab was suspended as if it had been halted in motion about a foot from the top of the landing.

Dust clogged the air, making it hard to breathe.

At the top they both stopped. Glancing around, Sara took a step toward the elevator. The hatch lay on the floor. Squinting through the opening, she peered down the shaft.

"My God, it's Ben," she gasped, swinging her arm behind her to draw Nick near. Bending over, he saw Ben's body, inert on the floor of the cab.

"Why didn't he jump and try to climb the cable?" Sara asked, puzzled. The cab was about seven feet high. Ben could easily have grabbed the cable and hauled himself out. She leaned farther over the edge. The lawyer lay sprawled in a corner, his legs extended in a curve behind him. "Ben," she called down the shaft, unwittingly reaching for the cable.

Then Nick saw the answer to her question. Needle-sharp wires protruded from the cables. His hand shot out in a flash to stop her. "No, Sara!"

Startled, Sara almost lost her balance. "What's the matter?"

Nick pointed. Mesmerized, Sara stared at the cables. The strands of flexible steel were frayed, ready to break. She pulled her hand back as if from a flame.

She looked imploringly to Nick. It was obvious that any weight would send the elevator cab crashing. "How are we going to get him out of there?" she asked in a hushed voice.

Nick had been wondering the same thing, then his gaze fell on a discarded piece of rope. Bending down, he fingered it thoughtfully. "I suspect this is the only way we can get him out alive—or in one piece."

Sara tried to follow his train of thought. They'd have to hoist him out, but Ben was unconscious. He wouldn't be able to tie the rope to himself. That left only one way. Her eyes darkening, she asked, "Are you thinking what I think you're thinking?"

Nick nodded, a grim expression in his eyes. "Yes. Have you had any survival training?"

"I've done some rappeling, if that's what you mean," she said briskly, referring to flat surface climbing.

"That's exactly what I mean. Except we'll have to use a variation of it. How much do you weight?"

"One-twenty."

He held up the rope, appraisingly. "And I weigh two hundred. Do you suppose . . . ?"

"Yes," she interjected quickly. "We can do it."

Despite the circumstances, he smiled his approval. He might have known she'd agree. "Good girl."

In an instant, Sara sat on the dusty, litter-strewn floor to remove her jacket and boots. "What about your arm, Nick?" she asked anxiously, glancing up. "Will you be able to handle the weight?"

While she was removing her boots, Nick had been running his hand along the inside of the doorway and the wall. Finding what he was looking for, he breathed a sigh of relief. Thank God. Sara was right. With an injured arm, he was going to need all the help he could get. "I think this is the answer, Sara," he finally responded to her question.

Now on her feet, she joined him. She peered inside the doorjamb. "A piece of metal?" she queried, seeing a two-inch bar of steel.

"An angle iron," he explained. "There's a bit of a gap between it and the wall. I can use it—"

"—to give you leverage with the rope," she said, with sudden comprehension.

"Right." Taking the rope in his right hand, he slid it under the angle iron. Sara caught the end, pulling it through until there was enough to make a loop. Deftly, Nick circled the rope, knotting it and testing it for strength.

Sara removed her holster, then stood, waiting. A thin line of perspiration dotted her upper lip as she looked at the hatch opening which she judged to be about two feet square. She'd just manage to squeeze through. But would Ben? She shoved the thought aside, her heart beginning to thump in her chest.

They could only try.

Nick was finished. "Are you ready?" he asked, facing her.

"I'm in your hands," she said with a smile.

Nick suppressed an automatic sensual response. There'd be time for that later.

He dropped as much of the rope as he could into the opening, holding some in reserve. "Go real easy, Sara," he cautioned. "Try not to touch the sides of the cab. I don't want to lose you, too." *Especially you,* he thought.

"You won't," she said airily, edging toward the opening. Nick positioned himself behind her, bracing his legs in preparation. His hands wrapped tightly around the rope.

Sara inhaled deeply, feeling the dust and grime tickling her lungs. "Now?" she asked, without turning around.

"Anytime you like, Sara."

Her pulse jumped. This was it. She waited a second, took another gulp of stale air and reached for the rope, steadying her grip. Then, heart racing, she bent her legs in. Go! She grabbed the hemp with her ankles and swung into the air through the opening.

The rope jerked convulsively as Nick struggled to take her weight. She weaved off balance for a few seconds, sliding farther down the rope. The only thing keeping her from crashing to the floor of the cab was the strength of Nick's arms. *Lord help him,* she prayed, closing her eyes. Then she felt the rope steady, and she opened her eyes again. She'd made it! Cleared the opening!

"Okay, Sara?" She heard Nick's breathless question above her.

"Fine," she replied hoarsely.

"Good. I've got you. Go ahead."

Sara took another deep breath and began to shimmy carefully down the rope until she almost reached the loop.

Then she stopped. Ben lay sprawled beneath her like a contented child.

She heard him moan, and a silent plea welled up inside her. *Don't, Ben. Whatever you do, don't wake up. And don't move.*

"All right, Sara?" Strain altered Nick's voice.

"Yes," she managed, her voice muffled as she adjusted her position. Her heart began to hammer in a staccato rhythm. This was the tricky part. She'd have to hang on to the rope with one hand and bend over from one side to secure the loop around Ben.

"I'm going to let go," she said.

Nick's response was clipped. "Okay."

She flexed her left hand then tightened her grip. Fighting a surge of panic, she inhaled deeply, then released her right hand and swung in the direction of Ben.

Sara gasped as she felt herself swinging out of control. *No!* A mute scream lodged in her throat. She was unable to stop herself. With a jolt, she hit the side of the cab. A grating sound pierced the air and the elevator shuddered. She was going to fall! Above her, she heard the ping of snapping cables. "Nick," she cried out in desperation, her arm waving in a wild curve. She shut her eyes tight, bracing herself for the fall.

"It's all right, Sara. I've got you." Nick's voice was ragged from exertion and he was breathing hard. "Almost there, Sara."

Blood rushed to Sara's temples. Then she felt the rope go taut. She was all right. Nick was still holding her.

"So . . . rry . . ." she heard him gasp.

Opening her eyes, she saw the rope slacken with more give.

"Relax a minute, Sara." Nick's voice sounded anxious. Forcing herself not to panic, she drew air in through her mouth, taking a few seconds to quiet her beating heart. "Okay," she finally managed.

Calmer now, Sara looked at Ben, gauging the distance. Tentatively, she stretched out with the looped end of hemp.

She inhaled sharply. There wasn't enough rope. She needed another couple of feet.

"Nick..." Her voice was nothing more than a whisper. "Need...more..."

"Hang on."

Sweat poured down Sara's face. She hovered in the air, partially upside-down. Her skin was flushed. Licking her lips, she tasted perspiration.

"There, Sara..." Nick was panting now. In order to give Sara the extra rope, he'd had to stretch his arms over his head.

Below, Sara felt the rope loosen in her hand.

Gingerly, she began to position the rope under Ben's right shoulder. It was a painstaking process with only one free hand. When she was finished, her body was drenched with sweat. Slowly, she released him and he fell back. The elevator stirred a fraction, and she held her breath.

Starting again, she did the other side, then drew the rope around his chest. She didn't dare risk sliding the rope any lower on his body.

Ben still lay motionless.

Suddenly Nick's voice rasped a rough command. "Get out fast, Sara!"

"Tighten...first..." she muttered through clenched teeth.

"Then do it!" he ordered. "The cables aren't going to hold...and the rope's beginning to fray."

Responding to the worry in his voice, Sara nimbly secured the loop, then gasped as Nick jerked the rope. Righting herself, she began to climb back up, her head reeling from the quick movements as she scrambled over the edge.

Nick pulled her to her feet. His face was slick with perspiration, his shirt glued to his skin. "Sorry," he apologized. His breath was coming in ragged spurts. "But the angle iron is weakening the rope and the cables are going to break any second." He indicated the frayed edges above his head. Frantically trying to clear her head of the dizziness that was engulfing her, Sara glanced at the cables. Only threads of wire remained.

"You okay?" he asked, distracted.

"Fine," she croaked.

"Let's do it then." He galvanized himself into action. Then she saw his arm. Fresh blood was oozing from the knife wound. "Nick, your arm," she exclaimed.

"No time." He tossed her comment aside. "Help me with this rope."

Ignoring her concern for Nick temporarily, she followed his order and grabbed a portion of the rope.

A tearing sound reverberated in the elevator canal. The wires began to split apart.

"Pull, Sara," he yelled, wrenching on the rope.

With feverish concentration, Sara dragged on the rope, Ben's weight almost tearing her shoulders out of their sockets. Ahead of her, Nick's muscles strained as his shoulders also felt the weight. His shirt was soaking wet, the right sleeve fiery red.

The cable wires were snapping. The elevator cab gave a shuddering heave. Sara couldn't even see straight. Stars danced in front of her eyes.

Ben's body caught in the hatch opening. With desperate determination, they yanked as hard as they could, sending the elevator into a convulsive spasm. As the last wire split, they angled Ben's body through the opening and clear of the top edge. With thunderous impact, the elevator crashed to the ground.

LILLIAN HANDED THE GUARD the clipboard with the attached writing pad. "That's all I can remember," she said as if challenging him to dispute her word.

The guard looked at her warily. "Is this the whole formula?"

"No," she snapped. "I've forgotten the rest of it."

"He isn't going to like this," the guard warned.

"That's too bad. If he wants it all, he'll have to get Sara Brennan."

The man gave her a stupid look. Lord, he was dumb, Lillian thought. But she hoped he was dumb enough to believe her.

She was desperate. She had no illusions that once she gave them the formula her life or Ben's would be safe. She had to find a way for Sara to get to her.

If she could convince them that Sara knew the rest of the formula, then maybe they'd bring her here and she'd think of some way to get them out.

Suddenly, Lillian felt very tired and very old.

BEN GROANED, leaning his silver head against the upholstery of Nick's car. Sitting in the back seat, his eyes half-shut, he clenched and unclenched his fingers as if to convince himself he was alive.

"How did you ever find me?" Weary, his voice still managed to convey his surprise.

Sara swiveled around, tilting her head toward him. A small smile hovered on her lips. "It wasn't easy." She glanced over at Nick, who gave her a conspiratorial wink. "We paid a visit to Tess," she explained.

"Tess." Softly, Ben swirled the name on his tongue. He closed his eyes, searching for answers, but finding none, opened them again. A shudder ran through him at how close he'd come to being dead.

Watching him, Sara could feel his pain. "We'll explain it all on our way to the estate, Ben," she reassured. "How do you feel?" Disheveled and grimy, Ben created quite a different image from the meticulous, dapper lawyer she was accustomed to seeing. But her real worry was whether this ordeal had caused him any permanent damage. Ben was no kid, after all.

"Fine," he answered in grim response. "A bit sore. Some aches and pains. Otherwise I'm okay. I feel better than I smell."

Relieved by his attempt at dry humor, Sara and Nick both laughed. Through the rearview mirror, Nick smiled at Ben. "I doubt any of us smells that great," he replied. "Or looks that good."

"You can say that again!" Sara agreed, looking down at her once white turtleneck. She had raised a few eyebrows when they stopped and she ran into a drugstore to get bandages for Nick's arm. Buying water to wash the wound had proved even trickier, but somehow she'd managed to do it.

When the laughter subsided, Sara turned back to Ben, her expression serious. "Do you know who kidnapped you, Ben? Or where Lillian is?"

He shook his head disconsolately. "No. The guys who drugged me were just hired hands, I'm sure of that. But I know they've got Lillian."

"How?"

Ben twisted his wrists for them to see, holding it above the seat. "They took my watch, I think to prove to Lillian that they'd kidnapped me. As best as I can make out, I was a hostage. My life for the formula." His voice grew shaky as the grim truth resurfaced. Lillian's whereabouts and safety were still in doubt.

Nick's hands tightened on the steering wheel. He could see the scenario with deadly clarity. They couldn't very well kill Lillian until *after* they had the formula. And Lillian wouldn't give them the formula without proof of the danger to Ben. But now, that they'd delivered that to her...

"They'll kill her once they have the formula."

Hearing the conviction in Nick's voice, Sara shuddered.

"Unless we can find her first," she countered.

"How?" Ben jerked his head up. "We have no clues. I didn't get the license number of the car. I barely even caught a glimpse of my kidnappers before they drugged me. I'm afraid I won't be much help."

"There must be something you can remember that might help us," Sara persisted. Her hand pressed onto the back of the seat as she faced Ben. They couldn't give up! They just couldn't.

"Nothing." Ben let out a sigh. "Not a damn thing."

"But..." Sara protested, her voice rising, glancing between the two men. "We've got to—"

"What, Sara?" Nick's quiet voice interrupted. "What have we got to do? Turn Toronto and all the neighboring towns upside-down to find a woman we all love—with no clues, without the weight of the law behind us?" He shook his dark head sadly. "Ben is right. We're amateurs. We'd better leave this to the police."

Sara stared at him, shocked. What had happened to change his attitude? "You didn't think that this morning," she reminded, flashing him a dark look. "And we found Ben."

Nick's jaw was set into a determined line. "That was this morning, Sara. Now, there's even less time—and maybe even more danger."

"I'm not afraid of the danger," she challenged.

Nor am I, he felt like saying. *But I sure as hell am afraid for you, more than you are for yourself.* The events of the past couple of days had finally caught up with him. When news of Ben's rescue reached the top criminal's ears, Sara might be in even more danger than she was now. He wasn't sure he understood why that was true, but a sixth sense told him to be exceptionally careful. If something were to happen to Sara now, he didn't know what he would do.

"Courage isn't the issue, Sara," he said, his voice raised in exasperation.

"Then if it isn't, what about our loyalty to Lillian? Don't we owe her something?" she challenged.

Loyalty and love. Powerful emotions to Sara. She didn't have to get herself killed to prove them. He felt like shaking her, even though he respected those same qualities in her. God, this woman could turn him inside out.

He adopted a new tack. "You've done everything humanly possible to find Lillian—more than anyone could expect. There's nothing to feel guilty about."

"No? Not yet, you mean. But if I quit, I'll have plenty to feel guilty about." Pain flashed in her eyes. "Nothing you say will change my mind, Nick. *You* can stop looking for Lillian, if you like, but I won't—I can't. I'm going on with the search—with or without you!"

Nick's frustration had reached the limit. His fingers latched over hers painfully. "Not if I have anything to say about it, you won't," he told her.

Sara had heard that statement too many times in her married life. Something in her snapped. "Well, you don't," she ground out, wrenching her hand out from under his.

Nick took a deep breath. He could accept her stubbornness, but he wouldn't let her be foolhardy.

"That's where you're wrong," he rasped. "I'll personally stop you if I have to."

In the back, Ben discreetly slumped against the seat.

Sara arched her eyebrows in derision. What inalienable right did men think they possessed to issue orders and threats with such authority?

"Oh, and how will you do that?" she retorted. "Truss me up? Tie me to a bedpost?"

He was sorely tempted to do the latter. Where Sara was concerned, he wasn't going to take even one small chance that any harm could come to her.

"Stop it, Sara. That's enough."

Hearing his proprietary tone, Sara bit back a caustic reply. She wouldn't dignify his comment with an answer. She'd do what she damned well pleased! No man was going to tell her what to do. She'd had enough of that to last a lifetime.

Chapter Thirteen

He looked at the three stooges with disdain. Nothing more than hired muscle, he thought disparagingly.

He had barely been able to contain his rage when they informed him that they'd botched their second attempt on Sara's life.

But now. His green eyes narrowed with an emotion resembling warmth. Luck was with him.

This time their bungling had worked to his advantage. He needed Sara—alive.

"You say that Lillian Kingsley can't remember the whole formula?" he said, steepling his fingers in front of him.

"That's what she says," one of the men answered, cringing with anticipation.

He continued. "And that Sara Brennan knows the entire chemical breakdown?"

The man nodded reluctantly.

He fixed the man who had answered with a cold, calculating stare. It was highly probable that Lillian was lying. His fourth man hadn't returned yet, but now that Ben was dead, he had nothing to bargain with.

If Sara had the formula, he could trade Lillian's life for it. If she didn't, he'd bargain for Sara's life with Lillian.

One of the women would cave in. He was convinced of it.

"Get Sara Brennan and bring her here, but use your head this time," he cautioned. "She's outsmarted us once too often."

The man nodded and left. Alone now, he began to relax, a faint smile warming his mouth.

The prospect of bringing Sara and Lillian to their knees appealed to him immensely.

SARA RETREATED to her suite in silence, leaving Nick and Ben to drive to the police station. Detective Adams had already signed out for the day, so they gave their statements to the detective sergeant in charge of the shift. Nick, concerned about how exhausted Sara looked, had persuaded her that her statement wasn't needed right now. In tight-lipped agreement, she'd conceded.

At last, Nick and the lawyer stood in the foyer of the Kingsley mansion, Ben totally fatigued from his escapade, and Nick worried about his confrontation with Sara.

What had come over her? She'd exploded like a summer storm.

Beside him, Ben coughed nervously. "Nick . . ."

He turned, looking expectantly at the lawyer.

The strain of his ordeal showed in Ben's face and echoed in his voice. "Nick, I owe you an apology and thanks. You and Sara saved my life tonight."

Nick hesitated at the foot of the stairs. He smiled wanly at the lawyer, shrugging the gratitude aside. "Forget it, Ben."

"No, no. There's more," the lawyer interrupted. "I said some things to Sara about you. I think I was wrong. Charles . . ." He paused as if unsure how to explain.

But Nick could see what was coming. Ben, now realizing the extent to which Charles had distorted the truth, felt guilty for accepting Charles's version of events. A sense of gratitude to the lawyer for his attempt to put things right welled up inside him. The vindication was coming late in his life, but it was welcome nevertheless. Now, however, was not the time to delve into the past.

He interrupted quickly. "I know what Charles was like, Ben, and I appreciate what you're trying to say. But we'll sort it all out after this is over." He placed a reassuring hand on the older man's arm.

The lawyer took a deep breath and cleared his throat. "Okay. But we *will* do it, Nick. I promise."

The conviction in the lawyer's voice stirred Nick more than he might have believed it would. Attempting a smile, he found there was a catch in his throat when he answered. "I know we will. Now, why don't you get a good night's sleep? You look like you could use it."

Despite his tiredness, Ben grinned. "You too, Nick. You look pretty rough."

Nick's mouth twisted into a good-natured grimace. "I guess I do at that. Good night, Ben."

"Good night."

Nick watched him head up the stairs. Exhaustion washed over him, and he had every intention of hitting his own bed as soon as he could, but first, there was something he had to do.

That flash summer storm. Sara's reaction in the car. Had he been too rough? It was only because he was worried to death about her.

Tossing off his coat onto the banister, he went up the stairs to Sara's suite.

The door was ajar, and he could see her through the opening, sitting at the small coffee table, her head down, lost in thought.

He swallowed hard. Ever since he met Sara, he'd been falling in love with her, even when he'd suspected her of murder. *The heart follows its own destiny,* he couldn't help thinking. He'd never realized the truth of that statement until now. In the semilight, her shining hair created a halo of burnished browns and gold around her head. Her beauty, like everything else about her, was completely natural and lacking in artifice. She took his breath away.

He tapped gently on the door. "May I come in?"

At the sound of a male voice, Sara almost dropped the tea she'd been sipping. The cup and saucer rattled in her hand as she looked up, startled.

"Sorry," he apologized, crossing the room in two easy strides, without waiting for a response. "I didn't mean to frighten you. May I?" He indicated one of the chairs.

Sara placed the cup on the table, nodding. "It's all right," she answered tonelessly. "I'm just a bit jumpy."

That was the understatement of the year, she thought ruefully. Fear for Lillian's safety was gnawing away at her like a starved thing. She wanted to do something—any-thing—to try to find her. And Nick was trying to stop her. Domination. Was that all men could think about? Ten-sion banded her temples. *Admit it, Sara, you're scared. You don't want to fall in love with a man who'll do to you what Derek tried to do.*

Rousing herself out of her reverie, she raised luminous, shadowed eyes to look at Nick, only to find him watching her.

As if reading her thoughts, he began to speak, his voice soft, disarming. "Sara, about what happened in the car. Let me explain why—"

Sara wasn't sure she wanted to hear this. If she was ready to hear it. "You don't have to explain," she inter-rupted, tossing her hair back. Droplets of water from her recent shower fell on her robe. She brushed them aside. "Let's just forget it, shall we?" With a jerky motion, she stood up and crossed to the window, clasping her arms across her chest and turning away from him.

In an instant, he was on his feet. Sidestepping the table, he came up behind her, gripping her shoulders.

"Sara, what the hell's bothering you? I know you're worried sick about Lillian. So am I. But there's nothing we can do...."

She whirled around, facing him. He noticed she'd removed the bandage from her temple. He wished he could erase the pain the blue-black stain on her flawless skin must be causing her with a caress of his fingers. "I know that." Her gaze was resigned, the green eyes sadly dark. "Don't you think I can see what's staring us in the face?"

"Then what is it?" Confusion choked in his throat. "You flared up at me in the car for no reason at all."

A flash of anger replaced her sadness. "No reason at all? You call yelling at me no reason at all?"

"That's it?" he asked in a quiet voice. "That's what this is about?" He drew a deep breath. "All right," he conceded. "I'm sorry. I'll admit I'm not the most subtle male in the world, but I'm not going to apologize for trying to keep you from risking your life."

"It's my job," she answered, trying to control the trembling of her mouth. "Or haven't you noticed?"

Noticed? he thought with a grimace. The image kept him awake at nights. "I know only too well that the way you earn your living puts you at risk," he replied, trying to keep his tone even. "But that doesn't mean I don't want to protect—"

"Control, you mean," Sara corrected heatedly.

"Control?" he repeated, his voice tinged with lack of comprehension. "What does control have to do with what I'm feeling?"

"It's what all men want, isn't it?" Her voice began to rise. She felt her tenuous hold on her emotions slipping. "To control the women in their lives? To have them fit into the neat slots that *they* design." With a sob, she wrenched out of his grasp, her eyes misting. "That's what men mean when they say they want to look after you, protect you, cherish you...."

Nick looked at her, shocked. "Wherever did you get that idea?"

The tears began to fall then as she tilted her head to meet his gaze. "From Derek," she replied, her voice husky.

The he saw it. The very real pain mirrored in her glistening eyes. The residue of her unhappy marriage. He inwardly cursed his own insensitivity. He'd hit a raw nerve and it had unleashed all her pent-up resentment.

His arm circled her convulsively. "Darling," he whispered. She went to pull away, but he held her fast. "Darling, calm down. I don't want to run your life. In the car I was only terrified you'd try something and get hurt."

"But..." Her protest was muffled against his chest.

"No, Sara," he soothed. "I don't want you to fit into some neat slot that I create. You're a spirited, independent individual and I want you to stay that way. Those qualities are the very ones that attracted mc to you." He hugged her close, his voice suddenly becoming raw with emotion. "Don't you know I'm falling in love with you? I couldn't stand it if I were to lose you now."

Nick's words seeped through Sara's haze of bitterness. He was falling in love with her? Raising her head, she stared at him, her eyes reflecting the wonder his words triggered. "You're falling..." she began, surprise making it impossible for her to repeat the words.

"Right." His mouth quirked at the corners as his dark eyes took in her beautiful, stunned expression. "I'm falling in love with you. Don't tell me you hadn't noticed?" he teased.

"I—I—"

His fingers gently brushed the last of the wet tears on her cheek. He tilted her chin toward him. "I was also beginning to hope you might be feeling the same way, Sara." His gaze locked with hers. "Do you?"

There it was, she thought. Out in the open. The question she'd been asking herself. But was afraid to answer because she'd been terrified of loving another man like Derek. But Nick wasn't at all like her ex-husband. How could she have been so blind?

Suddenly, her eyes shone. "Oh, yes," she answered, the rightness of it swelling in her voice. "Oh yes, Nick Kingsley. I am beginning to feel the same way. I'm so sorry. You were right that day about my having a chip on my shoulder. I have become defensive...."

Nick had been holding his breath, waiting for her response. The joy that leaped through him at her answer was indescribable. "Shh..." His fingers came to rest on her lips, silencing her. "That husband of yours did a real number on you. How much, I didn't fully realize until tonight. When you described your marriage, you seemed distanced. But I should have recognized the tactic. I've used it countless times myself to hide the hurt," he admitted. "But..." His eyes darkened. "Sara, I'm going to lose my temper with you again. I care for you so much, and you're going to have to remember that's why I'm doing it and get used to it. Can you?"

"I'll try." Then she added softly, looking up at him, her eyes brimming with new trust, "I may need a little help, though."

Sara's openness filled him with primitive protectiveness. Removing his fingers from her moist lips, he cupped his hand around her neck, drawing her to him. "Lady, I'm going to give you all the help you want," he responded.

When his mouth came down on hers, all energy deserted Sara. The insistence of his kiss sent waves of weak surrender shuddering through her. Without thinking, without doubting, Sara groaned her compliance underneath his warm mouth. His tongue forced her lips open, and he played it seductively inside her mouth, touching, searching, wooing.

Dizzying fire burst inside her. Reaching for him, her hands entwined around his neck. His hand moved unerringly toward her breast, sure fingers finding and coaxing its hot hard peak.

With an effort, he broke away. His breath was ragged and his eyes bored into hers.

"Take off your robe," he told her.

She answered him by removing her hands from his neck and untying the loosely bound belt. With a toss, the robe landed on the floor.

"My God!" he whispered thickly, and quickly undressed without taking his eyes from her.

His lean, naked body filled her with hot urgency. Then she saw his arm. It was roughly rebandaged as if he'd done it in haste, and a stain darkened the outside. "Your arm," she whispered.

"Damn my arm," he growled. "I could make love to you with both arms injured. Lie down on the bed."

Sara obeyed immediately, stretching out on top of the cover. Nick lay beside her, and as if to prove his point, covered her lips with his without touching her, parting them with his intensity and probing. All her senses reeled, then his knees urged her legs apart and she felt the full weight of his heated body. Pleasure and need soared inside her. His naked skin on hers filled her with delicious abandonment, and she arched her body upward to meet him in joyful acceptance.

Moaning, he pulled his mouth from hers. "Not yet," he breathed. Grazing his mouth down the long line of her neck, he licked a trail of fire to each breast, tasting each nipple with his tongue, ripening each into a plump, sweet berry.

Her hands searched for him, touching, teasing, caressing. Groans of pleasure rumbled in his throat.

The night disappeared as their urgency increased. Fingers, tongues and lips became more confident, more giving. They became lost in the discovery of each other's body. The events that had brought them together belonged to another time, a universe remote from the one they created together.

Every part of Sara's body was ablaze. She'd never felt so right about loving a man, and when he probed the core of her, she opened herself willingly, wholeheartedly, with no reservations and nothing held back.

When at last he entered her, neither had ever known until then the joy of such a total union. Together they took each other to the brink of fulfillment, and when they passed the threshold into sheer ecstasy, both sensed the union bound more than their bodies. Two hearts and minds crossed the threshold at the same time.

Afterward, Sara nestled in the crook of his good arm, reveling in the sleekness of his skin. Raising her head, she asked tentatively, "Why have you been so patient with me?"

His mouth brushed against her temple. "Charles and your ex-husband had a lot in common. Trying to control in the name of love comes naturally to men like that. It's a horrible experience. I know. I went through it with Charles. I just wished I'd recognized the symptoms in you sooner." Edging her chin toward him with his hand, he stared at her intently. "Sara, promise me you won't go off on your own looking for Lillian."

She snuggled back into the warmth of his body. "I promise."

His arm tightened around her as he planted a light kiss on the top of her head. "Sara, when this is all over..."

"I know," she whispered against his chest, understanding.

When this is all over, we'll have time for each other.

Chapter Fourteen

Like a waking kitten, Sara stretched languorously in the soft bed, a smile of enchantment sweetening her mouth. She'd never before realized how joyous lovemaking could be—how giving, how sharing. Not for one second had she felt any loss of self in Nick's arms, only an expression of who she was. She relished the power he seemed to have over her to make her feel, just as she relished the power she seemed to have over him. The mutual fulfillment had left her breathless with wonder.

Automatically, she reached out a hand to feel for Nick. Her fingers spread on the sheet came away empty.

Suddenly wide awake, her eyes flew open and she turned on her side. The indentation of his large body still marked the sheets. Confused by Nick's absence, she sat up, just as a knock came to the door.

Nick! Her heart skipped a beat. Patting her tumbling hair away from her face, she called out, "Come in."

Edie tentatively pushed the door ajar. "Morning, Miss Brennan. Sorry to disturb you."

Sara, trying to conceal her disappointment, reassured her. "That's all right, Edie. What is it?"

"There's a police officer to see you."

Sara's eyes widened fractionally, and she swung her legs over the side of the bed, ready to get up. "There is?"

"Yes. I told him you'd be a few minutes. But he seems anxious. He wants you to go to the police station."

News of Lillian? A glimmer of hope flickered in her, then she remembered Nick's comment from the night before. If the police wanted her at the station, likely they needed a corroborating statement from her. Her optimism flagged. She mobilized herself into action, reaching for the robe on the floor. "I'll be right there," she promised. "Tell him to give me ten minutes."

"All right. And Mr. Kingsley left you a note."

Sara stopped tying the belt of her robe to take the piece of paper Edie extended. Rapidly she scanned the contents.

"Couldn't sleep. Went to check for clues at Edward Metals. Wait for me. Love you. Nick."

Bless him. A rush of warmth spread through her. So, he wasn't going to just sit back and leave it all to the police. Love you. *Me too,* she thought with a delicious shudder. *If I had my way, I'd wait for you, right here, in this warm bed. If anyone other than the police wanted to see me, that's where you'd find me, Nick Kingsley.*

Smiling to herself, she folded the note and tucked it into her pocket. "Thanks, Edie. Will you tell Mr. Kingsley I had to go to the police station and I'll be back as soon as I can?"

Edie nodded. "I'll bring you a cup of coffee. You can drink it while you're getting dressed." She paused at the door before leaving, "Oh, by the way, last night while you and Mr. Kingsley were out, that Detective Adams came by with a search warrant and checked the house."

Sara's eyelashes fluttered, the news surprising her. A routine investigation? Searching for clues to Lillian's whereabouts, she concluded, then began hurriedly to get dressed.

Not quite fifteen minutes later, she ran down the gracious front staircase of the house, recognizing the back of Constable Tom Canfield as he hovered in the foyer. He turned quickly at the sound of her footfall.

"Hello, Constable." She extended a hand. "Sorry to keep you waiting."

The officer wasn't a tall man, but chunky and solidly built. His brown eyes were unsmiling as he returned her greeting. "Good morning, Ms Brennan."

"Any news of Lillian?"

The officer's response seemed a little more guarded than usual, she thought. "You'll have to discuss that with Detective Adams," he replied, staring pointedly at her. Releasing her hand, he moved closer, his fingers coming to rest on her left forearm.

Sara gave him a sharp glance. Anyone would think he was going to arrest her. Officers usually established physical control when they were about to take somebody into custody. Her gaze rested on his face.

The officer cleared his throat. "Ms Brennan, I'm arresting you for murder. It's . . ."

"Murder?" she gasped. "But that's impossible. Nick Kingsley and Ben Short gave statements to the police last night," she exclaimed, her eyes widening with horror. "Don't you have them?"

The constable halted her flow of words, his fingers tightening on her arm, as he continued, "It's my duty to inform you that you have the right to retain and instruct counsel without delay. Do you understand the charge and what I'm saying?"

Sara's horror gave way to a flash of anger. Of course she understood the customary arrest procedure. But she'd be damned if she was going to wake up Ben after his ordeal of the previous day. This was just a mix-up. The detective on the evening shift likely hadn't brought Detective Adams up to date yet. That was all, wasn't it? Her anger became uncertainty again. "Where's Detective Adams?" she asked testily.

Constable Canfield replied in even tones. "He's been called to court. You'll be able to talk to him at the station."

Adams would be at the station? Had *he* ordered her arrest? Surely Adams wasn't behind this? He couldn't believe she'd killed Lillian. With a supreme effort, she tried to dispel her fears as unfounded. Once she got to the station, she'd reemphasize to the detective her role in Lillian's charade, and then this ridiculous charge would be dropped.

The constable's voice interrupted her confused thoughts. "Will you please follow me, Ms Brennan?"

Sara bit back a retort. The young officer was only doing his job. "Yes," she managed in a tight voice. He hesitated as if expecting her to exercise her right to call a lawyer. If he didn't know there was a lawyer in the house, she had no intention of enlightening him. She could handle this herself without disturbing Ben.

"Ready?"

She nodded abruptly, wondering if she should at least talk to Edie before she left, then deciding against it. Edie knew she was on her way to the police station. No point giving her any more details. She'd only worry.

"Would you like to get your coat?" he invited.

"Yes, thank you," she replied. He stood aside while she retrieved her raincoat from the walk-in hall cloakroom, then let her precede him through the front door.

Sara breathed a sigh of relief. At least he wasn't handcuffing her. Not that female prisoners were usually handcuffed, but you could never predict how cautious an officer would be, she thought.

In the circular driveway, Sara saw the white police car with its distinctive red stripe and York Regional Police emblem on the door. As he maneuvered her toward the car, she tried to distract herself by trying one more question. "Has there been *any* progress on the case, Constable?"

But he obviously believed that a prisoner wasn't entitled to any real response. He held the door open for her. "Not that I know of," he told her bluntly, before she climbed into the back seat of the four-door Chevrolet.

Sorry I asked, she felt like saying. Instead, she settled in the back seat, watching him get into the driver's seat. A Plexiglas screen separated them, and she could only just catch a glimpse of his hat in the rearview mirror, shading his dark eyes. She stretched uncomfortably. There wasn't much room in the back of a police car.

Her long legs were drawn up in front of her. She noticed that the ashtrays, door handles and lock buttons on both doors had been removed, as was usual. The doors could only be opened from the outside.

Leaning back, she watched the fall countryside speed by in myriad golden colors, then closed her eyes for a few moments.

The Aurora detachment was only a twenty-minute drive from the estate. They'd be there in no time. The faster they reached the station, the faster she could get back to the mansion—and Nick.

"BUT I DIDN'T KILL Lillian Kingsley. I keep telling you that," Sara protested. This just couldn't be happening. Her heart pounded against her chest. She tried not to focus on the salmon-colored walls of the Newmarket Identification Branch. Constable Canfield had taken her there instead of to the Aurora detachment office. Her body temperature had dropped to a chilling point when she first saw the depressing building. It meant she was going to be processed as a criminal. She could still barely comprehend the reality. The walls seemed to swim in front of her eyes; "confession pink" police cryptically called the faded color. She forced her eyes away from the walls toward Detective Adams. "You have to believe me," she pleaded.

The detective sighed, leaning back in the hard chair of the basement quarters. A desk separated him from Sara. "We've found Lillian Kingsley's will. Other than bequests to Nicholas Kingsley, Ben Short and some of her servants, she names you as the prime beneficiary." With a deft movement of his wrist, he slid a piece of gray embossed stationery toward her. "Take a look at that."

While one trembling hand reached for the sheet, Sara's other hand clutched the edge of the desk. A film of perspiration dampened her palm. "I didn't know it existed," she whispered in a hoarse voice, her gaze taking in Lillian's sprawling, spidery signature but ignoring the contents.

"Oh, it exists all right. We found it last night in the top drawer of one of Mrs. Kingsley's night tables," he explained. "Admittedly, it's handwritten and short, but as far as we have been able to check, it *is* valid. Tell me, Sara—" he watched her intently "—where is Lillian's body?"

"I don't know," she groaned. Her thoughts raced in circles. Why had Lillian written a will? She looked at Constable Canfield for some kind of nonverbal support, but the officer standing by her side remained impassive. "This is all a terrible dream," she gasped, placing her head between her hands. "I didn't kill Lillian Kingsley."

"It's more than a bad dream, Sara," the detective corrected in a jaded voice. "It's first-degree murder." He paused to let the statement sink in. "Do you want to change your story?"

Sara shook her head, tears misting her eyes. "I can't. I'm telling you the truth. When last I saw Lillian, she was alive. I think she's been kidnapped. Please, Detective Adams..." In desperation, she dropped the will and reached to grab his hand. "You have to believe me. Lillian could be in danger."

The detective stood up slowly, breaking Sara's hold. His face bore a visibly distant look. "I'm not totally discounting that possibility, because I can't afford to, but quite frankly, I think you committed the murder. I also suspect that lawyer friend of yours might have been an accomplice. He's just lucky I haven't got enough evidence yet to prove a connection."

"Ben's innocent!" Sara objected, hysteria creeping into her voice.

The detective shrugged. "Maybe. Maybe not."

Sara's eyes flashed. "Ben Short didn't kill, or conspire to kill Lillian Kingsley, so you can forget that, Detective."

Adams's eyes narrowed as he poised by the edge of the desk. "Your loyalty's admirable, Sara. Too bad you weren't more loyal to the memory of your father."

At the mention of her father, Sara stiffened. "And what's that supposed to mean?"

The detective regarded her closely. "I knew your father. There isn't an officer on the Metro or Regional forces who didn't respect him."

"I respected him too, Detective," she said tartly, her face flushing. "And everything he stood for."

Detective Adams's gaze became hooded. "It's a bit late for that sentiment, Sara," he replied acerbically. "Now, don't you think you'd better exercise your right and call a lawyer. You're going to need one."

"I don't need you to remind me of my rights," she snapped.

"No," he replied rhetorically, "perhaps you don't. But I don't want some smart lawyer catching us on a technicality."

"Is that why you cleared the station before I came in?" she retorted.

The detective exhaled audibly. "You know the rules, Sara. When you bring in a murder suspect, get everyone else out of the way, so there's no possibility of communication between the suspect and anyone else."

"Continuity," she replied in a flat voice, understanding the process.

"Exactly. Now, since we've already done the arrest form, we can get on with the other procedures. I'm sure you're just as familiar with those." His brows rose in a questioning curve.

Sara's heart sank. She knew the other procedures, but accepting them was another story. Oh God, they *really* were going through with this. Detective Adams wasn't convinced of her innocence. She nodded. "I'd like to make one call first," she announced, her voice dry.

"Of course." He nodded abruptly, then in a brusque tone, addressed Constable Canfield. "Let Ms Brennan make her call, then book her." With that, he gave a tired sigh. "See you in court, Sara."

In seconds, he'd disappeared from the windowless basement, heading through a doorway to the back of the building. Sara's mouth clamped shut with nervous tension. Every hope of getting out of the Newmarket facility disappeared with the detective's departure. But she was through with begging. She was innocent, dammit. Lillian wasn't dead. Oh God, was she? Pain lapped at her temples. How could she help Lillian if she was in jail?

"Ms Brennan." Constable Canfield's voice commanded her attention as he edged the phone toward her.

"Thanks," she managed. The officer discreetly withdrew to a bank of filing cabinets. With trembling fingers, Sara began to dial the phone number of the Kingsley estate.

AROUND ELEVEN IN THE MORNING, Nick slipped back into the Kingsley mansion, his eyes burning from exhaustion. closing the door behind him, he stood uncertainly in the foyer, running his fingers through his hair.

Edwards Metals had produced no clues. Not that he'd really expected to find any. But Sara's concern for Lillian haunted him, and he'd been willing to give it a try.

With reluctance, he'd dragged himself from her bed, forcing not just his body, but also his mind to focus on other, more pressing realities. Making love to Sara had unleashed a torrent of emotions inside him. Emotions he'd long kept to himself. Emotions he now wanted desperately to explore and express. But they'd have to wait until this was all over.

He hovered in silence, unwilling to find Sara and tell her he'd found nothing. He wished he could spare her the frustration of waiting, but he didn't see how he could.

Fact were facts.

Muttering an oath under his breath, he turned and was about to head toward the kitchen, when a sound on the stairs caused him to look up. Expecting to see Sara, he saw Ben instead.

Ben was holding up one arm, as he reached the bottom step. "Hope you don't mind," he said, indicating the shirt he was wearing. The cuffs on the oversize shirt were rolled into neat folds above his wrists. "Edie loaned me one of yours."

Despite himself, Nick grinned. "Not at all." Taking another look at the familiar item, he couldn't help adding, "At least you picked one that's been ironed."

Ben's mouth twitched at the corners. "Even as a boy, neatness was never one of your strengths, Nick."

Nick chuckled. "Guess not." Then his face became serious as he glanced past Ben up the staircase to the second-floor landing. "Have you seen Sara?"

Ben shook his head. "No. I just got up." The fact that Nick had apparently just walked in the door and wore a beaten expression suddenly seemed to register with Ben. "Where've you been, Nick?" he asked anxiously. "Did you stay up all night?"

"Not quite." Nick began removing his trench coat. "But almost," he continued, fidgeting with a sleeve. "Sara's worrying about Lillian began to get to me, so I decided to check out Edwards Metals, but I'm afraid I didn't turn up anything."

"I see." The lawyer's gaze narrowed behind his wire-framed glasses. Now the argument in the car between Nick and Sara began to make sense. *So, that's the way the wind blows,* he mused privately. Inexplicably he found he was pleased. "And now I suppose you hate to tell her?" he posed in quiet speculation.

Nick halted his movements for a few seconds, Ben's interest surprising him. Charles could never have even asked the question, let alone been curious about the answer. Ben's fatherly interest softened the isolation he was feeling. Grateful, he admitted, "Something like that."

A slight smile crossed Ben's face. *Happens to the best of us,* he thought to himself. *You fall in love and then you can't do enough for the one you love. I ought to know.*

"C'mon." He touched Nick's arm in a companionable gesture. "You'll be better able to tell her after a cup of coffee."

Pulling himself together, Nick tossed the coat over the banister. "You're right. Let's go."

"Morning, Edie," he said to the housekeeper's back, as seconds later he swung through the doors into the kitchen, Ben behind him.

"Morning, Mr. Kingsley." Edie whirled around at the sound of his voice, then her mouth dropped open as she saw his exhausted face. "Were you in a fight?"

Nick grimaced, easing himself into a chair. "Do I look that bad?"

Edie planted herself next to him, her hands akimbo on her hips. "Worse," she told him.

Ben suppressed a grin. "Give him a coffee, Edie."

"Looks like he needs a sleeping pill," she muttered, but moved toward the stove and the bubbling pot of coffee.

Nick's gaze followed her movements with desultory interest. "Is Sara up yet, Edie?"

Juggling the coffeepot and two mugs, she plunked the latter on the table. "Long gone," she answered airily.

Nick's lackluster interest turned acute. His hand snaked out and grabbed Edie's arm. "Long gone? What do you mean, long gone?"

"Mr. Kingsley!" Startled by Nick's action, she let the pot shake in her hand, coffee spilling in an ebony arc onto the white laminated table.

Nick forced himself to calm down. Sara had promised! Loosening his grip on Edie, he steadied the pot in her hand, and relieving her of it, placed it on the table. "Sorry, Edie. I'm a bit stretched out." He breathed in hard, trying to quell the queasy sensation in his stomach. "What did you mean, she's gone?" he repeated, a little more quietly this time.

Damn Sara's determination and independence! Didn't she realize how deadly a game these thugs were playing? Why hadn't she waited for him?

Edie collected herself, nervously straightening the two mugs. "She went to the police station," she managed.

"You mean that's where she told you she was going, but not necessarily where she went." He couldn't restrain the distrust and disappointment in his voice.

"Oh no, Mr. Kingsley." Edie shook her head vigorously. "She went with a police officer."

"What police officer?" His eyes bored into Edie.

Edie rushed to answer. "The one who came here this morning at eight o'clock. He said he wanted to talk to her at the station."

Nick's mind raced. When he and Ben had talked to the desk sergeant the night before, he hadn't said anything about there being any urgency to speak to Sara. His gaze flew to Ben, confused. The lawyer's expression was equally perplexed.

Suddenly, the phone on the wall rang and all three occupants of the room exchanged startled glances. Nearest to it, Edie quickly reached for the receiver.

"Hello...yes...yes... He's here.... Just a minute..." Edie's voice was flustered. Hearing her response, Nick immediately stood up, but she shook her head distractedly, holding her hand over the mouthpiece. Nick stopped, a questioning, worried expression in his tired eyes. "For Mr. Short..." Edie explained, her voice trailing.

The lawyer hurriedly stood up and practically wrenched the phone from Edie's shaking fingers.

"Ben Short," he said brusquely, then he gasped, "Sara, what's going on?" While talking, he looked at the other two, shock masking his face. Then he fell silent, listening quietly, the shock collapsing into grimness.

As he watched Ben, Nick's stomach wrenched. "What is it?" he rasped, moving toward the phone. "Let me talk to her," he commanded, reaching for the receiver, but Ben pulled back, holding up his hand. Ben continued to say nothing, only listen and nod his head occasionally.

Finally Nick could stand it no longer. "Goddammit, Ben. What is it?" He reached again for the phone, but Ben twisted away, blocking Nick with the left side of his body. "Yes," he eventually answered. "I'll tell him. We'll be right there." He hung up the phone hastily.

When Ben turned, Nick's face was livid with fury. "Why didn't you let me talk to her?" he stormed at the lawyer. "What's happening? Why is she at the police station?"

Ben took a deep breath, with effort. He stared directly at Nick. "She's at the police station because she's been arrested."

"Arrested?" Nick repeated incredulously. "On what charge?"

Ben breathed in again, trying to control the pain he felt. "Murder, or to be more precise, first-degree murder."

Nick reached a hand to the nearest kitchen chair for support. "But that's ridiculous. There's no evidence. They have our statements—yours and mine—they..." Nick reviewed all the arguments he could think of, but Ben interrupted tiredly.

"Yes, all of that is true. Everything is circumstantial. But the evidence doesn't have to be overwhelming to charge someone, providing the officer can prove he or she acted in good faith. Don't forget, you filed an initial statement saying you suspected Sara of murdering Lillian. It sounds like they're not taking any chances. The worst that can happen from the officer's perspective is that the judge will throw it out of court. Adams won't lose anything, and in the meantime, he's probably hoping for a confession."

"Well, she can't confess to something she didn't do," Nick replied tersely. Damn. Why had he gone to the police with his suspicions? Why hadn't he just waited until he could get the truth from Sara? "What about our rescuing you, Ben? Surely the police will believe your statement? There's no body. No motive. No will . . .''

A soulful sigh escaped Ben. He placed his head in his hands. "I'm afraid that isn't true, Nick."

"What are you talking about, Ben? You didn't draw up a new will. Lillian *didn't* make a will. Dammit, she didn't, did she?" Leaning over Ben, he clasped the older man's shoulder.

Ben's eyes were glazed as he raised his head to face Nick.

"Lillian apparently made a handwritten will, Nick, and the police have found it."

"And . . ." Something in Ben's expression gave Nick the answer.

"And—" Ben's breath was ragged "—it was dated the day she supposedly died. It names Sara as the main beneficiary."

"My God!" Nick released his hold on the older man, and slumped on the chair next to him. "Ben, what does this mean—really mean?"

The lawyer's blue eyes seemed to have faded to a dull gray. The feathery lines in his face notched into deep grooves. "It means that because there's a will, there's strong indication of motive. According to Sara, I'm also under suspicion as an accessory. In Canada that means I could be charged with the original crime. It also means that Adams might not believe my statement of last night."

"But there's no body," Nick repeated his earlier comment. "Even if this ridiculous charge should ever go to trial, surely you can't get a conviction without a body?"

Ben sighed tiredly. "You've seen too many movies. I'm aware of at least one case in Canada where there was a conviction without a body. Anyway, there's something you haven't thought of, something far more serious. . . ."

Nick tensed. "What?"

Ben chose his words carefully. "Lillian's body could turn up somewhere. After all, we don't know that she's alive. All Adams would have to do then is find evidence connecting Sara."

"But there wouldn't be any," Nick objected.

"We can't be sure of that. So far none of Lillian's charade has gone according to plan. And there's something else...."

"Yes," Nick snapped.

"If the police are convinced that Lillian is dead and that her body has been hidden somewhere, they might stop treating it as a kidnapping and their efforts to look for her..."

"...will stop," Nick supplied, his stomach lurching.

"Exactly, so it isn't just a question of what could happen to Sara. If Lillian's alive and the police aren't looking for her, how long will she remain alive? Until she gives the criminals the formula?"

Nick struggled to understand it all. Sara was in jail. Lillian was still in danger. Or was it over for Lillian? He wouldn't believe that. They had to find Lillian and arrange for Sara's release.

"Can we at least get Sara out on bail?" he asked Ben.

Ben shook his head. "Not when it's a murder charge. Not without the go-head of a Supreme Court judge and that takes time—lots of time. I'm afraid that's one commodity we just don't have."

"Ben, we've got to do something!" Nick rasped.

"I can get Sara one of the best criminal lawyers in the province. He's a friend of mine. Then we can go to Newmarket and ask to see her."

"Newmarket?" Nick repeated, puzzled. "Isn't she at the Aurora station?"

Ben shook his head again. "With a murder charge, she'll have to appear in court tomorrow morning for a show-

cause hearing. That means the onus is on her to demon-
strate she's entitled to bail. The hearing has to take place
within twenty-four hours of her arrest, so they'll keep her
overnight. The jail's in Newmarket, not Aurora."

Jail. The word hit Nick hard. Damn, there had to be
some tack they could take.

In the meantime, Ben was addressing Edie. "I almost
forgot. Sara asked if you could pack a few things for her."

Edie's gaze seemed misted, but she managed a brisk
nod. "I'll do it right now," she said in a jerky voice, and
walked past them toward the back stairs. Ben watched her
leave, then turned back to Nick.

"This lawyer is superb, Nick. We've been friends for
years. He..."

"Too bad he isn't a Supreme Court judge, Ben. Don't
you know any of those?" he retorted, then could have
bitten his tongue as he saw how his remark had stung the
lawyer. Quickly, he added, "I'm sorry, Ben. I'm just so
damn worried. I can't believe this is happening."

Ben managed a wan smile. "Forget it, Nick." Then his
eyes widened and he spoke with an edge of excitement in
his voice. "Just a minute, I *do* know a Supreme Court
judge. An old buddy of mine..."

A glimmer of hope surged in Nick. The idea of Sara
being locked up sickened him. The fact that he was partially responsible for it was torture. "Do you think you
could get him to do something to rush the process?" he
interrupted in a desperate voice. "Make a decision? Set
bail?"

Ben thought for a moment. "I don't know. I'm not a
criminal lawyer, but maybe. Jack's pretty approachable.
He might just give me a hearing."

"Great! Let's do it."

Ben nodded, his own hopes rising, then he cautioned, looking at Nick, "I should warn you, in a murder charge the bail set is usually quite high."

In an instant, Nick's eyes had darkened to a turbulent brown, and his mouth had tightened into a solid stubborn line. For a split second, Ben was reminded of Charles Kingsley. Charles had possessed none of Nick's more humane instincts, but he'd nevertheless been a strong-minded man. His toughness had been something to respect as well as fear. The same toughness now flashed across Nick's face.

"If it takes every cent I've got, you can have it, Ben. Let's just get Sara out of jail."

"Arrested?"

The man whirled away from the view of the wooded ravine, which was changing color under autumn's sway, and with his back to the window, he faced the thug. Carl? Was this one's name Carl? What difference did it make? he thought irritably. He fingered the edge of his cashmere sweater absently, the fabric soft beneath his touch.

"Are you trying to tell me that Sara Brennan's been arrested for the murder of Lillian Kingsley?"

"She's been taken to the jail at Newmarket, you know, the one on Prospect Street," Carl offered helpfully.

No, he didn't know. How could he know? He didn't fraternize with criminals—except for expedience. He gave the man a scathing look. When he didn't answer, Carl went on.

"What do you want us to do now?" the heavy-set man asked.

"I have to think about it," he retorted. "Just wait outside." Dismissing the man with his eyes, he turned back to the window and stared out. Behind him, the door shut noisily, and he flinched. Thug, he thought. Clumsy thug.

Was there any way to use Sara's arrest to his advantage?

If he had the complete formula, he could just kill Lillian and let Sara take the fall for it. Plant the body where the police could find it. Maybe even leave behind some incriminating evidence, something that would substantiate the police's suspicions. But he needed Sara to complete the formula—or did he?

Was Lillian playing games with him or not? Lillian had always been a wily creature, giving to manipulation and cunning. She could outmaneuver any man. He's seen her do it. Living with Charles had only honed her skills. But damn her, she wasn't going to do it to him.

He broke into a smile. He still had two very strong options. He could get rough with Lillian and scare the formula out of her, assuming she was lying about having forgotten part of it, then he could kill her and let Sara get convicted. Or, if Lillian wasn't lying, he could kidnap Sara, get the balance of the formula and kill both of them. Either way, he couldn't lose.

But first, he had to play another hand with Lillian.

A METAL BED. No mattress. No blankets. No sheets. God, how was she ever going to stand this—even for one night? Fighting a fresh wave of panic, Sara edged herself onto the cold metal pallet that passed for a bed. There was no window in the cell. No chair. Just the bed, toilet and sink, and three bleak walls—walls that were threatening to close in on her. Taking deep breaths, she struggled to control the hysteria rising in her. How would she stand it? How *could* she stand it? Like Ben, she hated being confined.

Desperately, she concentrated on the bars. Across from her was the bull pen, a holding area for group arrests of twenty or so people. Better to look into space than into barricades, she thought, trying to find relief in the expanse outside the cage. She inhaled gulps of air raggedly. *Stay calm, Sara. Stay calm.*

A sudden clang sounded, and with a start, she jumped up. They were going to let her out. Thank God.

"Ms Brennan."

"Yes!" She grasped the bars excitedly. A young constable opened the door for her.

"You have a telephone call."

"Telephone call?" That was it? That was all? They weren't releasing her?

"You're not freeing me?"

The officer shook his head. "Just a call. Detective Adams said you could take it."

It was better than nothing, Sara reasoned. Less time to spend in the cell. Suddenly, the small reprieve seemed enormous. "Thank you," she managed.

Seconds later, she picked up the receiver sitting on the desk in the room where she'd been booked. "Hello," she answered breathlessly.

"Sara, oh my God, can you forgive me?"

"Nick?" Relief washed over her. No voice could have been more welcome to her at this moment. "Sara, this is all my damn fault. I should never have filed that first statement."

"It's all right, Nick," she whispered. "I'd have probably done the same thing in the circumstances. Don't blame yourself."

"But I do." The raw anger in his voice brought back to her the image of his dark, tousled hair and scowling face. Suddenly, the vision was so endearingly familiar that she managed a smile.

"Where are you?" she asked.

"In a telephone booth," he growled. "Ben and I tried to see you at the station, but they don't allow visitors. Are you—are you all right?"

"I'm better now," she answered huskily. "Since you called."

There was a slight pause as if Nick was catching his breath. "Sara, we're doing everything we can. Ben's talking to a Supreme Court judge, a friend of his, to see if we can get you released on bail."

A wet mist veiled Sara's eyes. She clutched the receiver tightly. "Thank you, Nick," she replied in a soft voice.

"God, Sara..." Her simple thanks seemed to unravel Nick for a moment. "There's so much I want to say to you..." he started.

Beside her, Sara felt a nudge and turned to see the constable indicate her time was up. "Nick," she interrupted, "I've got to go now."

"Sara, I'll make this up to you. I promise."

Sara knew he would. A man like Nick would keep his word. "I know you will, Nick," she whispered into the phone. "I'd trust you with my life."

Her words sang through Nick like a concerto gone wild. "I'll see you tomorrow, Sara, at the court hearing," he said in a gruff voice. "Think of me tonight. Think of us."

Sara didn't need the admonition. Nick was the only welcome thought available.

SARA WAITED AT THE BACK DOOR of the red brick Newmarket station. She was being transferred for her court hearing, and she'd never been so relieved in her life to be in the fresh air, no matter how damp and chilly it was.

The police cruiser stopped in front of her, and an officer jumped out, coming toward her. Pale eyes, a strange mixture of blue and green that reminded her of a changeable sea glinted at her.

"Please." Waving a hand, he directed her toward the back of the vehicle, and she went gladly. Anything was better than the inside of that cell—anything!

Soon, she'd be at the courthouse. With any luck Ben had been able to arrange bail and she'd be released—into Nick's arms. The thought warmed her, and almost cheerfully, she arranged herself in the back seat of the police vehicle.

Anytime you're ready, she felt like saying to the corporal, then realized she hadn't even checked the officer's insignia. *Oh well, what difference does it make? I'm going to be free....*

With that thought in mind, she paid hardly any attention to their departure from the rear garage bay. Leaning back, she closed her eyes and enjoyed the sensation of motion. Enforced inactivity gave new meaning to simple pleasures, she thought absently. Opening her eyes a fraction, she checked her watch, then lowered her lashes again....

SHE WOKE WITH A START, glanced at her watch, feeling disoriented. She must have dozed off. Nine o'clock. She and the officer had left the station at eight. Quickly, her gaze scanned the landscape for the provincial court building. It was only a five-minute drive from the station. Instead, she saw the car was driving on an unpaved country road, banked by trees.

Surprised, she leaned toward the silent bulk in front of her.

"Where are we?" she asked the back of his head, then looked in the rearview mirror. The officer's eyebrows arched upward, but he didn't answer.

Suspicion settled on her and her skin cooled. "Where are we?" she repeated, demanding an answer now.

The pale eyes just dismissed her, concentrating on the road ahead.

Alarm began to spread through her. She hooked her fingers into the grill separating them. "What's going on?" she hissed.

Silence greeted her.

"I demand to know what's going on," she said more loudly.

In reply, the officer accelerated.

She tried to wiggle her fingers through the grill to get at the uniformed figure. But it was futile, she knew, to even try. The car was designed to prevent that from happening.

Without thinking, she reached for her gun, then remembered it wasn't likely she'd be carrying it under these circumstances. Damn!

Panic mounted. Frantically, she peered out the windows at the flashing scenery. They were driving through a natural cathedral of trees, and branches arched in curves over the road. Even had they been in busy traffic, struggling would be a waste of time. Anyone seeing her would only imagine she was a prisoner trying to escape.

Clever. She gritted her teeth. Cold logic now told her the man driving the car was no more a police officer than she was a killer. She prepared herself, waiting for the inevitable.

It happened sooner than she expected.

The car suddenly swerved to the right. Twisting her head she saw that the driver had wedged the vehicle into thick brush at the entrance to a bumpy dirt road, only wide enough to accommodate one car. It was the kind of road that people designed for their country retreats—functional, but only just.

Branches trailed along the side and front windows, making a scratching sound as they were bent backward by the moving vehicle.

Sara held her breath, wondering what lay ahead.

She soon found out. The car turned again, this time into a small clearing, circular in shape, and she saw two big men standing by an oak tree. One of them had been pacing, and stopped when the car entered the clearing. Turning, he reached for something in his pocket. A flash of white caught her eye.

What was it? Her heart sank at the size of the men. She hadn't a chance of outmaneuvering them! One, maybe. But three? In such an isolated setting?

Her breath became ragged. The car came to a stop, and the two men drew closer, moving swiftly.

The driver jumped out and came around to the door she was lodged against. Quickly, but uselessly, she knew, she slid across to lean against the other door. One of the men blocked that exit, while the man with the white object in his hand joined the driver.

The door opened. A rush of cool air greeted her.

Her eyes widened. Not a sound was spoken as the man poured something on the white cloth he held in his hand.

Chloroform!

She'd be out in three seconds!

The man climbed into the car. Using the door as a springboard, Sara kicked out, fury giving her energy. Her booted foot found his breastbone. A vicious curse splintered the air, and he lunged for her. The driver ran to the other side and unlocked the door.

Suddenly, she felt someone grab her arms from behind, but still she fought, squirming to evade her attackers.

She could smell the anesthetic. One of her assailants jerked her head back by reaching under her chin.

No! she screamed in silence. The white shape came closer, the smell nauseating. She tried to twist away, but rough fingers held her in position.

The fabric grazed her cheek and then a hand clamped down.

Darkness hit her in an instant.

"WHAT DO YOU MEAN, she's disappeared? People don't just disappear from the back of a police cruiser," Nick roared.

At his side, Ben nudged him in the elbow. "Please, Nick. Take it easy." Turning, he directed his attention back to the Detective Adams. "Detective, if you don't mind, could you tell us what happened?"

Detective Adam's face wore a weary expression. His hazel eyes narrowed in confusion on the lawyer. "I don't know. She was supposed to be transferred here for the show-cause hearing, but when the officers assigned to transport her arrived at the Newmarket station, she'd already escaped."

"Escaped?" Nick ran his hands through his disheveled dark hair in disbelief. "Escaped?" he repeated in a loud voice. The long center hallway of the provincial court building was packed with police officers and civilians. More than one head swiveled at the husky sound of the Australian accent, and the words that echoed in anger. "She hasn't escaped, Detective! Unless she's got an army of well-trained commandos behind her, she's been kidnapped. Do you understand? Taken against her will, and more than likely, she's in mortal danger. Now, what are you going to do about it?" The challenge whistled through the air.

The detective emitted a long sigh. "Everything we can, Mr. Kingsley. We don't like this any more than you do."

"Everything!" Nick prepared himself to launch another verbal assault, but was interrupted by the stern voice of the detective, who addressed his instructions to Ben.

"Mr. Short, I think I should warn you that you're under suspicion, but in the meantime, I'd appreciate it if you could get him out of here." He jerked his head toward Nick, then glanced quickly around the entrance of the building. "This is enough of a zoo without Mr. Kingsley adding to the confusion."

"Adams..." Nick's voice was a low growl as he stepped forward, but this time Ben's polite nudge turned into a strong armhold.

"That's enough, Nick," the lawyer spoke quietly. "Detective Adams is right."

Nick halted, rigid with anger. The detective tossed a look of gratitude to the lawyer, then spoke to him. "Remember what I told you. You're not off the hook, Short. Don't go anywhere that I don't know about. Now, please, get him out of here." With that, he turned sharply on his heel.

Nick fumed. He didn't give a tinker's damn how many people heard him. All he cared about was Sara.

HOURS LATER, Nick paced the library like a tethered panther, always coming back to the silent phone on the desk, as if expecting it to ring with news of Sara. It was six o'clock and the evening light was already fading to black.

"Have a drink, Nick," Ben encouraged from the seat by the fire. A tray of decanters and glasses sat on the table beside him. Reaching for the whiskey, he said, "It might calm you down."

Nick stopped by one of the windows, looking out. "No, thanks, Ben," he answered in a rough voice. "Nothing will calm me down except finding Sara." He talked almost to himself, edging aside the curtains, seeing a crescent-moon curved in the sky.

It seemed his whole life he'd been searching for someone to love, a woman with whom he could share his dreams, his anger, his peace. He knew he had a hunger for love and laughter, private smiles and a family...children, a partner, a wife. He knew beyond a shadow of a doubt that Sara was the woman he wanted to spend the rest of his life with—if she'd have him.

And now? Pain closed his throat. *Dear God, keep her safe until someone finds her.*

He almost jumped when the library door opened. He whirled, an expectant look on his face, but Edie dispelled the surge of hope with a quick shake of her head. "Nothing, Mr. Kingsley." Her face creased with concern. "I'm sorry." She adjusted the bag of dry cleaning on her arm. "I just came in to see if either of you needed anything."

Shaking his head Nick turned back toward the window, then he heard Ben ask, "What's that?"

Something in Ben's tone made him swivel around again. Ben was staring at the cellophane garment bag in Edie's arms and pointing.

Edie gave the lawyer a perplexed look. "Just Sara's suit. The cleaners dropped it off on their last run."

Nick recognized the navy-blue suit Sara had been wearing the night her car had almost run off the road.

"No, not that." His voice excited, Ben waved his hand. "What's hanging in front of it?"

Nick was alert now. Coming over to stand by Ben, he touched the older man's arm. "Ben, what is it?"

Edie raised up the bag so she could see it better. "You mean the ribbon?" she asked, looking back at Ben.

"Yes, the ribbon!"

Nick's eyes clouded when he saw the bluish-green piece of fabric, hanging in front of the suit. "It's Sara's ribbon," he offered slowly. "I saw it in her pocket the night her car crashed."

"No, it isn't!" Ben interrupted in a loud voice.

Both Nick and Edie stared at Ben in confusion.

"Then whose is it?" Nick asked.

"It's Lillian's . . . except it isn't. It's . . ."

Taking Ben by the shoulders, Nick spun him around. "What are you talking about?" Nick's voice was husky with fatigue and tension.

Excitement animated Ben's features. "Sara didn't tell me about the car crash, remember? You did. So consequently she didn't tell me about the ribbon. That's it! That must be it!"

"What, Ben?"

Ben looked at Nick directly. "Didn't you tell me the car crashed the same day that Sara visited the condominium where Lillian was supposed to be?"

"Yes, but . . . ?"

"Then I think I can guess what happened," Ben replied. His words began to tumble out. "I remember that ribbon. Years ago, we—that is, Lillian and a number of her admirers—were at a country fair. We were only in our teens. There were races. Lillian agreed to take the ribbon from her sunhat and give it to whoever won the race. If Sara found that ribbon in the condo, then the man who won the race could have visited her and dropped it by accident. Maybe—just maybe—he's the one who kidnapped her."

Hope surged in Nick. "Do you remember who that was?"

Ben could no longer control his excitement. "Oh, yes, I'll never forget. He beat me by a fraction. It was Graydon Lewis, Dr. Graydon Lewis."

Nick stared, stunned. A doctor. He and Charles could have easily discussed the formula. "You're sure?"

"Completely. And—" Ben's voice rose now "—he wouldn't have to kidnap Lillian. She'd go with him willingly. She'd never suspect Graydon of wanting the formula. That's likely why there was no sign of a struggle."

Nick's mind processed the information. In a brusque tone, he asked, "Do you know where Graydon lives."

"Yes. Not far from here."

Nick didn't dare allow himself to believe this was the clue they needed. If Lillian was with Graydon, was Sara also? Were they alive?

Trying to control his excitement, he fixed Ben with an intent look. "Are you game to go there?"

Ben's response, although grim, had a determined edge. "You bet."

"Good man." Nick let out a sigh of thankfulness. He turned to Edie, who stood in silence, looking from one to the other. "Edie, call the police and tell them where we're going." He pulled out the card he'd used previously. "This is the number. Try to get Detective Adams. He's the officer I talked to earlier. It'll take less explaining. Do you know..."

Edie bobbed her head before he could finish. "Yes, Mr. Kingsley. I know where Dr. Lewis lives."

"Good." He turned back to Ben. "Ready?"

Ben nodded. As they went to pass her, Edie stopped them. "Good luck Mr. Kingsley, Mr. Short."

Nick clutched her arm in response, giving her a grim smile. "Thanks, Edie. Say a prayer."

Say a lot of prayers.

Chapter Fifteen

Sara tried to raise her head, but it seemed an impossible task, as if bricks were weighing on her temples.

Her shoulders ached. And her arms felt as if they were on fire, a mass of tiny pinpricks of heat.

What had happened to her arms? Flexing, she tried to inch them out of the vise that strapped them. Pain shot to her neck muscles.

"Sara." A distant, hazy voice breathed her name.

She struggled to move her head again.

There. There it was. Coming back to life, like the agony of first movement after a terrible cramp.

She ran her tongue inside her dry mouth, testing the sensations, and then worked her jaw open. Feeling began to return, and with feeling, the first cloud of consciousness.

Fighting a wave of dizziness, she tried to open her eyes. Shapes whirled in front of her.

"Sara. Thank God!" she heard.

In painfully slow motion, she turned in the direction of the sounds, blinking hard to focus. A fuzzy, colorful shadow began to take form.

"Lillian," she managed at last, her voice an odd mixture of query and statement. A print dress began to take definition. Blurred features began to form, the elements of

Lillian's aristocratic face. "You're alive," Sara mustered in a raspy voice that seemed to abrade her throat.

"You too," the spunky widow replied. "For a while there, I wasn't sure."

Slowly, Sara began to get her bearings. Sparks of pain splintered across her shoulder blades as she glanced around. She and Lillian were in a small sitting room.

"Where are we?" Her voice was slurred.

"Graydon Lewis's house," Lillian spit out.

"Graydon?" Sara's head whipped back to Lillian, the action spreading a fiery ache to her neck and down her spine. Trying to ease the spasm, she hunched her shoulders. It was then she realized why she hurt so much—her hands were tied behind her. Looking down, she saw that she was tethered to a straight-backed chair.

"I'm afraid they tied you up as soon as they brought you in here," Lillian explained in a quiet voice.

By now, Sara's vision was clearing. Her dark green eyes focused on Lillian. The Kingsley matriarch was in a similar position. "Are you all right, Lillian?" she asked, worry creasing her forehead. Now that she could see properly, she noticed Lillian's features were drawn, almost haggard, and that there were a number of bruises on her face. Despite that, Lillian's blue gaze snapped back at her, as bright as ever.

"Fine. Graydon tried roughing me up yesterday. Until then it wasn't too bad, but I think he's getting desperate. I've only been tied up since they brought you in here—a couple of hours now."

Sara struggled against her bonds, but to no avail. Frustrated, she gritted her teeth. "Lillian, how is Graydon involved?"

Lillian's eyes darkened with disdain and her body tensed against the ropes that held her. "He wants the formula. He kidnapped me, then when I stalled him, he kidnapped

Ben." Suddenly, her voice choked, her small, neat head falling forward. "Ben! Oh my God!"

In a flash, Sara realized Lillian couldn't know that Ben was safe. She interrupted quickly to reassure her. "He's all right, Lillian. Ben's fine. We rescued him."

Lillian's head shot up again, tears of relief shining in her eyes. "Thank God! I've been so worried about him." Then she stopped, a puzzled look on her face. "We?"

"Nicholas, your nephew," Sara answered in a soft tone.

"Nick—here?" Lillian's voice was incredulous, then her eyes clouded. "Oh, Sara," she groaned. "I've got so much to make up for."

"Please, Lillian." If Sara could have thrown her arms around the woman to comfort her, she would have. Her peculiar logic had gotten them all into this mess, but somehow, right now, seeing Lillian tied up, Sara could no longer feel any anger toward her. "Don't think about that now. We've got to concentrate on getting free."

"Free?" There was an unexpected note of defeat in Lillian's voice. "Free? We'll never be free." A sob caught in her throat. "Sara, I'm so sorry. I told them I couldn't remember all the formula, but that you knew it. And now he'll kill you, too. It was the only way I could think of for you to find me. I didn't think past that point!"

"Stop torturing yourself, Lillian," Sara assured, hoping to calm her. "We'll think of something. We've got to try."

In answer, racking, dry sobs shook Lillian. Sara struggled against the ropes again. She could feel her wrists chafing. "Lillian, please. Take it easy."

"Okay...I'm okay." Lillian started taking deep breaths. At last, she raised her head.

"Sara," she began in a halting voice. "Graydon will be coming soon to get the formula...and then..." Her frightened eyes widened, as she left the sentence unfinished.

Then. Sara fought now to calm herself. She knew only too well what would happen then.

Inhaling deeply, she put as much conviction into her voice as she could. "We have to get free, Lillian. One way or another..."

NICK AND BEN CROUCHED in the bushes surrounding Graydon's house. Peering through a break in the hedge, Nick surveyed the unusually structured two-story, modernistic, brick and cedar building. The design was based on a series of severe lines; two windows in the center extended the full height of the house. Sharp angles accentuated the overall austere effect. It was set on about four acres of uncleared land, and only a rim of earth around it had been tamed and trimmed. The mixture of wild shrubbery and trees gave them cover.

"Where do you suppose they are?" he whispered to Ben.

"My guess would be the second floor. The main floor is fairly open. Two prisoners would be hard to conceal there. Graydon has a small den on the next level," Ben answered promptly in a low voice. "If Lillian and Sara are anywhere, I would suspect it's there."

If. Nick concentrated on the house again to drive away any doubt. "Any suggestions how we can get in? There doesn't appear to be a basement."

"There is," Ben corrected him. "But you can't see the basement windows from the front of the house, only from the back."

"Let's try it," Nick replied tersely, dropping on all fours to slide through the dense underbrush.

A few moments later, they'd found a narrow window that was partially open. Taking out a penknife, Nick cut back the screen. "You'll have to go in first," he told Ben, his voice almost inaudible. "The opening's too narrow for me. Open that window over there."

Nodding, Ben followed the instruction. Panting a little from the effort, he eased himself backward through the window. His feet hit the floor with a thump as he dropped inside. Each man held his breath. Soon, Nick saw Ben's face at the larger window. While Ben opened it, Nick cut through the second screen.

The passage wasn't that much bigger and Nick had a difficult time squeezing through, but at last he landed on the basement floor, facing Ben. The lower level was functional only, containing a rudimentary washroom and what appeared to be a storage room at one end.

Ben leaned over and whispered, pointing at the room. "I'll bet this is where I was originally."

Nick nodded, remembering Ben had woken up in a basement shortly after having been drugged and kidnapped.

Cobwebs brushed his face. Absently, he pushed them aside. "Now, which way?"

Ben thought for a moment. "From what I can remember, there's a side stairway. I would imagine it's just beyond the basement steps."

"Okay. Let's go real easy. We can't afford to run into anyone. We'd better take off our shoes."

Ben's mouth set in a grim line as he removed his shoes. Turning, he saw Nick had already done so. Nick jerked his head toward the stairs. Ben nodded and led the way.

At the top of the wooden basement stairs, he clicked the door ajar. Then they both waited. All was silent.

"Okay," Nick mouthed.

Ben pushed the door open just enough for them to pass through. Nick found himself standing in a small hallway. Immediately to his right was another set of stairs, just as

Ben had said. Directly in front of him was a doorway into what appeared to be the kitchen.

"Up there?" He formed the words silently, his head inclining toward the bare cedar stairs.

Ben nodded.

Sweat had broken out on the lawyer's brow. Nick squeezed his arm in reassurance as he bypassed him, now leading the way.

Suddenly, above them, the sounds of heavy footsteps broke the silence. A door slammed. They both froze on the stairway, flattening themselves against the wall. Muffled voices echoed through the floors. Nick thought he heard a female voice among them.

Sara? Lillian? His heart beat faster. God, he hoped it was both of them.

"The den?" Again, he formed the words silently.

At first Ben couldn't read his lips, then he bobbed his head vigorously at Nick's second try.

Nick waited for further sound from above, then jerked his head to indicate he was continuing up the flight of steps.

Ben gave a nervous nod of agreement.

Soon they were at the top of the stairs. Ben's hand shot out to point down the second-floor hallway at the second room. At the far end of the passageway, Nick saw another staircase that he assumed must be the main one.

Quietly, he tested his foot on the landing, and waited.

Nothing happened, and he turned to urge Ben forward.

The lawyer quickly followed suit.

Like a rap of thunder, a door slammed on the first floor, and male voices sounded, engaged in discussion. Nick's stomach almost heaved. He stood motionless, Ben beside him, equally silent, except for his ragged breathing.

The louder voice seemed to approach the stairs, and then they both heard footsteps on the uncarpeted surface.

Ben's eyes widened with panic. Quickly, Nick looked down the hall. He waved frantically to the first closed door, and in two agile steps, had reached it and eased it open. Ben shuffled in behind him, his breath now coming in gulps. Nick clicked the door shut, and they both braced themselves against the wall of a small bedroom.

Ben was sweating profusely. Watching him, Nick could feel the sweat trickling down his own spine.

As they waited, they both heard the door to the next room being unlocked. Exchanging glances at the sound, they held their breath. The door locked behind whoever had entered and a female voice said something. Neither of them could catch the words.

Straining, Nick turned and pressed his ear to the wall. A man and a woman were talking, and then... He almost gasped as a second woman's voice joined in. Sara's voice. He was almost certain.

Ben looked at him expectantly as he pulled back.

"Sara and Lillian," he mouthed.

Ben signaled relief with his eyes, then posed a silent question with them.

Nick remembered seeing balconies on the second level. More decorative than functional, they might be just what he and Ben needed. Cautioning Ben to maintain silence, he went to the window and carefully looked out.

A balcony stretched across the room they were in and continued to the den next door. Not large, but certainly large enough for Ben and him to walk on.

Turning, he waved Ben toward him. Once Ben had reached him, his gaze traveled between the balcony and Ben in mute query.

Swallowing hard, Ben nodded.

Nick stretched out a hand to slide the door open, but before he did, his fingers grasped a heavy jade Buddha sitting placidly on a French provincial desk.

IN THE DEN, Graydon Lewis brandished the Savage .303 rifle at Sara. Still uncomfortably perched on the hard-backed chair, her arms aching, Sara glared back at him.

"You really have been the proverbial fly in the oint-ment, Sara," Graydon said, smiling but only with his mouth. His hazel eyes remained cool and dispassionate.

"Don't you think this is all a bit much?" Sara retorted, twisting against the rough rope. Her gaze strayed to the rifle, which although antique, looked to be in superb working condition.

"A bit much?" He raised his eyebrows in a contemp-tuous arc.

"The gun. Tying up Lillian," she responded.

He sat down with casual grace as if he were selecting a chair at a concert, and patted the rifle across his thighs. "The gun is necessary, Sara. A sign of control. Power, if you will. Everyone respects that, don't they, Sara?" he posed in a soft voice.

A glint of fire flashed in Sara's eyes.

"Ah yes," he answered with a knowing nod of his head. "I can see that control and power are familiar to you." Then he gave a quiet laugh. "I can also see that you don't like those qualities. I, however, have a great fondness for them."

He leaned back in the soft chair, adjusting the lapel of his navy three-piece suit absently, and watching her. "As for tying up Lillian, I couldn't very well leave you alone together, unless I did that. I have no illusions that Lillian wouldn't release you first chance she got. Now, Sara—" his voice became threatening "—it's time for the for-mula."

"You have no right to it," she retaliated, almost top-pling the chair in her efforts to break free.

"On the contrary." Graydon stood up, cold anger dis-torting his handsome features. "I have every right."

Sara knew she was only buying time, delaying the inevitable, but it seemed vitally important to stall Graydon for as long as she could.

"What right?" she challenged.

Graydon rested the rifle against the arm of the chair. Straightening up, he waved disdainfully toward Lillian. "Her husband wouldn't have known where to begin with that formula if it hadn't been for me."

The widow thrust her jaw upward in a display of mutiny. Graydon took a deep breath as if controlling himself.

Watching his eyes, Sara saw a demented light in them. Obsession, she thought. Wild obsession. "You worked with Charles on the formula?" she asked, not taking her eyes from him.

"I gave it to him," he spit. "I gave him the base, and then he, arrogant bastard that he always was, just ran with it. When I challenged him, he laughed at me." Bitter remembrance tinged his voice. "*Charles* laughed at *me*," he repeated in disbelief. "Told me I had no proof."

"If you gave him the base, why didn't you just keep experimenting with it?"

"I didn't have the facilities or the money. Charles had all that. Besides, he'd already made a breakthrough. It was so much easier just to steal it, even if I had to wait ten years to do it. Mind you, the formula almost became lost to me completely. My threats to Charles made him so nervous he decided to go into production with the formula before it had been fully tested."

So that was the reason for Charles's haste, Sara thought. Her eyes flickered questioningly. How did Nick fit into all of this? But Graydon answered that question himself, before Sara could pose it.

"If it hadn't have been for Nicholas, Charles might have been successful at bringing the formula onto the market,'' he continued, his dry, sarcastic voice filling the air. ''Nick was, unwittingly, an accomplice.''

Beside her, Sara felt Lillian shiver. Sara was sorry Lillian had to find out this part of the story like this.

''How?'' Lillian finally spoke up, her voice subdued. Sara sent her a quick glance. The strain was beginning to show on Lillian, the fine lines around her mouth now more pronounced. If they didn't soon escape, Sara wasn't sure how much longer Lillian's natural gutsiness could hold out.

Graydon turned to Lillian with an arrogant smile. ''He stalled Charles. Or didn't you know that, Lillian?'' Lowering his voice, his tone became silky. ''There's a lot you didn't know about that husband of yours, Lillian.'' He cocked his head sideways, as if to gauge her response.

The older woman flinched, but held her head high.

''Still proud, eh, Lillian?'' His eyes narrowed. ''Did you know he told me just before he died that he was going to give the formula to you? He taunted me with it, believing that I wouldn't harm you. He was right about that, but for the wrong reasons. I didn't need to harm you to get it. All I had to do was get someone to kidnap you. You need never have known that I was behind the attempt. But then you hired her.'' His eyes darkened and he glared at Sara.

''I waited ten years to find out where the formula was. Then you came on the scene.'' His mouth twisted into an ugly line, then broke into a sardonic smile. ''Fortunately, however, you and Ben fell in with Lillian's ridiculous scheme.''

Sara arched her brows. ''How did you know about the scheme?''

Graydon was obviously enjoying himself. A contemptuous sneer crossed his face. ''You, Sara. You let the cat out of the bag. You told Shane Cameron that Lillian had died of a heart attack, and I overheard you.''

Sara recalled the conversation. She hadn't told Shane exactly that, but when he'd posed the question, she hadn't denied it either. Graydon had jumped to conclusions—the right conclusions.

"So you assumed . . ." she began.

"Not assumed, Sara. Knew. Remember, I'm a doctor. I knew enough about Lillian's medical history to know she's always had a strong heart. Your comment at the funeral made me think, so I took a chance and followed Ben. Before he entered his condo, I noticed the lights were on. When he left the condo, they were still on. On a hunch, I telephoned from a pay phone and Lillian answered."

"I thought it was you, Sara," Lillian interrupted in a hushed voice.

"So," Graydon continued, after glancing up briefly at Lillian's interjection, "I immediately hung up. In the meantime I had one of my stooges follow Ben to Tess's house. He overheard the conversation between Ben and Tess."

Which gave Graydon the idea of how to use Tess to get to Ben, Sara thought, suddenly understanding.

"So you kidnapped Lillian," she prompted.

Graydon chuckled, relishing how he'd outwitted them. "I didn't have to," he replied disdainfully. "Lillian has always liked male attention. Years ago, she had given me a ribbon as a memento, and I saved it. So I took it to the condo, told her I'd cared for her all this time and asked her to spend a few weeks with me. Her vanity got the better of her, and she told me the whole story, at the same time agreeing to come with me."

The ribbon! God, why hadn't she paid more attention to it when she'd found it in the suite? Sara glanced quickly at Lillian, and saw that the older woman had bowed her head, embarrassed.

"I'm sorry, Sara," she murmured.

Sara glanced back at Graydon. "That's disgusting," she spit out.

"No, just perceptive," he corrected. "As much as Lillian has always appreciated men, she has also always underestimated them."

Lillian's head snapped up. "I didn't underestimate you, Graydon. You were always self-serving," she said, her old spirit returning.

"Ah, but how much, you didn't know, eh, Lillian," he replied.

Lillian's eyes blazed. She had no answer for that.

While Lillian and Graydon had been talking, Sara had focused her thoughts on a means of escape. As long as she and Lillian were tied up, they had no chance. She had to get Graydon to free them. But how? Then a thought occurred to her. If she didn't miss her guess, Graydon was overly confident. It was a slim chance, but he might just go for it.

Trying to sound calm, she interrupted. "All right, Graydon. You win. I'll give you the rest of the formula, but you'll have to untie me."

"What for?" he snapped irritably. "You can just dictate it."

Sara shook her head. "No. I have to see it written down. When Lillian told me, I wrote it down and I have a visual memory—not an oral one. Untie me and I'll write it out for you."

Chapter Sixteen

On the balcony, edged in between the wrought-iron rail and the exterior of the house, Nick breathed a congratulatory, "Good girl."

Next to him, flattened against the wall, Ben looked perplexed. He'd been able to make out some of Graydon's words, but not all of them.

Nick had heard most of what had been said. So that was how Graydon knew about the formula and why he wanted it. He considered himself the original architect. Ben's fingers tugged at his sleeve in query, but Nick shook his head, declining to answer. There'd be time to bring Ben up to date later. All he allowed himself was a whispered, "They're going to untie Sara, and then we move. Okay?"

Ben wasn't sure what that meant, but he nodded.

Nick edged his head around the casing and saw Graydon turn away from the women toward the guard at the door. Sara and Lillian were partially facing the window, and at that moment, Sara happened to look up. Her eyes widened when she saw Nick, but recovering quickly, she just flashed him a look of love and relief, and nodded before turning back to watch Graydon.

Graydon picked up the clipboard from the table by the guard and carried it back to Sara. His gun was still balanced by the chair where he'd left it.

"No games, Sara," he threatened. "This is your last chance, and hers."

Sara shrugged as best as she could. "You're going to kill us anyway," she acknowledged.

Graydon grinned, thrilling to the sheer power that he felt. "That's a chance you're going to have to take, but if you're cooperative, who knows?"

Looking back at the guard, he inclined his head. The guard, obeying his silent command, pulled a .38 revolver from inside his jacket and aimed it at Sara. She saw his fingers move and heard the click of the hammer. Satisfied, Graydon stepped behind Sara and began to loosen her bonds.

Beside her, Lillian stirred. "You'll never get away with this, Graydon," she rasped, watching him.

Graydon tossed his head with scorn. "Spare me the sermon, Lillian. I'll be in Europe within twenty-four hours, and then it'll all be over."

Sara casually sought out Graydon's gun, trying to calculate the distance. Graydon's cool fingers began to work on the last knot.

Lillian was tense, her stomach muscles balled into a tight fist. Sara didn't know the rest of the formula. What was she planning? Her heart began to pump furiously.

Sara considered her options. If she was going to reach Graydon's gun, she had to do it in one dive. Even then, she wasn't sure she would make it. The guard's gun was already cocked, ready for firing. He would shoot in an instant. Shifting slightly in the seat to line herself up with the rifle, she wiggled her fingers.

Misinterpreting her action, Graydon swallowed a sadistic chuckle. "Impatient, aren't we?"

But Sara barely heard him. Should she try for the gun? The guard could just as easily shoot Lillian as herself. Was Nick armed? Probably not.

She could feel the blood rushing back into her hands.

Now, Sara. If you're going to do anything, it's got to be now. While Graydon is relaxed.

Fighting back the nagging doubt, she made her decision.

ONLY THE HUNCHING of Sara's shoulders gave Nick any indication of what she planned to do. In a flash of intuition, he saw her body, the mass of tumbled tawny hair and, beyond her, the resting rifle.

Clenching his right hand around the jade Buddha, he shoved the sliding door open, just as Sara ducked, swandiving for the rifle.

Nick hurled the statue at the guard. Surprise gave Nick the advantage and the Buddha found its mark, knocking the gun out of his hand.

Graydon's head whipped around. Seeing Nick, he yelled in rage and, still half crouched, he threw himself after Sara, falling on top of her.

Sara gasped, her fingers locking around the rifle.

Nick raced across the room, tackling the guard as he rolled on the floor toward the .38.

Sara and Graydon engaged in a vicious embrace, each trying to wrestle the rifle from the other. Graydon's foot caught the leg of Lillian's chair and toppled it. She screamed as she hit the floor, still strapped to the seat.

Ben, hesitant until now, tore across the room toward Lillian. In that instant, Graydon hit Sara across the jaw, stunning her and gaining control of the rifle.

With a cry of fury, he stood up and butted the gun into Ben's midsection, knocking the wind out of the lawyer and sending him sprawling. Ben hit his head against the desk, and blackness engulfed him.

Nick's fists finally brought the bloodied guard to the floor. He fell unconscious, and Nick whirled around, chest heaving. Wiping his arm across his own bloodied face, he saw the guard's gun and grabbed it. Then he looked over at Ben and Sara. Ben was seemingly passed out, and Sara was struggling toward Graydon.

Scrambling, nothing of his grace and elegance in evidence now, Graydon was breathing hard. He righted Lillian's chair, throwing his free arm around the back of the seat and across Lillian's chest. Lillian's eyes were large with terror. Graydon jammed the muzzle painfully into her throat.

Sara and Nick froze.

At last Graydon spoke. "One move from either of you, and she's dead."

The night Sara had been used as a shield flashed in Nick's memory. But this time he had a weapon. "I have a gun too, Graydon," he announced, his voice cold.

Graydon nervously tilted Lillian's chin back with the gun. "Yes, but you're a lousy shot, Nick. Remember, I used to go hunting with you and Charles. You always hated it."

Sara's breath came in spurts. Still on the floor, her hands braced in front, her gaze flew between the two men facing each other with guns. The .38 was no match for the rifle, even if Nick was a superb shot. Behind Graydon, she could see Ben stirring.

Out of the corner of his eye, Nick also saw Ben. Quietly, he answered Graydon, waving the gun toward the ashen-faced doctor. "If I were you, lousy shot or not, I don't think I'd want to take a chance, Graydon."

"Oh no, Nick." A fine line of perspiration showed above Graydon's upper lip. "You're not going to outbluff me. You'd never risk hitting Lillian. Never." He shook his head in derision. "Now, I'm going to untie her and walk out of here, and you're not going to do a damn thing about it."

Ben's head was beginning to clear, and he watched the players, taking in the scene, then caught Sara's silent signal. For a moment he hesitated, then blinked, nodding slowly. Sara never took her eyes from him.

Suddenly, Ben moved, his hand snaking out to grab Graydon's ankle. Sara acted in a flash, shoving Lillian out of the way.

Graydon, losing his cover, let out a piercing howl of rage.

Lillian screamed. "Oh my God!" Still tied to the chair, she toppled to the floor.

Graydon scrambled to his feet, but in one swoop, Nick, taking advantage of Graydon's disorientation, closed the gap between them and swung out his right hand, knocking the rifle from Graydon's grasp.

Sara seized the heavy gun. Graydon's anger hissed through the room, a string of curses streaming from his mouth. He lashed out in panic, but losing his balance in the melee, he fell. Nick's foot came down on his chest.

Securing her grasp on the rifle, Sara jumped up, leveled the gun and aimed it at Graydon. Ben was struggling to his feet, reaching for Lillian's chair to right it.

"Ohh . . ." Lillian wailed.

Hearing her, Sara glanced over at Lillian. Annoyance at her lost dignity showed on Lillian's face. Sara suppressed a grin. It was likely one of the few times in her life Lillian had not being able to direct the scene she starred in. Lillian's predicament caused a bubble of amusement to catch in Sara's throat.

The sound caught Nick's attention, and he looked at her, their eyes locking over Lillian's head. The same amusement lit his eyes.

As Sara looked at him, she took stock. They'd made it. Together. They'd rescued Lillian, with Ben's help, found the criminal who'd been after the formula, and in the process, they'd found each other. The look she gave Nick turned to one of loving conspiracy. He smiled his understanding.

Then the moment passed, Lillian's voice interrupting their silent exchange.

"Nick," she said wonderingly, blinking in delayed disbelief. "Is it really you?"

Nick turned to his aunt. Grinning, he answered, "Yes, poor shot that I am." He tilted the gun toward Graydon. "It didn't seem to make much difference, did it, Graydon?"

The doctor went to rise, his chest heaving with agitation, his mouth opening to speak. Sara adjusted her aim. Graydon caught her motion, and sending her a scathing look, clamped his mouth shut.

Behind Lillian, Ben leaned over and began to untie the ropes. "Lillian—" he began.

Taken by surprise, her head snapped back, and she stared at the lawyer in shock, her eyes filled with new respect. "Ben . . . ?"

Nick went to move closer to help Ben, but Sara put out a restraining arm. Stopping, he gave her a perlexed look.

Turning her head, but still aiming the rifle at Graydon, she whispered conspiratorially, "Let Ben have his moment of glory. Lillian loves a hero!"

Nick stood still for a moment, then looked over at the couple. Ben was murmuring something low, and Lillian, free at last, was turning toward him, her arms outstretched.

Nick's dark eyes lit with merriment and comprehension. With a great roar, he leaned back his head and laughed, then transferred the gun to his other hand and threw his right arm around Sara. He pulled her tightly into his embrace.

The laugh was infectious. As he looked down at her, his eyes filled with love and joy. Sara cherished the sound and freedom he was expressing with his laughter.

Freedom from suspicion and deception.

The realization that it was all over struck her with full force.

They *were* finally free. Free to love each other.

A surge of sheer pleasure shot through her, and she began to chuckle.

His fingers tightened on her arm. His eyes on hers were bright, dark, filled with promise.

Her chuckle gave way to deep-throated laughter, which only encouraged Nick all the more.

Together, they stood, holding on to each other, the sounds of their shared happiness reverberating in the room.

DETECTIVE SERGEANT JOHN ADAMS, a twenty-year veteran of a number of police forces, surveyed the four occupants of his office. Absently, he tapped a sharpened pencil on the edge of his desk. Taking a short breath, he turned his head toward the older woman.

"Mrs. Kingsley, how old are you?" he asked abruptly.

"Sixty-two," came the jaunty reply.

Detective Adams started at the quick response. "Don't you think you're a bit old for this kind of nonsense?" he asked dryly.

Lillian bristled perceptibly. "Certainly not," she snapped. The rustle of her dress on the hard chair was a warning the other three recognized only too well. Ben lowered his head. Sara blinked rapidly, and Nick picked a convenient spot on the ceiling to stare at.

"I see." The officer paused for a moment, then turned his attention to Ben.

"Tell me, Mr. Short, do you really believe a lawyer of your stature should be engaging in such charades as this?"

Ben blushed. "I . . ." He stalled but was unable to complete the sentence.

Satisfied that he'd made his point, the detective glanced at Sara. "And you, a deputy chief's daughter . . ." He shook his head in resignation. "Too bad you don't take that heritage a little more seriously, Sara."

"I do take it seriously," Sara retorted. Beside her, Nick couldn't stifle a small groan. Having one headstrong woman in the family was bad enough. Having two was damned dangerous!

Ignoring Sara's reply, the officer quickly looked at Nick. "You might well groan, Mr. Kingsley. While you have my sympathy for your companions here—" he waved his hand in the direction of the other three people "—you by no means have my sanction. You're just as guilty as they arc."

"Now, just a minute," Lillian interrupted, squaring her slim shoulders. "Nick wasn't even in the country."

"A moot point, Mrs. Kingsley," the officer pointed out in acid tones. "The fact remains," he continued, standing up, "that you're all as guilty as hell. By the way . . ." He stopped at the edge of the desk and positioned himself against it. "Just for interest's sake, Mr. Short, would you mind telling me how much the coffin you supposedly buried Mrs. Kingsley in cost?"

Ben cleared his throat nervously. "Ten thousand dollars."

"My God!" Nick's eyes flew wide. Even Sara gasped. The detective's mouth twitched in surprise. All of them looked at Lillian.

The widow's gaze flitted from one to the other. "Well," she said, sniffing, "I do, after all, have a position to maintain."

Nick almost choked. The detective managed to regain his composure. "Something perhaps you should have thought about more carefully at the outset, Mrs. Kingsley. A police record isn't going to do much for your standing in the community."

Lillian let out a cry of outrage. "You wouldn't dare!"

"For God's sake, Lillian." Ben jabbed her in the ribs, whispering hoarsely, "Keep quiet."

"Good advice, Mr. Short," the officer allowed sarcastically.

"I'll say whatever I like," Lillian snapped, tossing the detective and Ben each a scathing look.

"Not in my office, you won't, Mrs. Kingsley," the detective rasped. "That's enough." Lillian went to respond, but another sharp jab from Ben changed her mind. She sat in tight-lipped silence.

The detective pushed his body away from the desk. "I could book you all, but the amount of energy and paperwork required just isn't worth the effort. This case will be complicated enough once Dr. Lewis is brought to trial." He let out an audible sigh. "It might come as quite a surprise to you to know that police departments all around the world manage quite nicely, without—and I stress *without*—creative help from amateur volunteers. I would certainly appreciate it if you would all bear that in mind in the future." He gave a tired wave of his hand. "That's it, you can all go now."

Sara expelled the breath she'd been holding. All four stood up. Lillian led the way with her cane, as Ben escorted her carefully across the office.

"Oh, by the way..." Detective Adam's voice stopped them. They all turned.

His eyes found Lillian. "Mrs. Kingsley, normally I'm a reasonable man, but even I have my limits. If I ever catch you doing anything more dangerous than knitting, I'll arrest you.''

Lillian's eyes flared, but Ben physically propelled her out of the office before she had a chance to respond. Outside, she could barely contain her rage. No sooner had Sara and Nick joined her and Ben in the hallway than she gave full vent to her anger.

"Knitting?" she sputtered in a voice that could easily have reached the ears of half of the York Regional Police force. "The nerve of the man! I wouldn't be caught dead knitting!"

Epilogue

With one last glance at the letter in his hand, Nick shook his head in disbelief, passing it to Sara, who sat next to him on the library sofa. "I would never have expected this of Charles."

Across from them, Ben stood up. "I guess being on his deathbed gave him a change of heart, but being Charles, he just couldn't give it to you right away. He had to make you wait."

"Amazing, isn't it?" Nick said to Sara, who hastily scanned the letter confirming the contents. Charles's will had specified that on November 15, 1987, his letter was to be opened. Today. The letter concerned the disposition of the formula. In it, Charles directed Lillian to give the formula to his nephew, Nicholas Kingsley. The missive was terse and concise with one small concession to human emotion.

"Nicholas is entitled to the formula. Tell him good luck with it."

Sara suppressed a whistle of agreement. "It certainly is amazing. He could have saved us all a lot of anguish if he'd just left it to Nicholas in the first place, as they'd agreed." She tossed her head, angry at the absent Charles whose love of power had endangered so many lives.

Ben shrugged. "That was Charles—always making you jump through hoops. But thank God, it's over." He cast a speculative glance at Nick. "Does Graham Marshall still want to buy the formula from you?"

Nick nodded. "Yes, but we're both going to wait and see if Graydon launches a lawsuit, claiming some right to it." He gave a sad shake of his head. "Graydon could have spared himself a criminal record. Had I known he had any kind of claim on the formula, I would have ensured that those rights were respected, whether I owned the formula, or Lillian owned it."

"He probably thought you were cut from the same cloth as Charles," Ben offered. Then his tone changed. "Do you think Lillian's still in danger?"

Sara answered. "For a while, she might be...."

"But I intend to make a public announcement about the formula and its current side effects. That should alert most companies in other countries," Nick finished for her. "It's not foolproof protection, but once Graham is able to continue the experiments, the composition of the formula will change, which will invalidate Lillian's knowledge."

"Good." Ben seemed pleased. Standing up, he faced Nick, his hands behind his back. "You and Lillian have covered a lot of ground in the past few weeks, I gather?"

Nick smiled, knowing what he meant. Circumstances had forced Lillian to face certain facts about Charles and to reevaluate her relationship with her nephew. It had been painful at first, with Nick trying to spare her some of the details, but Lillian was nothing if not strong. At last, with tears in her eyes, she'd merely said, "I'll make it up to you, Nick." It was a proud but gracious concession, and Nick suspected she wanted now to forget the past as much as he did.

Lillian had also explained why she'd written the will. It was a simple explanation. At the last moment, it had occurred to her she only had one heir—him. His lack of interest in claiming the estate when Charles left it to him had made her think he wouldn't be interested in anything else from the Kingsley fortune. On the off chance something might happen to her, she'd quickly handwritten a will in Sara's favor and shoved it in her night table drawer. She'd apologized for not including Nick in the will, but she'd been peeved, she admitted, when he hadn't returned to the estate after Charles's death. She'd believed he wanted nothing more to do with her. Now she understood his reasons for wanting to maintain his emotional distance. She was writing a new will, she avowed, with three beneficiaries this time. Nick guessed they were Ben, Sara and himself. But the important thing was that he and Lillian could establish a relationship without Charles's interference now. He was looking forward to that, he had to admit.

He pulled his thoughts back to Ben's question. "A lot," he agreed, still smiling.

"Well, I hope this has taught her a lesson," Ben sniffed.

"What has taught me a lesson, Ben?" Lillian's imperious voice wafted from the doorway.

All three occupants of the room looked up quickly as Lillian tapped her cane on the floor, walking toward them. It hadn't taken her long after her kidnapping to bounce back to her usual regal style. Stopping in front of Ben, her vibrant eyes gazed at him in mock innocence.

Immediately wary, Ben stiffened. "You know very well what we're talking about, Lillian. You and your schemes. In the past couple of months, you've developed a real knack for getting into trouble."

Lillian gave a coquettish sigh, tilting her head, which barely came to Ben's chest. "I never was very good without a man, Ben."

Ben snorted. "Then find one. God knows there're enough out there. Even for you, Lillian."

Lillian softened her voice, giving him a meaningful look. "I think I've already found one, Ben."

Ben drew back, scandalized at her overture. "Oh, no, Lillian. Not me." His eyes narrowed as he shook his head.

"Now, Ben—"

"Lillian," he cut her off, "I managed to elude you when I was twenty-two and I have every intention . . ."

Sara and Nick exchanged quick amused glances. "Let's get out of here," Nick whispered.

Nodding, her eyes bright, Sara stood up quietly. Unobtrusively they closed the door on the rest of Ben's objection, and in the hallway, burst out laughing.

"She never gives up!" Nick announced, his eyes twinkling.

"You can say that again!" Sara leaned against the wall, trying to contain her amusement. "She's one tough lady."

Nick's mouth curved upward in a smile. Taking advantage of Sara's position, he leaned forward, planting a hand on either side of her, so that she was imprisoned between his arms. They barely touched her, but she could feel the warmth of him.

"Talking about tough ladies, I know one who could give Lillian a run for her money."

"Oh," she replied archly. "And who might that be?"

"You, lady. You're one hell of a package of fire and torment. Ever since I met you, my stomach's been in knots." Removing one hand from the wall, he trailed a finger along the curve of her jaw, tilting her head upward. "Being close to you is hard on a man. I've been falling in love with you ever since first meeting at the cemetery."

A gasp of pleasurable surprise caught in her throat. "I thought you hated me."

"I hated what I thought you had done. But the way you stood up to me—" he shook his head in wonderment "—all I thought of was how incredible it would be to have a relationship with a woman who was that direct. That beautiful."

"But you were so angry with me," she whispered.

"Of course I was. I thought you'd killed my aunt. That all you were interested in was money." Suddenly, his expression turned serious. "Sara, how could I have known otherwise? You didn't trust me either."

"I know." She sighed. Then she reached up a hand and touched his finger with one of hers. "Then I found out differently and began to see qualities in you other than your bull-in-the-woods routine."

Nick grimaced. "You're not exactly the sweet, domestic type either, my love."

"More's the pity," she answered in a quiet voice.

His eyes widened, a flash of fire brightening them. "Don't ever say that. I like you just the way you are. Courageous. Strong opinions. Loyal. Sara, I want a real woman. Not a wind-up doll."

Sara's eyes became moist. She was beginning to believe that Nick meant what he was saying. "You do?"

His eyes locked with hers. "I do."

A wave of need spread through her. Nick aroused every feminine instinct she possessed without forcing her to sacrifice her individuality. What woman could ask for more? Not subjugation. But exultation in who she was.

"Oh, Nick." Her eyes glistened with tears of love.

Seeing the incredible joy shining in her eyes, Nick's chest constricted, then his gaze darkened. "Do you still think I'm a bull in the woods?"

Sara grinned. "Absolutely."

He looked startled. Then Sara drew his hand into hers, and gently kissed the tips of his fingers.

"But, you know—" her green eyes flashed with mischief "—I've suddenly developed a real passion for take-charge men."

Nick smiled, then pressed his body against hers, so that their thighs were touching.

His mouth stopped barely an inch from hers.

"Enough of a passion to marry one of them?"

Sara's heart soared. "More than enough," she answered in a raw voice. "Whom did you have in mind?"

"Me," he replied, his voice a husky whisper. Then his mouth captured hers.

A delicious shudder raced through her. *Thanks, Lillian. Maybe your scheme wasn't so bad after all.* Those were her last thoughts before she gave herself over completely to Nick and to her love for him.

ATTRACTIVE, SPACE SAVING BOOK RACK

Display your most prized novels on this handsome and sturdy book rack. The hand-rubbed walnut finish will blend into your library decor with quiet elegance, providing a practical organizer for your favorite hard-or soft-covered books.

Only $9.95

**Approximately
16" x 8"
when assembled**

Assembles in seconds!

To order, rush your name, address and zip code, along with a check or money order for $10.70* ($9.95 plus 75¢ postage and handling) payable to *Harlequin Reader Service*:

Harlequin Reader Service
Book Rack Offer
901 Fuhrmann Blvd.
P.O. Box 1396
Buffalo, NY 14269-1396

Offer not available in Canada.

BKR-1A

*New York and Iowa residents add appropriate sales tax.

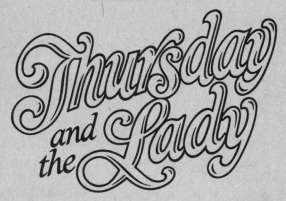